Look for these other Dog Lover's Mysteries
by Melissa Cleary!

A TAIL OF TWO MURDERS Jackie finds a beautiful dog with a bullet in its leg . . . and, not much later, the dead body of her boss at the Rodgers U. film department . . .

DOG COLLAR CRIME Dog trainer and basset hound devotee Mel Sweeten is killed with a choke collar—and Jackie and Jake have to dig up the facts to find out whodunit . . .

HOUNDED TO DEATH Mayoral hopeful Morton Slake has the morals of an alley cat—but when his girlfriend is found dead, Jackie and Jake prove that every dog has his day . . .

SKULL AND DOG BONES An ex-screenwriter says good-bye to Hollywood after someone spikes his bottled water . . . and Jackie's on her way to L.A. to solve the case!

FIRST PEDIGREE MURDER After Mannheim Goodwillie's voice hit the Rodgers U. radio airwaves, he hit the floor—and now Jackie and Jake are trying to pick up the signals of a killer . . . "Absorbing . . . quick and well-written." —*Armchair Detective*

DEAD AND BURIED Walter Hopfelt's job was keeping the Rodgers campus safe from crime. But now the security chief's career is over—along with his life . . . "Mind candy for dog lovers with a fondness for mysteries." —*Sun-Sentinel* (Florida)

THE MALTESE PUPPY Jackie has her hands full finding a home for Maury, Jake's gigantic and badly behaved puppy. It's even harder when she's trying to solve a murder case at the same time . . .

MURDER MOST BEASTLY The bizarre death of a Palmer zookeeper proves to Jackie that not all the so-called animals are behind bars . . .

OLD DOGS An elderly woman's tale of a long-ago bank robbery leads Jackie and Jake into a present-day puzzle . . .

AND YOUR LITTLE DOG, TOO Jake and Jackie investigate the "accidental" death of a homeless woman—and become foster parents to her orphaned pooch . . .

IN THE DOGHOUSE

MELISSA CLEARY

BERKLEY PRIME CRIME, NEW YORK

IN THE DOGHOUSE

A Berkley Prime Crime Book / published by arrangement with the author

PRINTING HISTORY
Berkley Prime Crime edition / January 2000

All rights reserved.
Copyright © 2000 by The Berkley Publishing Group.
This book may not be reproduced in whole or in part,
by mimeograph or any other means, without permission.
For information address: The Berkley Publishing Group,
a division of Penguin Putnam Inc.,
375 Hudson Street, New York, New York 10014.

The Penguin Putnam Inc. World Wide Web site address is
http://www.penguinputnam.com

ISBN: 0-425-17311-9

Berkley Prime Crime Books are published
by The Berkley Publishing Group,
a division of Penguin Putnam Inc.,
375 Hudson Street, New York, New York 10014.
The name BERKLEY PRIME CRIME and the BERKLEY PRIME CRIME
design are trademarks belonging to Penguin Putnam Inc.

PRINTED IN THE UNITED STATES OF AMERICA

10 9 8 7 6 5 4 3 2 1

CHAPTER 1

"Quiet on the set!" A woman's voice rang out over the sounds of whispered conversations and the scraping of chairs against the cement floor of the warehouse. Marti Bernstein, the assistant director of *Under the Dog Star,* repeated her request for silence and stepped back out of the shot. Jackie Walsh signaled her German Shepherd, Jake, to silence with a finger to her lips. "Roll 'em!" the director ordered, and "Rolling!" came a voice from behind the camera.

"Action!"

Jackie's dog, Jake, watched quietly from his accustomed place near Jackie's feet. Lorraine Voss, the actress playing the lead role, walked across the warehouse floor and pointed a gun at a tall, menacing man in an overcoat.

Jake had finally learned not to growl every time he saw either Lorraine or Kurt Manowski, the actor who had played hundreds of thugs and gangsters over a long career in movies and television, holding a gun during the shooting of scenes. Right now he seemed to be keeping a close eye on Lorraine's gun, and moving his head back and forth between her and Kurt.

Although Kurt's gun wasn't visible at the moment, the

position of the man's hand inside his coat was enough to
signal to the ex-police-service dog that there was reason
to suspect he had one. Jake rolled his eyes in Jackie's
direction as though he might be hoping she'd give him
permission just this once to intervene, but she caught the
look and shook her head firmly. "No, Jake," she whispered. Jake sighed and put his big black muzzle down
between his paws.

The actress moved forward a cautious step. "I don't
want to have to shoot you," she said to the man.

The man shrugged. "That's okay," he said in a gravelly
voice. "I don't want to have to die."

"Then put both your hands where I can see them,
and . . ." The actress sighed and gestured helplessly with
the gun.

"Cut!" came a man's voice from a few feet away. John
McBride, the director of *Under the Dog Star,* rose to his
feet with a sigh of barely contained exasperation. This was
the third take of this particular shot, and on a young independent filmmaker's stringent budget, Jackie knew that
he really wouldn't want to do more than five takes of any
shot if it could be avoided.

"Line," John prompted.

A script supervisor in a nearby chair read the line without inflection. "Then put both your hands where I can see
them, and face that wall over there."

"Thanks, Daphne. Is that okay, Lorraine?" John asked.
"Can we take it from the top?"

"No, it's not okay," Lorraine Voss snapped. "I've been
working for two hours under these lights without a break,
and I'm sweating buckets and I've got a headache, and
nothing is okay right now!" Her voice broke slightly on
the last of the sentence.

John nodded and looked at his watch. "That's my fault
for trying to push this shot," he admitted to the actress.
He turned to the assembled cast and crew. "We're all a

little tired. I think we should call lunch and be back here at two o'clock."

"So you're the director—call lunch, already," one of the crewmembers quipped.

John threw both hands over his head. "Lunch!" he shouted. There was a ripple of tired laughter. Lorraine Voss tossed her gun onto a nearby chair, put a hand on the back of her neck, and walked toward her trailer, still frowning.

The rest of the tight group of people gathered in the center of the warehouse began to break apart into twos and threes, heading for the doors. Kurt Manowski gave John a mock salute, handed his gun, butt first, to the waiting prop master, and wandered toward the warehouse doors with a few crewmembers with whom he had had a standing poker game since the first day of shooting.

John came over and sat down on the floor beside Jackie and Jake. He wore a buttoned-up flannel shirt over an R.E.M. T-shirt, and a pair of khaki shorts. His green eyes, dark blond hair, and easy smile had been a distraction for many of Jackie's female students, and probably a few male ones as well. None of that had changed since he had graduated in June—he still turned heads on the street, though he never seemed to notice. He was working on a mustache and goatee since the beginning of the film shoot, which still didn't quite make him look twenty-one, and he was actually a year or two older.

"Well, Lorraine's not especially happy with me right now," he said, rubbing his stubbled face. "What do you think? Should I be at her trailer door on my knees, begging her forgiveness?"

"Give her a few minutes to chill," Jackie told him. "Then offer to buy her lunch."

"Great idea." He sighed wearily. "Would you mind telling me again why I decided I could actually make this film?"

Jackie pretended to think on the matter. "Um . . . Because you didn't have anything else to do this summer?"

"That couldn't be it," said the young director, idly scratching Jake between his huge black ears. "I could have taken a job and actually made money."

Marti Bernstein came over and sat down on the floor beside John, smoothing out the folds of her multicolored gypsy skirt. "Then how about because you've maxxed out all your credit cards, taken out loans from your parents and all your other relatives, and told everyone you know you were going to take the Judges' Prize at the Central States Film Festival this fall?" she suggested.

John groaned. "I actually said that, didn't I?"

"There are witnesses," Jackie agreed. "But there's a real reason, you know."

"Tell it to me quick, before I tell all these people to go home and do something meaningful."

Jackie looked at John with real sympathy. He was the best student she'd ever taught, and she'd always hoped he'd stay in Palmer, Ohio, long enough for her to watch him make his first film. Now she was getting her chance. "Okay," she told him. "The real reason is that you're the best natural filmmaker Rodgers University has seen in thirty or forty years, and this is going to be your chance for some real recognition."

"She's right," Marti agreed, twisting her sandalwood beads around one finger. "I've taken every film class ever offered at Rodgers—"

"Bernstein, you've taken every class of any kind ever offered at Rodgers!" John countered.

"Let's have some respect here, boss," Marti demanded, giving the director a backhanded slap on the arm. "As the oldest professional student at Rodgers University, I claim both standing and expertise. Ms. Walsh is absolutely right. You're an awesome filmmaker, and for you to do anything else with your life would probably be a crime."

"Right this moment"—John sighed again—"crime seems like an acceptable alternative."

John's movie, a *film noir*–style detective thriller, was loosely based on Jackie and Jake's real-life adventures, as they had found themselves involved, often against their will, in a number of murder cases over the past four years in Jackie's hometown of Palmer. He had shown Jackie the script some months before, hoping she'd agree to play the part of the film's protagonist, Shannon O'Neill.

"I haven't acted since college," Jackie had told John, "and if you really want to know, I wasn't all that good at it even back then. What I think you ought to do is sink some of your budget into hiring a name actress for the part. Maybe someone who hasn't worked in a while. Hungry actors tend to work for a more reasonable rate."

There's a formula in Hollywood, which Jackie knew well, that states that ninety-five percent of all actors are unemployed at any time, and not only willing but eager to work. Of the five percent who are actually working, this formula goes on to state, ninety-five percent of them would like to have lead roles, but aren't able to get them. Sometimes, she knew, it's worth it to an actor to take less money to get a shot at a leading role, even in a small, low-budget film. Lead roles look good on an actor's résumé.

Acting on Jackie's advice, John had put out feelers with a number of Los Angeles talent agents, and turned up Lorraine Voss, whose private-detective television show, *Eyes of the City,* had run five seasons in prime time, but hadn't yet been picked up for syndication.

Lorraine had also worked in feature films in earlier years, but never seemed to get lead roles anymore. Barely in her mid-thirties, she seemed to be on her way down from feature-film and television stardom to roles in middle-sized stage productions in middle-sized cities. That sort of thing tended to make former stars a bit desperate, especially ones who hadn't invested their money wisely when they had it coming at them from all directions.

The grapevine had it that Lorraine was being considered for a solid supporting part in an upcoming big-budget project—the kind of role that Oscars are made of—but things had a way of turning around suddenly in the film industry, and tentative offers had a way of evaporating as quickly as they materialized. Lorraine's luck hadn't been all that good of late. Even given the need to spend several weeks in the sweltering Midwest summer, and the modest amount she'd earn playing the lead in a low-budget independent film, she had seemed agreeable to the idea, and John had been overjoyed to sign her. If he could wrap shooting on time and finish postproduction quickly enough, he'd have a shot at winning a spot in the Central States Film Festival taking place in Palmer this fall. If the film was well received this close to home, he might get a shot at a screening at one or more of the major festivals every young director dreamed of.

Kurt Manowski had been another lucky find for John's movie. The burly, middle-aged actor was instantly recognizable to millions of moviegoers who couldn't have told you his name, owing to thirty years of steady work in films large and small, and hundreds of episodes of television dramas. A lifelong drinking problem had gotten steadily worse over the years, and his formerly unblemished professional reputation had likewise gone downhill as he began showing up drunk or late or not at all on shooting days. He had also grown more and more belligerent toward his fellow actors, and toward the directors and producers who were hiring him, or increasingly, as it happened, not hiring him.

Following a conviction for aggravated assault on a fellow actor, Kurt had signed himself in for a prolonged stay at a well-known Southern California clinic known for sobering up the rich and famous. He declared himself clean and sober upon his release, but the good parts in the good films hadn't materialized after that, and he had been happy to accept the role of the heavy in *Under the Dog Star*.

Everyone concerned liked John's script, and they all seemed curious to know how much of it was fiction and how much fact, since the model for Shannon O'Neill was none other than the owner and wrangler of their canine costar. Jackie had lost track of how many people had asked her about this since shooting began. She went out of her way to assure all of them that she was flattered to have a part in the picture, but her own adventures were nowhere near as exciting as John's depiction of them.

Of course, Jackie had insisted John change the names and the more telling details of his story. "To protect the guilty?" John had asked, grinning.

"To protect *me*," Jackie had replied. If there was anything she didn't need, it was to have more attention drawn to her unusual involvement in some of Palmer's most infamous murders. As it was, people around here had a habit of trying to involve her in crime investigations despite her frequent protests, and if her fame were to spread outside Palmer, she might have to change her name and go into hiding just to get some peace and quiet. To avoid that she had asked John to undertake some script changes to make her and the plot a lot less recognizable. "Just make sure it's fiction," she had told him, "and I won't have any problem with it." John had made a lot of changes, including setting the story in the 1940s to justify an economical switch to black-and-white film. The present story bore almost no resemblance to any actual case Jackie and Jake had been involved in, and Jackie liked it that way.

"And you're okay with Jake playing himself?" John had asked.

"Who better?" Jackie asked. "I'll even sign on as dog wrangler." Jackie's mother and son had other plans for the first month of summer, and she and Jake would be on their own. It had been a while since she'd taken any kind of active role in the production of a film or teleplay, and the idea interested her more than a little.

All the other roles had been filled from the ranks of local stage actors and Rodgers University students and instructors. Ral Perrin, a young Hollywood cinematographer who had come to Rodgers to teach a couple of years back, had been happy to accept the job of director of photography. Andy Fry, John's roommate and another of Jackie's students, was the producer. There was a third roommate in the big, run-down house in Central Palmer that John had inherited from his grandmother. Katie Nolan was an art major at Rodgers, and had agreed to lend her artistic abilities as production designer. As more and more commitments of time and energy came through, the dream had finally begun to approach reality.

Andy came up to them now, waving a clipboard with a thick sheaf of papers attached. "Hi, Ms. Walsh. How's the dog-wrangler business?"

"Booming," said Jackie. "I've decided to give up teaching film and take Jake straight to Hollywood."

Andy smiled, then the smile faded into a frown. "I sure hope you're kidding, Ms. Walsh. Hey, we need to go over these production boards, my man," he told John. "It'd be a big help if we could do it today."

John took a deep breath, let it out slowly. "Would tomorrow be too late?" he asked his friend.

"Nope. But day after tomorrow will be."

"Get me up early and I'll look at them with you over breakfast," John said. "I'm sure they're fine anyhow. I trust your know-how, Andy."

"Well, this *is* the first thing I've produced outside of a student project," Andy reminded him.

"I'm here to tell you it won't be the last, buddy," John

told him. "Today the Central States Film Festival, tomorrow the world."

"No, today the waterfront warehouse setups, tomorrow the exteriors with the nice doggie," Andy reminded him, stooping to give Jake a friendly pat. Jake panted a canine smile and wagged his long black tail. He seemed to like all the new friends he'd been making this summer, and Andy was known to carry dog biscuits in his pockets. He pulled one out now and, after Jackie had nodded her permission, gave it to Jake. "Just one, big guy," he told the Shepherd. "Wouldn't want to spoil your lunch."

"Don't you go eating the rest of them yourself, Mr. Producer," said John to his roommate. "Go out and get some lunch with everyone else. You look to me like you could use some."

"Ah, I'm going to skip it," Andy said. "I'm not feeling so hot today. Stomach flu or something." He saluted Jake and his two friends with the clipboard and walked back toward the corner of the warehouse, where he'd staked out an office for his production department. The warehouse was serving as production headquarters for the film as well as providing space for several interior sets.

"Hey, have you seen my car keys?" John called after him.

"Nope," Andy replied. "Where did you see them last?"

"In my shirt pocket," said John.

"Real men keep their keys in their pants pockets," Andy teased, patting his pocket. "Hear that? I always know where they are. You took your shirt off about an hour ago and threw it into some corner or other like you always do." He walked off shaking his head.

"That's not true," John protested to Andy's retreating back. "Some days I throw it over the back of a chair."

Katie Nolan had been standing behind Andy, waiting her turn for a moment of the director's time. "Got a minute for me, Captain?" she inquired. Her tone was flip, but

Jackie saw the same stars were in the pretty young bru-
nette's eyes that were there every time she looked at the
director.

"Sure, Katie," John replied. "What can I do for you?"
John never seemed to notice Katie's feelings for him,
though he was always as friendly and comfortable with
her as he was with Andy.

"Can we go over these paint and fabric samples for the
Shannon's apartment set? I've had to completely rethink
all the colors since you decided on black-and-white,
'cause a lot of colors just don't photograph right. I thought
maybe you might be free for lunch . . ."

"I wish I was, but I've got to butter up my leading lady.
You know how it goes. Can we look at them at home
tonight after we wrap?"

"Oh, sure. Tonight would be just fine." Katie was good
at hiding her disappointment, but Jackie wasn't fooled.
John had just broken up with the girl he'd been going
with for most of the past school year, and Katie had probably been hoping to step into the gap. It didn't look like
she had much of a chance if she couldn't get John to pay
any more attention to her than he was paying to the latest
batch of fabric samples.

"See you tonight, then," said Katie, turning away. "Am
I giving you a lift home?"

"I brought my truck today," John told her, "but maybe
we could carpool tomorrow?"

"It's a deal," Katie said with a smile that Jackie had no
doubt was sincere.

"Maybe you'd better go talk to Lorraine now," Jackie
suggested to John. "Blow some of your stupendous budget
buying her crêpes at Suzette's. Make her feel like a movie
star. Maybe you should get her an air conditioner for her
trailer while you're at it. I think the heat's making her
cranky."

"Good idea," John agreed. "I guess I should spend more

time socializing with the cast, but to tell you the truth I'm afraid to leave the set for fear someone else will get sent to the hospital." On the first day of shooting, a grip had dropped a prop telephone onto an electrician's head and sent him to the emergency room for twelve stitches. Even though John had taken out a thorough and expensive insurance policy on the shoot and the electrician's medical expenses had been covered, he hadn't stopped worrying since the incident had happened.

"It might be you that gets hit if you don't start kissing up to your leading lady," Jackie told him. "Jake and I are going to take a walk around town. We'll see you at two o'clock."

CHAPTER 2

Jackie wasn't terribly surprised to meet up with Mercy Burdeau, the chairman of the Palmer Film Commission, less than a block from the set as she and Jake walked toward Cockrill Park.

"Jackie! How's it going?" Mercy inquired with her usual good cheer. "I was just on my way over to visit you on the set."

Jackie was pretty sure Mercy had actually been on her way over to visit Ral Perrin. Jackie could have sworn she saw big blue sparks the first time they'd met only a few weeks previously, but Ral had been too shy to do much of the pursuing, and Mercy had been out of town since then doing some pursuing of her own: Hollywood producers for Palmer.

"Checking up on our DP?"

Mercy's liquid brown eyes sparkled. "Does he need checking up on?"

"Well, coming from you I think he'd welcome it," Jackie assured her. "And while you're there you can gather all sorts of good info to take back to your employers about what a boon to Palmer commerce this production is. It might help the next impoverished independent filmmaker who comes along."

Although the Palmer Film Commission had been officially in existence for over a year, there hadn't been much happening until Mercy was hired on to promote the town to Hollywood filmmakers as an unspoiled small-city location with lots of beautiful old buildings. The city government had issued its first permits to John McBride and Andy Fry only a few months before, enabling them to shoot on city property. The film commission wasn't exactly doing a booming business yet, but it was a strategic move on the city's part—if there was a Palmer Film Commission and an advertising campaign in the Hollywood trade publications, surely films made in Palmer would follow, or that was the plan, anyhow. Now that Mercy Burdeau was on the job and actively chasing after productions, it looked like that actually might happen, and soon.

"The set's pretty empty right now," Jackie told her. "Most of them are either gone to lunch or out in the parking lot playing poker with Kurt Manowski. I think Ral might still be hanging around, though. By the way, how'd the latest L.A. trip go?"

"I think I've sewn up that Paramount project," said Mercy with her characteristic dazzling smile, "thanks to Leo McTaggart's photos of the Market District and some tap dancing on my part. I just talked my tail off as usual, and convinced them it'd be tough to find a more authentic-looking location for the kind of period piece they're doing than right here in Palmer. Especially for the price."

"So the neighborhood's going to be overrun with movie stars, huh?"

"If I have anything to say about it, yeah."

"Everything still on track for the film festival?"

"Absolutely. And with Palmer hosting its first festival, it'll be good to have a Palmer film in the running for the prizes. Everything still on track for our movie?"

"Absolutely," Jackie told her. "Right on schedule, thanks to our producer. Well, Jake and I are on our way to the park for a bag lunch"—she held up the bag in question—"so I won't keep you. Maybe I'll see you after lunch?"

"Bank on it," Mercy told her with a little wave of her hand, and walked off in the direction of the old warehouse, where the handsome young cinematographer was waiting, unawares.

Jackie let out an involuntary sigh. Romance was everywhere, and Tom Cusack, her own choice in matters romantic, was two thousand miles away with his daughter, Grania, and Jackie's son, Peter, spending a month in California. Her old school chum Marcella Jacobs was seen everywhere these days on the arm of Palmer's chief medical examiner, Cosmo Gordon, who'd never seemed younger or handsomer himself, though he was closing on sixty nearly as fast as Jackie was sneaking up on forty. The Palmer Police Department's newest detective, Bernadette Youngquist, had taken up with Joseph Rayney, a dog trainer who worked for Tom, and the one who was single-handedly running Cusack Kennels while Tom was away. The two of them had started out with mutual affection for a scruffy little terrier named Arlo, and the rest just happened.

Even Jackie's mother, Frances Costello, was away for the summer, visiting her friend Bara Day in Florida. Her letters and phone calls were increasingly full of mentions of a certain Mr. Dennis Mallon, a retired gentleman who had taken to sitting in on their card games every day since Frances had arrived, and off whom she had won forty-five dollars so far at penny-ante poker, with the likelihood of more to come. Mr. Mallon was a lousy poker player, but a "real dish," according to Frances.

Jackie sat down on a wooden bench and unwrapped an egg-salad sandwich for herself and one for Jake. It was only three weeks, she reminded herself, and meanwhile she could keep herself busy helping out on John's film. Well, maybe not busy, exactly. A wise person once said that the most exciting day of his life was his first day on a movie set, and the most boring day of his life was the second.

The vast majority of people had no idea just how dull a day on a typical movie production actually was, Jackie knew, but at least her experience writing for television in Los Angeles years ago had taught her what to expect. When Jake wasn't working or getting ready to work, there was little to do but sit and watch while scenes were being shot, or sit and read while they were being set up, which took a great deal more time than the shooting.

Jackie fumbled a paperback book out of her handbag and opened it with one hand while managing the sandwich with the other. Jake, having wolfed his sandwich in two bites and having looked around fruitlessly for more, lay down at her feet. A nearby squirrel gave him the eye from two feet above the ground on a tree trunk, but earned nothing more for his trouble than a tired "whuff" from the big German Shepherd. "You *are* getting old, Jake," Jackie told him, laughing.

In fact, Jake was getting on in years for a dog of his breed, but he was still healthy and active, and entirely free from most of the typical health problems that plagued German Shepherds. Besides, he had a young ginger cat at home, or perhaps the cat had him, who kept him young and playful. Charlie wouldn't hear of Jake lying about when he wanted to run in circles around the living room and kitchen, endangering anything that wasn't nailed down in Jackie's townhouse apartment. He liked to chase up and down the wrought-iron spiral staircase that led to Jackie and Peter's bedrooms, too, but Jake usually drew the line at that, being ten times Charlie's size and weight, and with a much stronger sense of dignity.

When her watch told her it was nearly two, Jackie slipped the book back into her handbag and picked up Jake's lead. "Time to get back to work, old boy," she told her dog. "I think you've got some pickups to do this afternoon. Ready for your close-up?"

Jake seemed to recognize a question even if none of his favorite words was contained in it. He barked once in his version of an answer. This trick had fooled any number of people into suspecting that Jake actually understood English.

"Then let's fight our way through the throngs of autograph hunters and get back to the set."

When Jackie and Jake were closer to the warehouse, they could see an orange-and-white Palmer Memorial Hospital ambulance pulled up at a hurried angle outside the big double doors onto Indiana Avenue, with a knot of people standing nearby. They walked toward it as the attendants climbed inside and closed the doors.

Jackie could see John McBride and Lorraine Voss standing at the rear of the ambulance as it pulled away into the light afternoon traffic. Katie Nolan stood on the other side of John. Ral Perrin and Mercy Burdeau, along with Marti Bernstein and a few of the other crewmembers, were a few feet away, talking worriedly among themselves.

"What happened?" Jackie asked, almost afraid to hear the answer.

"Andy had some kind of attack," John replied. "They're taking him to the hospital."

"Attack?"

"I think it's probably appendicitis," Lorraine put in. "I'm sure he'll be all right."

"Yeah, after surgery and a couple weeks' recuperation." John sighed. "I'd better get over there."

He turned to his assistant director. "Marti, will you tell everyone we're done shooting for today? Tell them I'll call them tonight if I want them to come in tomorrow."

"Sure thing, boss," Marti replied. "That's it for today!" she called to the people standing outside the warehouse. "We'll call and let you know what's up with Andy when we hear from the doctor." She walked into the warehouse to inform anyone who might still be inside.

"John, would you like me to give you a lift to the hospital?" asked Katie.

"That'd be great," John said with relief. "I think I'm too distracted to drive without ending up in the hospital myself." He took off his backward-facing ball cap and ran his long fingers through his hair. "Hey, I'm really sorry about this, Lorraine," he said to his leading lady.

"Don't sweat it, John," Lorraine replied. "This kind of thing happens on the big shoots, too. You go look after Andy, and I'll expect your call tonight. We'll talk about those script rewrites." Lorraine's earlier pique seemed to have dissipated, or probably drowned in the wild mushroom cream sauce on one of Suzette's crêpes champignons. She patted John's arm and walked into the warehouse.

"Rewrites?" Jackie asked.

"Oh, Lorraine had some ideas for integrating some things from *Eyes of the City*. Just little detective tricks she seems to like. I told her I could write a few things into the scenes that haven't been shot yet. I just hope I have a movie to rewrite anything for in the first place. I'll call you later and tell you what's happening with Andy."

"I'll be at home," she told him. She put a hand on his arm. "You're worried about the movie, aren't you?"

John sighed deeply. "I feel like a jerk even thinking about it with Andy sick and everything, but yeah," he said. "Without a producer we're dead in the water. I might as well tell everyone to go home and forget about it. I can't do both jobs and finish this shoot on schedule."

"I've got some ideas on that," Jackie said. "Come by when you get through at the hospital, and we'll talk about it."

CHAPTER 3

"You think you can actually get Cameron Clark to produce?" John's astonishment at Jackie's suggestion was evident. "Jeez, Jackie, that'd be great! I mean, that guy's got credentials. Genuine Hollywood credentials, and lots of them!"

"Well, you're not exactly chopped liver yourself," Jackie reminded him. "Maybe you don't have twenty years of feature films to your credit like Cameron Clark, but your student projects have gotten a lot of favorable attention, and all the film instructors have been watching to see what you'd do, not just me. Besides," she added, "if Cameron Clark was such a hot ticket in Hollywood, what's he doing teaching film production at Rodgers University? We've got a pretty good reputation for a small school in Ohio, but we *are* two thousand miles from the real center of moviemaking in this country."

"Good point," John remarked. "I guess I never thought about it before, but what *is* he doing here?"

"I don't know," said Jackie, "and I *have* thought about it. But the important thing for you to think about is, we've got a shot at getting him."

"Have you ever worked with him before? When you were in Hollywood?"

"No, we were never on a project together. Remember, I did mainly television, and he did mainly features, so we never actually met before he came to Palmer, but we have a lot of mutual friends in the business, and he knows that. I'll call him tonight and arrange to go by and drop off a copy of the script."

"I'm sure he'll listen to you out of professional courtesy," said John, "but courtesy won't get him to sign on. I still think we're probably sunk."

"Don't you believe it," Jackie countered. "Sure, he'll let me talk to him about the film and your problems out of courtesy. He'll read your script out of courtesy, too. But when he does, he'll be sold. I'm sure of it."

"I'm sold," Cameron Clark said, putting the script to *Under the Dog Star* down on his desk with a snap. He smoothed his graying blond mustache in an unconscious gesture, then linked his hands behind his head and leaned back in his leather executive chair. "I have nothing on my plate for the next few weeks, and I think this is a project I could be proud to be a part of. I'll want a day or two to familiarize myself with what's already been done, but I think we could start shooting again on Monday."

Jackie looked at John McBride, who was staring at Cameron in disbelief. "Well, John?"

John closed his mouth. "Well, okay! I mean, thank you, Mr. Clark."

"That's Cameron, John," he said with a smile. "We're going to be working together closely for the next few weeks, so let's not let any formality come between us."

Jackie had called Cameron Clark the night before, after talking to John, and delivered a copy of the script early this morning. Two hours later he'd called back and asked her to bring the young director to his house for a discussion on the project. John had been a wreck, anticipation vying with apprehension about the fate of his film. If there was such a thing as luck, Jackie thought, John McBride hadn't been getting his fair share of it the last couple of days. Cameron's acceptance of the producer job was a needed upturn.

Cameron turned toward the doorway to his study where his wife, Sondra, was entering with a tray of cold drinks. "There you are, darling. Just in time to congratulate us on our new enterprise."

Sondra Clark was nearly half her husband's age, Jackie guessed—probably not much older than John. Cameron had met her soon after he came to Palmer, and married her after a whirlwind courtship, if a dating relationship in Palmer, Ohio, could truly be called by such a glamorous name. She was a beautiful woman, nearly as tall as her husband and even blonder, with deep blue eyes and striking features. She'd had some modeling experience in Chicago before moving back to Palmer, where she'd been born and raised, and rumor in the film department had it that she wanted to be an actress. Rumor also had it that she had assumed Cameron would be packing up and moving back to the excitement and glamour of Hollywood after his first semester teaching film production to Ohio college students, and that she'd be on her way to stardom. Unfortunately for Sondra and her ambitions, Cameron seemed perfectly content to stay right where he was.

He was not nearly so content with his new wife's spending habits, it was said around campus. She favored designer labels in her clothes and exquisitely expensive handmade Italian shoes, and had recently treated herself to a red Miata courtesy of Cameron's savings account. It didn't seem to bode well for the long-term survival of the marriage, and in fact, bets had been placed on the matter by several instructors. As far as Jackie knew, Cameron was unaware of the "Cameron and Sondra" pool, and she herself had declined to buy a chance on more than one occasion.

"You're going to produce the movie? That's wonderful!" Sondra flashed a wide smile at John and handed him an icy glass of lemonade. "I'm so glad you and Cameron are going to be working together," she breathed, and Jackie could swear she actually batted her eyelashes. Sondra had been unable to tear her eyes away from John McBride since he walked into the house. It was no surprise to Jackie that John seemed to have that effect on women, but Sondra Clark was certainly no actress, Jackie mused, if she couldn't hide her interest in another man any better than that, and in front of her husband, besides.

"Let's drink to our project, shall we?" said Cameron. He either didn't notice Sondra's behavior or wasn't willing to admit he did in front of guests. He passed out drinks to Jackie and Sondra, then took the last glass for himself.

"To *Under the Dog Star*." Cameron raised his glass.

John raised his in turn, then withdrew it suddenly. "You do understand I can't pay you?" John asked him.

"I understand the limitations of your budget," Cameron replied. "I'll take the same percentage deal you offered Andy Fry, of course, less what Andy's already earned by producing up to this point. The important thing is to get the film made. Then we can all bask in your reflected glory." He flashed John a brief smile of even white teeth and held his glass high again. "To making a movie."

"To making a movie!" chimed the other three.

Cameron took a drink of his lemonade and frowned. "This is too sweet, Sondra."

Sondra had nothing to say to that. She was too busy making eyes at John.

"So, are you having any problems with Kurt Manowski yet?" Cameron asked, setting his glass down on a polished stone coaster on top of his desk.

"No," John replied. "No problems at all."

Cameron's expression turned dark and sour. "Trust me," he said, "you will. I've known that character for almost as long as I've been making movies, and he's nothing but trouble. Consider yourself forewarned."

As Jackie had told John, she knew Cameron Clark by reputation only, and his reputation in Hollywood was that of an operator. He'd never been one of the major players, but it wasn't for lack of trying on his part. He'd had a long string of commercial and critical successes up until nine or ten years ago, but then came a string of bad choices and bad luck, and since then he'd had to content himself with making films that raked in a modest amount of money and no critical notice whatever. Although he'd seemed to be making a fair amount of money at it, at some point he'd started putting out feelers for teaching jobs. When a recent opening in the Rodgers University communications department had presented itself, Cameron had been offered the job teaching film production, and to the surprise of everyone in the department, Jackie included, he had accepted.

Cameron's reputation as an instructor was likewise solid but undistinguished. He showed up for his lectures, unlike a few people Jackie could think of at Rodgers, and he taught his own classes, unlike quite a few more. His teaching was widely considered to be serviceable but uninspired, and his salary was solid but hardly princely, if department scuttlebutt was any indicator. His main value to the university seemed to be the number of times his name had appeared a foot high in the opening titles of big-budget feature films, and as to what Rodgers's value was to Cameron Clark, no one had the slightest idea.

Jackie would have guessed that to someone like Cameron, the position at Rodgers would be such a long way down from wheeling and dealing with actors and directors in Los Angeles as to be entirely undesirable, but maybe he had just tired of the rat race, as she had years ago. Maybe he just wanted to live without the constant hustle,

without constantly having to watch his back. Jackie could
certainly understand that.

"A real movie, right here in Palmer!" Sondra gushed.
Jackie realized she'd been gushing for at least a minute,
but lost in thought, she had tuned her out. "Will I be able
to come and visit you on the set, dearest?" she asked her
husband with an unsubtle sideways glance at John.

If Cameron saw the look, he was still pretending not to
notice. "Of course you can, darling," he said, patting her
arm, "but you won't find filmmaking nearly as exciting
as it's been depicted, I'm afraid."

"I can vouch for that," Jackie told Sondra. "It's ninety-
nine percent boredom."

"Well, I guess I'll just have to hope for that one percent," Sondra said, rearranging a platinum curl against her
perfectly made-up cheek. "Have you finished the casting
yet?" she asked John.

"Uh, yes, we're a week into the shooting, actually."

"Oh," said Sondra, a bit crestfallen. "I was hoping there
might be a part I could test for."

Cameron relieved her of the tray. "Enough about acting, darling," he said, "what we're here to discuss is production. And success." To Jackie, it seemed that he wasn't
trying too hard to hide his impatience with his new wife's
career ambitions. Or just possibly the real source of his
impatience was the way Sondra was throwing herself at
a good-looking man a lot closer to her own age than he
was.

Jackie sneaked a look at John. He had noticed nothing,
of course, deep in thought about getting his movie made
despite the hard knocks he'd been dealt so far. Jackie told
herself with some satisfaction that she'd been able to
make a difference: it looked like now he finally would.

CHAPTER 4

Jackie stepped out onto her front porch and bent down to pick up her morning *Palmer Gazette*.

" 'Morning, Ms. Walsh," called a neighbor from the next building. It was Mr. Culbertson, who liked to sit out on his porch to drink his morning coffee. "Why don't you just have that dog of yours go out and get the paper in the morning?" he inquired cheerfully.

" 'Morning, Mr. Culbertson," Jackie called back. "I tried that, but he has a bad habit of hogging the sports section. Still keeping the birds happy?"

Mr. Culbertson picked up the three-pound coffee can full of birdseed that he liked to keep on his porch. "You bet. They keep the bugs out of my flowers."

Mr. Culbertson got so much pleasure from the birds who gathered around to get fat on his birdseed that Jackie never had the heart to tell him that seed-eating birds weren't all that interested in bugs, and vice versa. She was sure the bug-eating species found their way to his garden on their own, and who was she to deprive a finch of a nice breakfast of millet? She picked up the paper.

LOCAL FILM CARICATURES LOCAL CITIZENS, read the feature teaser above the headline, MARCELLA JACOBS RE-

PORTS. After that, who cared about Wall Street, the latest war in the Middle East, or the Indians' losing streak? Shaking her head in disbelief, Jackie carried the paper inside, with a distracted good-bye wave to Mr. Culbertson. The phone was ringing.

"Hello?"

"What's this about that movie of yours being—wait a minute, here it is. Oh, yes—'a thinly-disguised portrait of the real Palmer, Ohio'?"

"Good morning, Jane," Jackie said with less than total good humor to the mayor of the real Palmer, Ohio. "First, it's not my movie, second, I haven't even read—"

"Well, I have!" Jane Bellamy shouted through the phone. Jackie winced and moved the receiver eight inches from her ear. "It's wrecked my entire morning and made my city into a laughingstock!"

"First, it's not your city—" Jackie began, but it was doubtful Jane even heard her—she was too busy shouting her next statement.

"I'm appointing a commission to look into this affair," she went on. "You and your movie people had better be ready to deal with them!"

"Jane, you already have a film commission," Jackie said. She pitched her voice to a calm, reasonable tone, the better to set a positive example for Palmer's fearless leader. "Maybe it would save a lot of time and trouble if you—"

The phone went dead.

Jackie laid the paper down on her 1950s-vintage dining table in shades of pearl gray and bright red with bright chrome upholstery tacks studding the chair backs, and dug a box of Weetabix out of the cupboard. She was just going for milk and a carton of vanilla yogurt when the phone rang again.

"Hello?" Jackie said into the mouthpiece, a bit more tentatively than the last time.

"Jackie, is it true what they're saying about *Under the Dog Star*? This time it was the new president of Rodgers University, Tanner Maxwell—Max to his intimates, of which Jackie was not one.

"I don't think Marcella Jacobs constitutes 'they,' Dr. Maxwell," Jackie told him. "At least I hope she doesn't. I haven't read the story yet, but I'm sure it's exaggerated. Marcella has gone a while between juicy features, and it's starting to show."

"Then you're sure the university won't have any cause to consider taking legal action against the production company?"

"Absolutely certain," Jackie assured him. At least as of the most recent script rewrite, she thought to herself, but there was no particular need to share that with Dr. Maxwell. "Even if the story's true, and I hasten to point out it isn't"—she rushed the last over the sound of indrawn breath that told her Dr. Maxwell was reacting to the possibility that Marcella was onto something—"there's no point in getting upset unless something actionable happens. And it won't." She winced to herself and waited for a reply.

A moment of silence from the other end. "If you say so, Jackie. You know how seriously I take Rodgers's reputation." Tanner Maxwell had only been on the job for the past semester, having been hired away from a prestigious school in New England, but he planned to be here a long time, and often bludgeoned innocent bystanders with his sincerity about his adopted school.

Jackie had been hoping it wouldn't actually come to this, but now it had, and there was nothing to do but bite the proverbial bullet and break the bad news. "I'm pretty sure the university is never mentioned in the film, Dr. Maxwell," Jackie informed him.

"It's not?" There was no mistaking the disappointment

in the old professor's voice. "But isn't Mr. McBride a
student of ours?"

"Well, technically, no. He graduated several weeks ago
with a bachelor's degree in film."

"An alumnus, then. Surely he'd want to make some
mention of his alma mater in his film . . ."

"Well, if he does," Jackie told him with as much seri-
ousness as she could muster under the circumstances, "I'll
remind him to be sure it isn't libelous."

"Thank you, Jackie," Dr. Maxwell said, and Jackie
could clearly hear the relief in his voice. "I knew I could
count on you."

Jackie groaned and hung up the phone. She took two
steps across the kitchen, then turned back and removed
the receiver from its cradle. Time for a nice, peaceful
breakfast, if her old pal's story didn't manage to wreck
her appetite entirely.

Marcella had stopped by the set three days ago, Jackie
recalled, on Cameron Clark's first day on the set. Accompanied by her faithful staff photographer Werner Benz,
she'd interviewed Lorraine Voss, Kurt Manowski, Cameron, John, and any number of crewmembers and local
actors. Her editor at the *Gazette* wanted a series of five
feature articles, one each day from then until Sunday, and
if the first had caused this much reaction already, Jackie
was thinking about moving out of town before the *Gazette*
had a chance to publish the other four.

And what's more, Jackie thought to herself as she
poured low-fat milk on a crunchy whole-wheat biscuit,
Cameron's first day on the set had been the good one. It
had been the second and third days that had seen actors
at the boiling point, crewmembers threatening to walk out,
and in general made spending a day on the set like doing
time in movie hell. Even Jake seemed disappointed with
the change in producers, but that probably had as much

to do with missing Andy and his doggie treats as anything else.

Cameron had generously allowed the cast and crew a grace period of one whole day before starting to throw his weight around, act like a Hollywood big shot, throw out all of Andy Fry's preproduction work, refuse to approve any of Katie Nolan's set and costume sketches, and declare John's choice of camera equipment and film stock completely substandard for a feature film. To complete the Pretentious Producer image, he never went anywhere without his cell phone, and seemed always to have an important call to make or to take. He seemed unwilling, thank God, to badger John into reshooting the scenes that were already in the can, but after throwing out all Andy's and Katie's work and nearly reducing Katie to tears in front of everyone, he'd made an overnight trip to Chicago. The next day he'd returned with a new and more expensive camera and a lot of high-priced sound equipment, along with a couple of cases of premium thirty-five-millimeter film stock, courtesy of John McBride's rapidly shrinking production budget.

All this Hollywood posturing hadn't exactly filled John with joy, a fact that surprised no one, and he and Cameron were spending a lot of time glaring at one another, and very little time communicating about the needs of the film. John was worried about the budget and the shooting schedule, and Cameron's main concern seemed to be what was left of his reputation and what harm he might be doing it if he couldn't manage to turn John's film into something a little more ambitious than the young director had intended.

Jackie also knew Cameron's mood hadn't been helped along any by Sondra's behavior, or by the fact that John had written a minor character into the script for her to play. It was a small thing in itself, and not unheard of in Hollywood, where script rewrites came daily or even hourly, and characters sometimes came and went like streetcars, but this wasn't Hollywood. The crew and local actors seemed to put a suspicious cast on John's motivations for writing Sondra into the film, and the way Sondra hung on John's every word and looked for excuses to be as close to him as possible didn't exactly make them feel they'd been mistaken.

Cameron ignored his wife directly, but appeared to be taking out his frustrations on others. He wrangled with the crew over every detail of their work, and repeatedly insulted the local actors' abilities and professionalism. As if that weren't problem enough, he and Kurt Manowski were beginning to act like a couple of alpha male wolves on the verge of a major dogfight. Jackie wasn't certain which of them could be called the aggressor, but Cameron's general attitude toward Kurt, never really good to begin with, had deteriorated considerably since that first day when everything had seemed so promising.

The local actors were grumbling, several crewmembers had already threatened to quit, and it was all John could do to hold on to them day by day. It was anybody's guess if the crew would remain intact for the three weeks remaining on the shooting schedule, and unlikely any of them would still be speaking to the producer by the time the shoot wrapped—even the ones who were still students of his at Rodgers.

Jackie was thankful, at least, that Marcella's visit had occurred on the one day when the production had been a model of peace, organization, and general harmony. Maybe Cameron had even been on his best behavior for the press—he'd had plenty of practice making himself look good to tougher audiences than Marcella Jacobs and the *Palmer Gazette*.

Or maybe that had been Marcella's problem, Jackie mused as she ate her cereal and turned the pages of the newspaper without really seeing them. When there hadn't seemed to be anything unusual to report, perhaps Marcella's imagination had started working overtime. Jackie decided she'd give her old pal a call. She crossed the kitchen to the phone, hung it back up, and picked it up again quickly, lest any more angry citizens of Palmer get through on her line. Then she dialed Marcella's number at the *Gazette*.

"Marcella Jacobs's office," said a man's voice on the other end.

"Is this Marcella's personal secretary?"

"No, this is Bruce from copy. I think her ladyship's in the powder room."

"If you value your job, Bruce, don't let her catch you calling her that," Jackie advised.

She heard Marcella's voice in the background: "Give me that! What are you doing answering my phone, anyway?"

"Marcella, it's me. Jackie."

"Jackie, hi! What's up? Have you read my first article on the movie?"

"Well, I haven't actually had time to read the whole thing yet," Jackie told her. "I've been too busy answering the phone and dealing with the people who have."

"It's causing quite a stir, isn't it?" There was no mistaking the pride in Marcella's voice.

Jackie couldn't bring herself to burst her friend's balloon first thing in the morning by complaining about the trouble her article had already caused her or the trouble that was likely to be added to that by the time the series finished running on Sunday. "It certainly is," was what she managed, finally. "Are you free tonight, or have you got something going on with Cosmo?"

"Well, he usually calls before lunch, and more nights than not we have dinner together, but if you want to do something, I can always tell him I'm busy. Cosmo's a dear, but it won't hurt him to be reminded I've got a life aside from him."

"No, probably not. I was thinking drinks at Prince Charlie's."

"Why not the Michigan Grill?"

"Because that's where Lorraine Voss hangs when she leaves the set every evening, and we'd never get a table for all the locals who want to be seen drinking with a movie star."

The Michigan Grill, an attractive and usually quiet place on Michigan Street in downtown Palmer, was referred to on the set as the Star Bar since Lorraine had taken to spending her evenings there. A less upscale local watering hole on Indiana Street—the Crow Bar—had been renamed the Crew Bar since Kurt Manowski and his buddies on the crew had made it their own. The Crow Bar was a little on the noisy and smoky side, and Jackie had no desire to fight Kurt's share of local autograph hunters for a quiet table only to find she couldn't breathe the air. Her own favorite hangout, Bridget O'Malley's, was too working class for Marcella's tastes, and to make it worse, Martin the bartender got no end of pleasure out of making fun of the fancy, sweet drinks Marcella favored.

"Prince Charlie's, then," Marcella agreed. "Is eight okay?"

"Is that a time, or the number of Fuzzy Navels you're planning on putting away?"

"Be nice to me or you'll have to drink alone," Marcella warned.

"Oh, okay. If I must. See you at eight."

CHAPTER 5

Jackie approached the warehouse on Indiana Street with a sense of dread, which Jake seemed to reflect with a nervous attitude of his own. Things on the set were going downhill day by day, and Jackie dreaded another day of watching Cameron Clark throw his weight around with the cast and crew. These were the people John needed to hang together for him, and they were growing increasingly discontented.

She and Jake had walked to the set from the apartment on Isabella Lane, enjoying the brief coolness of the morning all the more because it wouldn't last until nine o'clock. A pigeon landed on the sidewalk in front of them and startled Jake, who barked at it. "Cool down, old guy," Jackie told him as the pigeon flapped away. "Don't let my lousy mood rub off on you. One of us has to act like a professional, anyhow."

Jake had already done several major scenes and any number of minor pickup shots, and although he was not a movie dog by trade, Jackie was impressed by the way he followed directions and remained patient in the face of retakes and endless delays for lighting and setups. He seemed genuinely to enjoy the added attention he received on the set whether he was working or not, but typical of his breed, he didn't go out of his way to show it.

Jackie had to acknowledge that Jake was noticeably happier when he had something to occupy his intellect, or at least something more challenging than chasing a kitten around her apartment. Life as a retired dog didn't suit him all that much, and he really shone when he had work to do. She also had to admit that if Jake weren't a working dog on this film, only her loyalty to John McBride would have kept her coming back to the set day after day to watch Cameron Clark make enemies left and right. Even then, she wasn't entirely sure how long that loyalty would have been enough.

Now she stood outside the big double doors on Indiana Street, took a deep breath, and walked inside. The relative darkness after the bright sunshine of the street outside, and the fact that none of the interior sets were lit just now, made the warehouse seem dark as night. For a moment Jackie couldn't hear anything, then Cameron Clark's voice cut through the silence: "I've had it with your attitude, Manowski! I'm not going to put up with any lip from you on this shoot. There are plenty of hungry losers out there looking for work, and don't think for a minute I'm not just looking for an excuse to jack you up and stick another washed-out, unemployed actor where you used to be."

As Jackie's eyes adjusted to the change in light, she could see Cameron and Kurt squared off in the center of the warehouse floor, surrounded by the rest of the cast and crew.

"Like you did the last time, right?" Kurt said, his voice tight with anger, fists clenched at his sides.

"You'd better believe it," said Cameron, his words dripping with malice and self-satisfaction. "*Just* like I did the last time."

Jackie turned to Ral Perrin, who was perched behind the camera, chin on hand, watching the confrontation.

"What's that all about?" she whispered. "What does he mean by 'the last time'?"

"Tell you later," Ral whispered back. "I called up Matt D. last night, and we talked for half an hour. I've got truckloads of good gossip for you."

The two men in the center of the floor edged closer to one another, bodies inclined forward, eyes locked. John McBride was watching from the sidelines, Sondra Clark holding on to his sleeve, eyes wide with alarm. John shook off Sondra's arm, stepped forward, and put out his hands. "I don't think you two ought to fight over this," he said quietly. "At least not here. We've got a movie to make, and time is passing us by while you guys decide whether or not you want to kill one another."

Cameron shoved John's hand aside. "Don't you try to tell me how to run a film shoot, punk," he said, turning toward him. "I've been doing this longer than you've been toilet-trained."

"You've been doing it longer than he's been *alive*," said Sondra. She gave her husband a look of pure disgust and walked away through the knot of people. A few heads turned to watch her go.

"John's right," said Kurt, relaxing a bit, "This isn't the time or the place. Sorry, boss." He gave John a little smile, shot a look of pure malice at Cameron, then walked away and took a seat in a canvas chair near Lorraine Voss. Lorraine reached out and patted Kurt's arm, leaning over to talk quietly to him.

Cameron stared at John for another few seconds, then turned and went into the production office, slamming the door behind him. The corrugated metal walls of the little room rattled like a cheap movie sound effect for thunder.

"Hey, I've got a great idea, everybody," said John, his voice shaking just a little. "Let's take twenty and loosen up before we shoot this next scene."

"Think twenty'll do it?" Marti Bernstein asked him out

of the corner of her mouth. "I was thinking maybe the rest of the week."

John lowered his head and looked up at her. "Call twenty, Bernstein."

"Twenty!" Marti shouted, and the crowd dispersed to the outer edges of the warehouse, the drink tables, and the eternal poker game. The smokers headed for the door to the alleyway between Indiana and Michigan streets.

"Did I miss something?" said a voice behind Jackie. It was Mercy Burdeau. "Hi, Jackie. Hi, Ral."

"Hi there, Mercy," said Ral, brightening visibly. "What brings you here today?"

"Oh, I just wanted to see if everything in that *Gazette* article was true," said Mercy with a barely controlled smile. "The shoot Marcella Jacobs was writing about seemed so different from the one I was familiar with, I wondered if maybe another film production hadn't sprung up around here without my knowing about it . . ."

Mercy shook her head, and her dark curls flew out and settled back down prettily. Jackie was certain she heard Ral gulp. "As Director of the Palmer Film Commission," Mercy went on, "I couldn't afford not to be right on top of the situation." She winked at Jackie. "So the visit is strictly official."

"Yeah, right," Jackie mouthed at her. "Well, I'll let Ral fill you in on the gory details," she said aloud. "I've got to get the Dog Star here ready for his next scene. Come on, Jake," she said to her dog. "Time for makeup."

Leaving Ral to whatever fate Mercy might have in mind for him, Jackie walked Jake to a corner of the warehouse where screens had been set up to define a hairdressing and makeup area. Linnie Mossberger, co-owner of Mossberger's Salon and Day Spa, had turned her shop over to her employees and signed on to be the production's makeup artist. Her sister Violet, the salon's other owner, had taken the job of hairstylist. John was paying them a nominal salary out of the film's budget, but the fact of it was they had begged him for the chance to do it, and they were good at it, besides.

"Hi there, Jackie. Is our boy ready to have that gray touched up?" Linnie asked as Jackie and Jake walked toward her.

"Well, I don't know if 'ready' is the word I'd use," Jackie told Linnie. Jake didn't care for the smell of the makeup that Linnie used to cover up the gray hairs on his muzzle, but he seemed to understand that it was required of him to submit bravely to having it applied, even if he wasn't quite capable of understanding why. He sat down and waited for Linnie to approach him with the sponge loaded with the dark liquid, shooting only one reproachful glance at his mistress.

"Hey, look what I got for our star!" Violet Mossburger was coming up to them holding a large, soft-bristled dog brush. "I figured there was no reason for Jake here to be the only actor whose hair I wasn't fussing with all the time, so I bought this for him. He does like to be brushed, doesn't he?" she asked Jackie.

"He adores it," Jackie assured her. She unclipped Jake's lead and Violet knelt down beside him and groomed his coat while Linnie finished the makeup job on his nose. "Now, that's what I call the real star treatment, Jake," Jackie told the big Shepherd. "You ladies let me know when you need me to take him away. I imagine you've got human customers waiting, too."

"Well, we've still got to touch up Ms. Voss," said Violet as she ran the brush through Jake's thick coat, "but I think we're agreed we like Jake better."

Linnie rolled her eyes in silent agreement.

"Is Lorraine being a problem," Jackie asked them, "or just a movie star?"

"Well, I never met a movie star before this," said Linnie, "but that woman is more particular than any customer I ever had, and I've had some doozies."

"If she's being rotten to you, I could probably have John talk to her," Jackie offered. "It looks like he's finally managed to get on her good side."

"Oh, it's nothing serious," said Violet with a wave of her hand. "She's just not a very happy person, I think, and it shows." Neither Violet nor Linnie was inclined to look for the bad in other people, so Jackie was pretty certain they were minimizing their problems with Lorraine Voss.

"Now, why don't you leave Jake to us for a few minutes," said Linnie, "and we'll call you when we're done with him. Why don't you go get some coffee or something," she suggested.

"What a wonderful idea," said Jackie, heading for the drinks table, where a large urn of hot coffee was always waiting. It was starting to get hot and not a little muggy in the poorly insulated warehouse, and the thought of a steaming cup of coffee was fast losing its appeal, but the tub of ice and soft drinks was beginning to look awfully good. Jackie picked a sparkling juice drink and twisted off the cap.

"Do you suppose we can get through another three weeks without Kurt and our producer strangling one another?" Lorraine Voss reached into the tub of ice for a cola and gave Jackie a weary half smile.

"I sure hope so," Jackie replied. "What's the story behind all that, anyhow?"

"Oh, they've got a history back in L.A.," Lorraine said with a wave of her hand, "but for that matter, who hasn't? I'd just like them to keep their hormones under control until we can wrap this damned shoot and jet back to the land of central air-conditioning."

She fanned herself with a copy of *Variety* and swigged some of the cola, then set the paper down on the table, reached into the pocket of her 1940s-vintage gabardine skirt, and pulled out a miniature bottle of Russian vodka, which she proceeded to pour into the remaining soda. She raised one eyebrow quizzically, as though waiting for Jackie to say something about it. "The pause that *really* refreshes," she quipped, picking up her paper again and walking back toward her trailer, which had been moved inside the warehouse doors to keep it from getting too hot, and fitted with a small window-mounted air-conditioning unit.

Jackie watched her go, wondering what kind of problems made a person drink vodka for breakfast, and feeling terribly grateful that whatever they might be, she didn't have them.

"Hey, Lorraine!" Cameron's voice boomed across the warehouse, and Lorraine spun around. Jackie was startled as well. Cameron leaned out the office door, one hand on the doorjamb, the other on the knob. His mood seemed to have lightened more than a bit—a grin spread across his face, and he gave Lorraine a wink. "I hear you landed the lead in Lawrence Spalding's new project. Congratulations."

Cameron's congratulations were echoed by cast and crewmembers still in the warehouse. This was the part Lorraine had been hoping to get—the one that might well jump-start her stalled career. Jackie turned around to add her own voice to the well-wishers, and saw Lorraine smiling thinly at an assistant cameraman who patted her on the back. She gave Cameron a look Jackie couldn't interpret, and went into her trailer.

Jackie hardly had time to wonder about Lorraine's peculiar reaction before Sondra Clark walked up to fill the spot Lorraine had vacated. "Sorry about that husband of mine," she muttered as she fished around in the ice.

"Oh, it's not your fault," Jackie told her. "I guess Cameron's just anxious for everything to go right." That

wasn't at all what she thought after several days of wit-
nessing his bullying and tantrums, but there was no sense
dissing the man in front of his wife.

"Well, he's working pretty hard to make it go wrong,
if you ask me," said Sondra. She pulled her hand out of
the ice, holding a can of diet soda. "Besides, his real problem isn't with Kurt, it's with me."

Jackie willed herself not to let her curiosity show. Of
course she wanted Sondra to elaborate, but she wasn't
going to allow herself to encourage it. It wasn't really any
of her business, was it?

She needn't have worried. Sondra was all too eager to
talk about the situation, personal or not. "He hates the fact
that John wrote in a character for me." Sondra handed
Jackie her soda. "Could you open this for me? I just had
my nails done." She held up two sets of perfectly polished
acrylic nails in a shade of red that Jackie was pretty sure
was an exact match for her new sports car.

"No problem," Jackie assured her, and popped the top
on the can, taking a fraction of a second to regard her
own less-than-perfect nails—unpolished, unaugmented,
trimmed short. She proffered the can.

Sondra took the can back and took a long drink. "I
mean, the character's only got a dozen lines, but Cameron
hates the whole idea anyway. He doesn't want me to be
an actress, you know."

"No, I didn't know." Jackie was still fighting the urge
to lead Sondra on, but she was fast losing the fight. She
wasn't investigating anything, after all, so she had no excuse, but curiosity was killing her. She drank some more
juice—casually, she hoped—and waited to see if Sondra
would continue.

"Cameron's determined never to go back to Los Angeles, and he's afraid if this film's a success, I might be,
too," said Sondra. "If I were offered work on the West
Coast, we'd have to go back there, wouldn't we?"

"I suppose so," Jackie said. "For a while, anyway. At least *you* would."

"So he's sabotaging it the only way he can," Sondra continued, "by making life hell for everyone else."

"But not for you?" Oops. That had just popped out, Jackie realized. But Sondra was so determined to talk about her problems with her husband, and it would be nothing less than rude to make her carry the entire conversation, wouldn't it?

"Nope. I'm surprised you haven't noticed, but I'm about the only person on the set he doesn't seem to be trying to drive off. That's how he is, see."

"I don't think I do, actually," Jackie replied, a bit confused.

Sondra gave her an impatient look. "Don't you understand? He doesn't like to admit that it's getting to him."

Jackie was dying to know what "it" was, but she bit her lip and remained on her best behavior.

"You know," Sondra went on, leaning in closer and dropping her voice, "John." She waited for a response, and when it didn't come, she continued as though it had. "Don't tell me you haven't noticed how attracted he is to me." She tucked one blond curl behind her ear. "He's hardly taken his eyes off me since the first day I walked onto the set! Anyhow, Cameron should be used to that sort of thing by now—it's always happening to me wherever I go. But that's his problem, all right. John McBride and me. That's what it's all about. No one knows Cameron any better than I do."

Sondra paused for breath. "Well, I've got to go get into costume. One of my two whole scenes is coming up today. It's with Kurt. He scares me a little. Don't you think he's a little scary?" She didn't wait for an answer. "Of course, if Cameron has his way, my second scene may never get scheduled. Oh, well." She gave Jackie a wave and walked away. "Good talking to you," she called back over her shoulder.

"Hey, anytime," said Jackie, still a little dazed. Apparently all one had to do was hang around the drinks table and the entire cast and crew would come by and reveal their innermost secrets.

"Is Jake ready for his scene?"

Jackie turned around to see John coming up behind her. So far, her theory was holding up. He poured himself a glass of ice water from a huge white plastic container on the table, cleverly designed to look like an outsized ice cube, which was already starting to sweat drops of icy condensation in the morning heat.

"He's still in makeup," Jackie told him.

"Well, we're still setting up," said John. "No need to hurry our star."

"How's it going, John?" Jackie asked him. "I mean, really."

John shook his head. "I think I liked it about five hundred percent better when I had a producer with acute appendicitis and no hope of finishing this movie."

"I'm really, really sorry about what's happened with Cameron," Jackie said, with feeling. "I had no idea it would turn out this way. I actually thought I was doing you a favor."

"You were," John assured her. "Hey, you had no way of knowing Dr. Jekyll was about to chug the alter-ego potion and grow hair on his palms."

"John, I know it's none of my business . . ." Jackie began hesitantly.

"What isn't?" John asked. "You know you can ask me anything, Jackie."

"Oh, it's just that I'd be willing to bet part of Cameron's problem is you and Sondra." In fact, she had it from the best possible source, but there seemed no need to go into that just now.

"Jackie, there is no 'me and Sondra,' " said John. "I'd have shot her down her first day on the set, when she started coming on to me, but I was afraid of making things worse if I told her how little interest I have in her. Believe me, I've tried everything subtle. Sondra doesn't do subtle."

"It doesn't help that you wrote her into the film," Jackie reminded him.

"At the time I thought it'd make Cameron happy if I gave her something to do. I'd already decided I needed that character anyhow, so I didn't really write it just for her. But I don't mind letting her play it—it's not exactly Shakespeare."

"That's probably a good thing."

"Yeah, Sondra's not a great actress, but I've seen worse," John added.

"There are worse out there," Jackie agreed. But there was none who was making a bigger problem of herself, she thought. Sondra made a big show of pulling her little red sports car up to the doors every morning and asking a grip to park it for her. She arrived well before Cameron, who always walked the distance between their house and the set and back again every evening, and she spent the entire day finding excuses to be near the director.

"Well, when Kurt Manowski walks off the set, and all his poker partners quit in protest," John told her, "we won't need a producer's wife, because we won't need a producer, because we won't have any cast or crew left. Then I can get a job and start paying back all the money I borrowed to make this movie."

"Let's hope it won't come to that," Jackie said. She wanted to reassure John, but wasn't sure how to go about it. Would it really be better to put up with another three weeks of Cameron Clark in order to get the shoot completed? Could they all take another three weeks? John would do just about anything to get his film made, but how long could he keep everything else together?

As if in answer to her question, Daphne Harris, the script supervisor, marched up to John and pulled herself up to her full five feet nothing. "I love you like a brother, boss, and I love your movie," she told John, "but if I have to put up with one more day of that Hollywood poseur acting like he owns this shoot, I'll go postal. Put a leash on that guy, or I quit." She turned and walked two steps, then turned back around. "And you know I'm not the only one."

"You don't suppose this movie is cursed do you?" John asked Jackie as Daphne walked away, and Jackie couldn't be sure he was joking.

"I don't know," she replied. "Did you check to see if this warehouse was built over an old Indian burial ground?"

"I guess I should have." John sighed with real feeling. "On the other hand, maybe we've used up all the bad luck possible for one minor low-budget film. He started ticking off the list on his fingers. "We've already had an injured electrician, a hospitalized producer, Sondra Clark thinking I've got the hots for her, and Cameron trying to incite one of my actors to homicide. What else could possibly go wrong?"

Jackie opened her mouth to say "Don't ever say that!" But before she could get the words out, there was a scream from the direction of Lorraine's trailer. Jackie looked over to see a plume of thick gray smoke issuing from the air conditioner that had been jury-rigged into the trailer's window opening.

"Let me out!" Lorraine screamed, and pounded on the inside of the trailer door. "The door handle's broken in here!"

Jackie and John sprinted for the trailer, but Jake shot past them like a black-and-tan rocket. He pawed at the outside door handle and the door flew open, sending Lorraine tumbling out onto the concrete, gasping and cough-ing. Smoke poured out the door, along with the unmistakable smell of burnt electrical wiring. Two crew members ran up with fire extinguishers and aimed them inside the trailer door. The rest of the cast and crew gath-ered around, talking in a jumble of excited voices.

John knelt down by Lorraine. "Are you all right?" he asked her.

"Not by a long shot," she croaked, tears rolling down her face. "I could have died there."

"Not while Jake's on the job," John assured her. "He's the one who opened the door."

"Thanks, doggy," Lorraine acknowledged, letting John help her to her feet. "My costar's a hero. Bet the local papers will have a field day with that, provided it doesn't get knocked off the front page by a bake sale." She reached into her skirt pocket and fished out another min-iature vodka bottle. This one she opened and drank straight in three gulps, not bothering with the cola.

"Oh, that's all we need!" moaned Marti Bernstein. "An-other visit from the *Palmer Gazette*'s ace feature reporter. Can't we just pretend this whole thing never happened?"

"Fire's out," said one of the impromptu firefighters. The air conditioner and most of the interior of Lorraine's trailer had been coated in a thick layer of dry white foam, and smoke had ceased to issue from anywhere in the vi-cinity.

"Thanks, guys," said John. "Well, it looks like we don't need to call the fire department, but Lorraine might want a doctor to look at her."

"Forget about it," Lorraine assured him with a wave of her hand. "Just call the shoot for the day and let me go home. I'll be fine in the morning."

"Your absolutely sure about that?" John asked.

"Why make a bigger deal of it than it was? Some bad wiring, Jake on the spot and no harm done." She straightened her clothes and hair a bit. "No point trying to salvage anything out of that mess," she said, pointing at the trailer. Who do I have to kill to get a hairbrush around this place?

Violet Mossberger picked up a brush from the hair-dressing table and brought it to Lorraine. Here's one of those little Wet-Nap things, too," she offered. "You've got some soot on your face."

"Oh, hell, I might as well go wash up," said Lorraine. "How'd you like to give me a lift home, John?" she asked. "Of course I might want to stop off somewhere for a stiff drink."

"I guess that's the least I can do after all you've been through," John told her. "I'll buy." Jackie caught sight of Katie out of the corner of her eye and saw the look of jealousy and disappointment she tried but failed to hide. Poor Katie. When was she ever going to have John to herself? Maybe never, Katie, she thought. Sometimes that's just the way things work out.

"Bernstein, let's call it," said John.

"That's it for today, folks!" Marti shouted to the crowd. "Same bat-time, same bat-channel tomorrow!"

John turned back to Jackie as Lorraine walked over to the sink in the makeup department, and the cast and crew dispersed, talking among themselves. "Was that me who just said things couldn't get any worse?"

"I'm afraid it was," Jackie said, patting his arm sympathetically. "But I think you've learned your lesson."

CHAPTER 6

Prince Charlie's was heavy with quaint English ambience, with Union Jacks and dartboards and high, dark wooden booths and lots of British beer on tap. Nearly a hundred varieties of single-malt Scotch whiskeys lined the wall behind the big antique bar. The menu mostly consisted of all sorts of things Jackie never ate, like steak-and-kidney pie, but that didn't matter tonight. Tonight she was here to unwind, and she had taken the precaution of walking over from her apartment so she wouldn't have to forgo a couple of drinks in her pursuit of sociable relaxation.

"I'll have a shot of your Glenfarclas twelve-year-old and a water back," she told the bartender. "You can send it to that booth over there." She pointed to a nearby empty table.

"You want that straight up?" the bartender inquired, turning over a glass and reaching for the bottle.

"Absolutely," Jackie assured him. She picked up a bowl of crunchy snacks from the polished bar top and claimed the empty booth. Marcella wouldn't be on time, of course, so she might as well relax and enjoy the place.

Prince Charlie's had been assembled in England, then taken apart piece by piece and shipped to New York in containers. From there it had come to Ohio by train and been reassembled on the site of a burned-down restaurant about a quarter mile from Jackie's apartment. It was suitably dark and cozy and friendly. Jackie's mother would have hated it, but then Frances never had much patience with anything that reminded her of the English.

Jackie wished she'd had a chance to get together with Ral Perrin and find out what he knew about Cameron and Kurt. But after a tense day on the set, and a busy one for Jackie and Jake, Ral had slipped off to have dinner with Mercy Burdeau, and Jackie had missed out on the promised gossip from Matt Darwin, a Hollywood director of quirky films who was most often described as a maverick, and next most often as an oddball. He and Ral had worked together on several projects during Ral's years in the movie business, and he was Ral's most trusted source of industry gossip. If there was anything worth knowing in that town, Ral always said, Matt knew it, and best of all, he knew which parts of it were true.

Well, she supposed she'd hear it all in good time, Jackie decided. It wasn't as if knowing the facts of Kurt and Cameron's feud was going to keep them away from each other's throat. Tomorrow was another day, and the way it had been going, it would probably be another day of tense words, dirty looks, and near fisticuffs. Since there was absolutely no way of avoiding it, she figured the least she could do for her mental health was to forget about it for a few hours.

A waitress came by with a tray full of drinks and placed Jackie's Scotch on a red, white, and blue Union Jack cocktail napkin. "You want to run a tab?" she inquired.

"Sounds like a plan," Jackie told her. After taking an appreciative sip of the whiskey, she picked up the copy of the *Manchester Guardian* that was lying on the table and began reading the front page.

Marcella breezed in about twenty minutes late and

threw herself into the soft booth, sliding across the seat and coming to rest near the rough-plastered wall with an exhausted groan. "Sorry I'm late, but you knew I would be," she offered. Marcella's reputation for never being on time having been secured years ago, she never even tried for punctuality anymore. Twenty minutes was hardly late at all for Marcella.

"Not a problem," Jackie assured her, folding the newspaper and placing it back on the table. "Unless you consider it a problem that I'm already one Scotch ahead of you."

"It's a problem I know how to remedy," said Marcella, raising her arm to signal a server who was cruising nearby. "I'll have a brandy Alexander," she told the waitress, "and a tray of cheese and biscuits. Heavy on the Stilton."

"I'll have another of these," said Jackie.

"Which kind?" asked the waitress.

"Surprise me."

"I'm starved," Marcella told Jackie when the waitress had gone to put in their order. "I came straight here from work."

"I thought you'd already written that whole series on the film shoot," Jackie commented. "That certainly ought to cement your reputation as a feature writer for another week."

If Marcella noticed the tone of Jackie's voice, she wasn't rising to the bait. "I don't want to be a feature writer for the rest of my life," she told Jackie. "I'm trying to break into news reporting. I've got a friend on the news desk, and I've been showing him my work and trying to convince him that I'm ready to write something important. He's promised to give me a break if I can get a story to him before one of his own reporters. All I need now is a hot story. Maybe a crime. Like one of your murders, for instance."

"First, they're not my murders . . ." Jackie began, then realized it didn't really matter what she said to Marcella when the latter was in one of these enthusiastic moods. Marcella wanted to believe that the investigating Jackie did occasionally was glamorous and fun, and nothing Jackie said in the way of actual fact was going to affect that. "Good luck," she finished lamely.

"I'll need some," Marcella allowed. "The managing editor doesn't think I have what it takes to report breaking news, especially crime. He's got me firmly fixed in his fluff category, and fluff's the only thing he'll ever assign me unless I can get in through the back door. If I get a byline on a real story, he'll have to start taking me seriously. Won't he?"

"I hope so for your sake," Jackie said. "I wonder what I'd do for a living if I suddenly decided I didn't want to teach film anymore."

"You could become a private detective," Marcella suggested.

"Or a pet-sitter, maybe."

"You could go back to writing for television, I suppose," said Marcella.

"I didn't enjoy it all that much," Jackie admitted. "And I'd never take Peter to live in L.A., which is where a series television writer really needs to live. The money is good, but the lifestyle doesn't suit me, the traffic is awful, and the air is virtually unbreathable. I think Rodgers University is stuck with me for the foreseeable future."

The waitress returned with Marcella's fruity drink and a snifter of black liquid. "That's my Scotch?" Jackie asked her.

"Loch Dhu," said the waitress. "It's sort of the Guinness of malt whiskies. You *said* to surprise you."

"And you did," Jackie said. She took a sip. It was delicious. "You can surprise me anytime."

After a couple of rounds and a long conversation about

nearly everything, Marcella's attention seemed to be drawn to something on the other side of the room. "Say, isn't that Cameron Clark over there at the bar?" She pointed to a slump-shouldered man with a glass of whisky in one hand and three more shots lined up in front of him.

"It is, but I wouldn't have recognized him," Jackie told her. It was true. The man sitting at the far end of Prince Charlie's massive oak bar, looking like he was racing to the hangover of the century, bore very little resemblance to the suave figure usually cut by the producer of *Under the Dog Star* and any number of better-financed feature films. His graying blond hair hung down over his eyes, and his hands were shaking.

"What's wrong with him?" Marcella asked.

"I don't know, but I guess I ought to find out," said Jackie. "Wait here for me a minute."

She walked down to the end of the bar and sat down on the next stool. "Cameron? Are you all right?"

Cameron looked up at her with red-rimmed eyes. His left hand nervously twisted a heavy gold signet ring on his right middle finger. "Not exactly, no," he replied.

"Is there something I can do to help? Maybe a ride home?"

Cameron laughed bitterly. "Thanks, Jackie, but I'm not drunk. Not yet." He lifted one of the full shots and drained it.

"If you don't want to talk about it, I'll go away and mind my own business," Jackie offered.

"Hell, why should you?" Cameron asked with a wave of his hand. "It'll be everybody's business tomorrow."

"Uh, *what* will be everybody's business, exactly?"

"Oh, just the fact that your fair-haired young director is sleeping with my wife."

"What makes you think that?" Jackie asked him. Of course it was no secret to anyone on the set that Sondra had been throwing herself at John for the past four days, but somehow Jackie had been certain that John had better sense than to take her up on it, especially after their talk earlier today.

"I don't even have to think," said Cameron, picking up another full glass. "She told me."

Jackie opened her mouth to point out the obvious fact that Sondra's confession could have been intended to make him jealous, but Cameron was ready for her. "I found his shirt behind the bedroom door," he said. "I guess he left in a hurry."

He downed the shot, set the glass down, and reached for another. "My wife the wannabe movie star." He laughed bitterly. "Well, I told her what her chances were of ever getting to Hollywood on *my* coattails," he said. "I'm never going anywhere near Los Angeles again, and neither is she as long as she's married to me."

"I could try talking to John," Jackie offered lamely. As though talking could do any good at this point.

"Don't bother," Cameron told her. He stared at his watch for a moment, then seemed to focus on it. "I've got some other business to take care of right now, and then I'm going to talk to him myself." He straightened his rumpled jacket and combed his hair back with trembling fingers.

"Cameron, do you think it's wise to force a confrontation just now?" Jackie asked him. "I know this is a pretty big issue, but you've got the film to think about. You threw out a lot of completed work and completely changed the shooting schedule, and you promised John the new one first thing tomorrow, and—"

Cameron drained the last shot of whiskey. "I think you've got a good idea what young Mr. McBride can do with his shooting schedule *and* his film," he said. "We're going to have this out tonight. Just him and me."

He rose carefully to his feet and looked down at Jackie. "If I'd never set foot on that set, none of this would have happened. Why the hell did I let you talk me into getting involved with this one-horse-town amateur film in the first place?"

Before Jackie had time to protest that he hadn't exactly needed talking into anything, he had turned and left, walking only slightly unsteadily.

Marcella was at her elbow before Cameron was completely out Prince Charlie's back door. "Did I hear right?" she asked breathlessly. "Your student is having an affair with Cameron Clark's wife?"

"No, you're not going to do a story about it," said Jackie flatly, though she had a good idea how much effect that was going to have on Marcella's decision. "I've got to call John right now, and warn him about Cameron."

Jackie fished in her pockets for a quarter and came up empty. "Damn!"

"Here," said Marcella, handing her some change. "So tell me—what's this going to do to your movie?"

"It's John's movie," Jackie reminded her, "and this might just be the end of it."

"Ooh! 'Sex on the Set. Palmer, Ohio's, First Feature-Film Production Ends in a Hail of Accusations and Jealousy,' " Marcella recited, half under her breath, as Jackie hurried to the pay phone on the wall and inserted coins into the slot. "Come on, Jackie. You can't tell me that wouldn't make a terrific story."

Jackie raised an eyebrow at Marcella as she listened to John's phone ring. "Of course it would," she told her, "but you can't believe it's worth John McBride's reputation for you to write it."

"Might I remind you that it wouldn't be my story that wrecked his reputation," Marcella replied archly. "He's the one who was sleeping with the producer's wife."

"Hello?" Katie Nolan answered the phone at the other end.

"Katie, this is Jackie. Is John there?"

"No, he hasn't been home all evening."

"Damn!" Jackie muttered again.

"Is something wrong?"

"You might say that. Cameron Clark's on the warpath and looking for John. He'll probably show up there at the house. Do you have any idea where he is?"

"No. He hasn't been around the house much the last few days."

Jackie cringed. "How about the last few nights?"

"He wasn't here last night for sure. I've heard him dragging in at three or four in the morning a couple of times lately. But I don't understand what that's got to do with . . . Oh. I see."

Jackie felt terribly sorry for Katie, knowing how she felt about John. "I don't know anything for sure," she said, hoping she sounded more reassuring than she felt. "I just know Cameron's suspicious, is all."

That, and he found a piece of John's clothing in his wife's bedroom, but there was no need to mention that to Katie. She felt bad enough already. There was also no need to mention what this was likely to do to the production, but she knew Katie would be able to come to that conclusion without her help. "If he does come back home, warn him about Cameron, okay?"

"I will," said Katie, her voice starting to break. "This is going to be it for John's movie, isn't it?"

"I don't know. Maybe. Or maybe there's something John could say that would convince Cameron to stay and finish the production." But would he want to? Jackie wondered. "Listen, Katie, is there something I can do . . . ?"

"I'll be fine," Katie told her. "I'll see you on the set tomorrow, Jackie." The phone went dead in Jackie's hand. She sighed and returned it to its cradle, then turned to Marcella. "I think I'd like to have another drink now," she suggested.

CHAPTER 7

The phone rang, startling Jackie from a long dream of confusion and conflict. She fumbled with the receiver and managed to get it somewhere in the neighborhood of her ear. "Hello?"

"Hi, babe. It's Tom."

"Oh," said Jackie, sitting up in bed and switching on the lamp on the bedside table. "I was wondering which of the many men who call me 'babe' was calling me at this time of night."

"Well, now you know. Sorry it's so late. The kids and I went to Disneyland today, and Grania insisted we stay until they shut the park down. I thought they were supposed to get blasé at her age."

"Soon enough, I promise. Look how blasé I am at my tender age."

"Case in point," Tom agreed, chuckling. "Do you miss me yet?"

"If I said I missed you before you were out of sight down the road, would you get the idea I was totally gone on you?"

"I might, but I'm sort of an optimist about romance," Tom said.

"Well, I'll try my best not to make a pessimist of you," Jackie told him as she propped both pillows behind her back and settled in for a long conversation.

"How's our boys?"

Jackie looked down at the foot of her bed where the big Shepherd and the young ginger cat were curled up together on the bedspread. "Jake and Charlie are fine, thanks. I'll tell them you asked." Jake looked up at the sound of his name, then laid his head back down next to Charlie's.

"How's the movie going?" Tom wanted to know.

"Don't ask."

"I already did."

"Oh, yeah. Well, it's been better." She proceeded to fill Tom in on the gory details of today's happenings on the set, followed by tonight's unpleasant revelation by Cameron Clark.

"Gosh, Jackie, I'm sorry it's turning out like this," he said. "I know you had such high hopes for John and his movie, and you were having fun being part of it, weren't you?"

"I was, actually, until Cameron's evil twin took over the shoot. But by this time he's probably already had it out with John, and already quit as producer. Andy Fry won't be ready to come back to work for at least two more weeks, and I don't think there's any way John can hold everyone together for that long."

"I'd imagine people have other projects lined up," said Tom, "especially the name actors."

"Exactly. I don't know about Kurt Manowski, but it sounds like Lorraine Voss has another project starting up right after this one—a real feature with a real budget and real air-conditioning, no doubt—and there's no way she's going to give that up for sitting on her hands waiting for the rest of a small-time shoot in the middle of summer in the middle of Ohio."

"So when does the axe fall?"

"Probably first thing in the morning, when everyone's on the set. Everyone but Cameron Clark, that is—I don't know whether he's planning on showing up or not." Jackie felt tears starting up behind her eyes. "It's just so damned sad, Tom. John really wanted this to work, and he's earned it, you know?"

"Yeah, but he also brought it on himself by messing around with Cameron's wife, didn't he?"

"I suppose you could say that," Jackie allowed. "It's just that it seems so unlike John to do that. I know Sondra was being awfully obvious about how much she wanted to get her hands on him, but I just thought he had better sense than to take her up on it."

"I don't think sense enters into that sort of thing," Tom told her.

"He told me he wasn't interested in her," Jackie insisted.

"That's the kind of thing people tend to lie about," said Tom.

"I guess you're right. It's just sad."

"You said that already," Tom reminded her.

"Well, it's so sad that once doesn't cover it, then." Jackie sighed.

"I'm sorry, babe."

"You said that already, Mr. Wiseguy."

"Then I'm so sorry that once won't cover it. I really am, you know. Would you like to talk about something else for a while?" Tom asked. "Something a little cheerier, maybe?"

"I'm sorry, Tom. After all that, anything would be an improvement, wouldn't it?"

"Hey, I don't mean you shouldn't talk about it if you need to, babe. I just thought you might feel better if you got off the subject you've probably been thinking about for hours."

"And dreaming about, I think. You're right. Time to change the subject. Tell me all about our teenagers and Disneyland."

After she and Tom hung up, Jackie tried to get back to sleep, but her mind wouldn't let her forget all the terrible things that were happening because of the affair between John and Sondra. There was the movie, of course, and the disappointment of all the people who were working on it. This also might be the end of Cameron and Sondra's marriage, not that Jackie thought it was such a great one in the first place. And what about poor Katie Nolan? She was going to be heartbroken by all this.

Abandoning sleep entirely for the time being, Jackie turned her lamp back on and reached for a book. She glanced at the clock: nearly two A.M. She was going to feel like hell in the morning, but then she didn't feel much better than that right now anyway.

When Jackie arrived at the warehouse with Jake the following morning, she found the cast and crew sitting around doing nothing much. Lorraine was nowhere in sight. Sulking in her trailer? No reason to be unkind, she supposed. Lorraine was a movie star, and that conferred sulking privileges.

Kurt Manowski and the grips were playing yet another hand in their eternal poker game, and a few of the local actors who'd been scheduled today were already in costume, reading the newspaper or talking with one another.

John was pacing, back and forth, up and down the warehouse floor with a murderous look on his face. Stomach tightening, Jackie brought Jake to heel with a backward gesture of her hand.

Marti Bernstein walked by and stopped to give the Shepherd a pat. "Hi, Jake!" she greeted him. "Guess what? I found Andy's stash of dog biscuits in his desk drawer. Come see me later, okay?"

Jackie nodded toward John. "What did Dark Cameron do this time?" she asked Marti, pretty certain that this time she knew the answer.

"Good guess, but as a matter of fact, he hasn't even shown up yet," Marti replied, "*and* he has the revisions to the shooting schedule that John needs."

If John was still expecting Cameron, and expecting his shooting-schedule changes along with him, that must mean that Cameron had never managed to meet up with him last night. Jackie didn't know whether or not she ought to be relieved.

"And he's not answering his phone, either," Marti added.

"Not even the one he has grafted to the side of his head?"

"Totally incommunicado," Marti informed her.

"Is it safe to approach the director?"

"Not without a whip and a chair," said Marti.

"That bad, huh?" Jackie asked sympathetically.

"Oh, he's not really taking it out on anyone," said Marti. "You know John—that's not his style. But he's upset all right. And I think he's got a hangover, on top of everything else. He's been chowing down pain relievers like after-dinner mints. I don't know what all is going on, but I know I wouldn't want to be Cameron Clark when he finally shows up."

Jackie thought that she wouldn't want to be John when Cameron showed up, either, but she decided against saying it. There'd be plenty of unpleasantness soon enough, she was sure. No good reason to hurry it.

Jackie saw Katie Nolan sketching at a drawing table John had set up for her near the corner of the warehouse that served as a wardrobe department. She walked over to her, Jake following obediently just behind her.

"Hi, Jackie," said Katie, looking up from her sketch. Her voice dropped to a whisper. "He didn't come home until it was light out," she said. "He showered and changed, and gave me a ride over here."

John caught sight of Jackie talking to Katie. He stopped pacing, and came over toward them, his frown softening a bit.

"Jackie, what's going on?" Katie asked her, too low for John to hear.

"I don't know, exactly," said Jackie, laying a hand on Katie's shoulder.

" 'Morning, Jackie. I don't suppose you've seen our producer," John said when he reached them.

"No," Jackie replied carefully. "Not since last night, anyway."

"No one's seen him," John almost growled, the full frown back now. "He's vanished into thin air."

"Oh, I've seen him," said a man's voice from the doorway onto Indiana Street.

Jackie and John turned to look. The man stood silhouetted by the sunlight from outside, unrecognizable except by his shape and size. Jackie's heart sank as she realized who it was. This could only mean some sort of deep, awful trouble.

"Is he all right?" she asked the tall, broad-shouldered shape in the doorway.

"As a matter of fact, he's not," said Detective Lieutenant Evan Stillman. He walked inside the warehouse and looked around at the people who stood and sat looking at him. "He's dead."

CHAPTER 8

There was a moment of stunned silence, then everyone started talking at once.

"Dead?"

"Jesus!"

"I don't believe it!"

"How?"

Evan Stillman looked around at the assembled cast and crew, his eyes going from one face to the other. "He was hit by a car. Knocked off the bridge over Little Canyon Creek."

John sagged into a nearby chair, white-faced. The buzz of shocked conversation stopped for a second, then resumed, louder than before.

Jackie's knees trembled just a bit. She wished she had a chair to sink into while her legs were still working. Evan's presence here told her that the police probably didn't consider Cameron's death to have been an accident. Or if they did, they were at least dealing with a hit-and-run.

"We're going to need to talk to everyone here," Evan continued, confirming Jackie's suspicions. The buzz quieted down and stopped. "I'm Detective Lieutenant Still-

man. Detective Sergeant Youngquist here will be taking
your names and other information." He indicated his partner, the blond and beautiful Bernie Youngquist, who had
entered the warehouse behind him. "We'll be conducting
some of our preliminary interviews right here, since
you're all so conveniently located in one place. Is there
somewhere we can talk to people in private?" he asked.
"A room with a door that closes?"

"There's an office in the corner over there," Katie told
him, pointing toward Andy's former production office, so
recently taken over by Cameron Clark. "I think the door's
unlocked."

"That'll do fine, thanks. We'll use that office, Sergeant
Youngquist," he said to his partner, pointing at the door
in question. Bernie nodded.

"These interviews we're doing are just preliminary
ones," Evan said. "Just so we can ask questions while
things are still fresh in everyone's memory. It's possible
we'll also want to talk to some or all of you at police
headquarters later on."

The people in the warehouse began to mutter again, a
dozen simultaneous conversations, none of which could
be clearly heard, but all of which together managed to
convey feelings of shock and confusion and not a little
crankiness at the sheer inconvenience of the thing. The
element that seemed to be missing was any sorrow at the
passing of Cameron Clark. Jackie supposed she wasn't
surprised, given Cameron's methods and attitude the last
few days. If he had any friends in Palmer, and she
couldn't think of one offhand, even in his function as an
instructor at Rodgers, he certainly had none within the
cast or crew of *Under the Dog Star*.

Evan noticed Jackie, and walked over to her, removing
his hat. "Well, well, well," he remarked, shaking his head
and almost smiling, though not quite.

"Hi, Evan," Jackie offered.

"If it isn't my own personal trouble magnet," Evan said, managing to look pained and amused all at once. "Don't miss this one, Sergeant Youngquist. We might want to interview her twice."

Bernie raised a hand in greeting. Jackie waved back. She could clearly remember a time not so long ago when she'd been not only overwhelmed, but downright intimidated by Bernie Youngquist's utter physical perfection. Eventually she'd learned to get beyond Bernie's intimidating surface to discover the intelligent and delightful woman underneath, and they'd become good friends. It hadn't been easy, but all it really took was for Jackie to grow up a bit along the way.

Evan walked up to Jackie and leaned down to give Jake a pat on the head. "How ya doin', old fella?" he wanted to know. Jake wagged his tail in response to the attention from his former coworker. Evan paused on his way to straightening back up to speak into Jackie's ear. "You know what I'd like just once, Jackie?" he asked.

Jackie bit back any number of smart remarks. "What, Evan?" she asked back.

"Just once in my lifetime I'd like to get somewhere in this town to investigate a homicide and not find you anywhere in the vicinity," he informed her.

"You're exaggerating," Jackie protested. "In a town this size there must be dozens of people who get murdered, and I'm not involved in the slightest."

"You're right, there are." Evan stepped back a bit. "And this next part may come as a surprise," he said, "but most of the people you could point out on the street out there"—he pointed out the doorway where the people to whom he referred supposedly walked the streets of Palmer, Ohio—"most of those people aren't involved in even one of those murders, not even once in their entire lifetimes."

His voice was rising a little as he got to the end of his

speech. Then he controlled himself and let out a careful breath. "Not one." He held up a single finger to illustrate his point.

Jackie hadn't set out to be the bane of Evan Stillman's existence, but she seemed to have attained the goal without ever knowing she was doing so. Evan and Bernie made up most of the homicide division of the Palmer Police Department, and although her dog had been in service to the department for several years, Jackie wasn't officially connected. She wasn't even unoffically connected since she had stopped dating Palmer Police Detective Michael McGowan a couple of years previously, which was the reason she and Evan had become acquainted in the first place.

Still, Evan had a reasonable point to make that Jackie seemed to stumble into a lot of his investigations. Often as not, she didn't just stumble out again, but stayed to do some investigating of her own. More to the point, Jackie supposed, on more of those occasions than Evan probably liked to admit, she and Jake had been of some material value in solving the case. She could also tell Evan liked her in his own cranky sort of way, though she was pretty certain he'd never admit it in a million years.

Now Evan seemed to notice a tall, broad-shouldered actor in a suit and tie not unlike the ones he was wearing, drinking coffee and talking to another actor in the uniform of a patrol officer. "Who's that?" he asked Jackie, a frown beginning to crease his forehead.

"That's Danny DeCastro," she told him. "A local actor—pretty well known. You may have seen him in *Coriolanus* last year at the Palmer Rep."

Evan cocked a wry eyebrow. "I mean who is he playing in the movie?" Marcella's juicy hints about a film à clef of Palmer's citizens hadn't been lost on Evan, apparently. He might not get out to the theater much, but he read the *Palmer Gazette,* all right.

"A detective," was Jackie's answer to that. There was no point at all in telling Evan that before she'd insisted upon certain script changes, Danny's character had been pretty nearly indistinguishable from the Palmer Police Department's own Detective Lieutenant Evan Stillman. Apparently he was still close enough to attract the attention of the original, even dressed in his 1940s-vintage suit.

"A detective," Evan echoed. "Would that be a police detective by any chance?"

"Uh-huh. So are you going to need to talk to me, too?" Jackie asked. She knew the answer, but it was the only thing she could think of at short notice to divert Evan's attention from Danny DeCastro and fictional detectives. It didn't work.

"He doesn't look too bright," Evan mused, not entirely happily.

"Oh, Danny's pretty sharp. I think he has a master's in theater arts," Jackie provided.

"That's not what I'm talking about," said Evan, then shook his head. "I've got an investigation to run here. Try like hell to stay out of it, will you?"

"You think it was homicide, huh?"

"Didn't you hear me just then?"

"Absolutely. Stay out of it. Gosh, Evan, why would I want any part of it? I didn't even like the guy, particularly."

"Did you not like him enough to paste him with a motor vehicle going about fifty miles an hour?"

"Let me rephrase that," Jackie suggested.

"Never mind. Just hang around and wait for me or Bernie to talk with you before you go running off, okay?"

"Okay."

Jackie shook her head as Evan walked away. What a day this had turned into. "As though I'd bother," she said to her dog. "As though you would either. As smashed as Cameron was last night, he probably stumbled in front of a truck." She looked up to see Kurt Manowski looking at her from the card table where he had been watching Evan and Bernie work the room while dealing a hand of poker. "I'm sorry, Kurt, I didn't mean . . ."

"No offense taken," Kurt rumbled. He raised his can of diet soda in a mock toast and gave her a little smile as he turned back to watching the two detectives. As always, Jackie felt a slight undercurrent of fear and suspicion around Kurt, and as always, she felt ashamed of it. She'd been conditioned by seeing him play thugs and murderers in films for thirty years, but she didn't want to judge someone only by their film roles.

Jackie turned around to see Katie Nolan standing beside her. "Who would have wanted to kill Cameron?" Katie asked, surprise and disbelief still evident in her voice.

"Oh, pretty nearly everyone who's been working with him the last few days," Jackie told her.

Katie's eyes got very large. "Everyone?"

"Oh, I guess I don't mean *really* kill him," Jackie amended. "I mean, I didn't at least, but you've got to admit he didn't waste any time making enemies around here. I think you'd have to admit that even you weren't that crazy about him."

Katie looked thoughtful. "I guess I actually hated him when he humiliated me in front of everyone," she acknowledged. "But I've gotten the same treatment from a few teachers between junior high and here, and I never killed any of *them*."

"Well, most of us don't give in to our impulses quite that easily," Jackie agreed, "but with those two homicide detectives here, you can bet someone killed Cameron, and the chances are very good that they think it was someone on this production."

"God, that's awful," said Katie. "That means it would have to be someone we know." She looked around at the assembled cast and crewmembers, gathered into groups, still talking to each other in hushed tones. "And it could be any of them. Anyone at all."

"I could use some coffee," said Jackie. "How about you?"

"Good idea."

They headed across the warehouse floor to the rented table that held coffee urns and soft drinks and aluminum-foil containers of breakfast rolls. Jackie was pouring herself a cup of coffee when John walked up and stood between her and Katie. "How're you two doing? Are you okay?" He looked back and forth between the two of them, concern evident on his face.

"I'm all right, " Jackie assured him. "Just deeply shocked, is all. I don't think the reality has quite sunk in yet."

"I'm okay, I guess," said Katie. "I don't think I ever knew anyone before who was murdered."

John touched Katie's arm in a reassuring gesture. "I can't believe any of this is happening," he said, shaking his head. "If I hadn't been so determined to make this film—"

"If a frog had wings, he wouldn't bump his ass all the time," said Kurt Manowski from behind them. "Don't kick yourself about Cameron." He pulled a diet soda from a tub of ice, popped the top, and picked up a cheese Danish. "You didn't kill him." He walked back to his poker game without waiting for a reply. The three of them stared after him for a moment.

"Did you see Cameron last night?" Jackie asked John.

"No. Should I have?"

"Maybe not. But he was looking for you," she said. "I saw him at Prince Charlie's around nine, and he was already drunk. I called your house to warn you, but you weren't there."

"Warn me?" John looked puzzled. "I don't get it. If he

was looking for me, why didn't he just call the house himself?"

Jackie wondered whether she ought to say anything to John about the reason Cameron Clark had been determined to see him the previous night, and decided that it was better left for a private conversation. It wasn't any of her business whom John was sleeping with, though Cameron had certainly gone out of his way to let her know. There'd be plenty of time to bring it up when there weren't so many people around, she supposed. She had a feeling no one in this room would be talking about any subject other than the life and death of Cameron Clark for days on end, and besides that, she figured Katie didn't ne. d the extra grief.

Bernie Youngquist came up to them. "Are you John McBride?" she asked.

"That's me," said John.

"Do you have a list of everyone in the cast and crew I can use to get started with these interviews?" she asked.

"Actually, that's the producer's—" John began, then caught himself. He took a deep, careful breath. "I'm sure there's one somewhere around here," he said, "but I don't know where it is."

"Cameron kept all those lists," said Katie, "and they might be in his office. If they're not, I think between Marti Bernstein—that's the assistant director—and me, we can probably help you put one together."

"Thanks," said Bernie. "You find Marti, and let's work on it in the office over there."

Just then a small, dark-skinned woman in a blue police coverall gestured to Evan from one of the outside doors. He went over to her, bending down to hear whatever she was whispering in his ear. It got very quiet as everyone seemed to strain to hear their conversation. Evan straightened up and looked at John for a long moment, then followed her out into the sunlight.

"Why was he looking at you like that?" Katie asked John.

"I'm about to find out," John replied as he put down his book and walked toward the doorway. Katie followed him, with Jackie behind her, bringing Jake along for good measure.

Outside, the uniformed woman was standing by John's pickup truck and pointing at some dents in the fender. "Those dents have been there since before I got it," said John as he walked up to them.

"This your truck?" Evan inquired.

"Yes."

"And you are . . ."

"John McBride."

"Well, Mr. McBride, *those* dents maybe you've had since you got the truck," Evan agreed, pointing to some old, rusty dents in the Chevy's solid steel left fender, "but not *these*." He indicated two fresher dents near the old ones, free of rust, the metal of the fender bright and fresh where paint had flaked away. More crackled paint lay near the edges, waiting for the action of air or water, or just plain time to remove it.

Evan bent down to examine the chrome-plated bumper where it wrapped around the lower part of the same fender. "And this scrape here looks pretty recent, too. It also looks like you just washed your truck," he remarked to John, straightening back up.

John was staring at the marks Evan had indicated, shaking his head. "I haven't washed this thing in . . ." he started to protest, but his words trailed off as he looked at the sparkling clean truck as though seeing it for the first time. "I didn't wash it," was all he could say, finally, and his voice barely rose above a whisper. "And I didn't make those dents."

Evan turned to the uniformed woman. "Gopalan, call down and get a tow truck with a slide back over here to get this thing to the city yard," he ordered. He looked at John as he spoke.

"Right," the woman replied.

"Have them put it up on the lift and go over every square centimeter of that undercarriage for blood, flesh, cloth—anything."

John grew noticeably pale.

"You'll want to match the height of that scrape against the one on the bridge railing," Evan went on, never taking his eyes off John, "and match the paint against those chips you found on the victim's clothing. But I think we've found our murder weapon."

"You can't possibly think I killed Cameron Clark," said John. "He was producing my film! Without him the whole production goes down the drain! If my truck was used to kill him, then somebody must have stolen it."

"Really?" Evan exclaimed in mock wonder. "Now, why didn't I think of that? Of course! Somebody stole your truck. Where was it when you went to get into it this morning?"

"It was in the carport beside the house," said John, looking like he might be sick at any moment.

"So this somebody stole your truck and was thoughtful enough to return it so you could get to the set on time this morning." Evan laughed unpleasantly. "I'll tell you, Mr. McBride, I wish all the car thieves in Palmer were that considerate. It'd save the city a whole lot of money." He looked in the driver's-side window. "Now, did this courteous car thief get in by busting your wind wing, or did he maybe have an extra set of keys?"

"There's only one set of keys," said John. "I lost the other set over a year ago."

"And you locked the truck up last night?"

John nodded. "I'm pretty sure I did."

"And as we can see, the window hasn't been broken, and I believe you'll agree the steering column hasn't been broken into, either, so the car wasn't hot-wired. That's a very subtle car thief we're talking about, McBride, in addition to those good manners we've already mentioned. Nope, I'm betting this truck ran down Cameron Clark about one o'clock this morning, and I'm betting that you were the one driving it. And just to back up that bet, I'm placing you under arrest for suspicion of vehicular manslaughter."

John's knees sagged, and he put his hands on the truck for support. Katie reached out to him, and he took hold of her arm, his knuckles white against her skin.

"Evan, you can't be serious!" Jackie protested, but she knew he was.

"That's the very least you can be charged with on account of leaving the scene," Evan continued, ignoring her. "But I think you can pretty much make bank on that charge being upped to first-degree murder."

CHAPTER 9

As the black-and-white pulled away from the warehouse with John handcuffed in the backseat behind Evan, Katie Nolan wiped tears from her eyes and turned to Jackie, her arms crossed tightly in front of her.

"He couldn't do anything like that, Jackie. Not John. He just couldn't." Her eyes begged for reassurance, and Jackie wasn't sure how much she could provide.

"They could be wrong about the truck, I suppose." Jackie looked up the street and watched the cruiser turn the corner and disappear. Her heart sank even further when the car was out of sight. "But I have to tell you, Katie, I know Evan Stillman. He's been on the job a long time, and he wouldn't have arrested John unless he was pretty certain he was right." She looked over at Bernie Youngquist, who was standing near the warehouse doors.

Bernie nodded agreement to Jackie's statement. "Come by the department around two o'clock—I should be done here before then," she said quietly, then walked back inside.

"He's not right," Katie said, her voice hollow. "He can't be." She turned and went back into the warehouse.

News of John's arrest had spread quickly through the

cast and crew, and many were still standing around outside, looking lost. Danny DeCastro rubbed an index finger
against his temple and looked around for someone in au-
thority. His eyes settled on Jackie.

"What now, Ms. Walsh?" One by one, heads turned
toward her, eyes expectant. This was what being a teacher
had gotten her—a bunch of otherwise responsible adults
were suddenly acting like schoolchildren in need of some
rules to follow. She looked around for Marti Bernstein,
and caught sight of a tie-dyed dress coming toward her
from inside the warehouse. Marti made eye contact with
Jackie, and her expression was grim.

"This is pure feces, Jackie," she growled, and stepped
out into the sunlight. Silver beads flashed at the ends of
three tiny braids that lay over her shoulder. In her arms
she held a clipboard with its usual sheaf of papers. "We
both know John didn't kill anybody. And what are all you
guys staring at?" she challenged the crowd.

"The troops are looking for leadership, Bernstein, and
it looks like you're it."

"No director, no producer, no movie," Marti said sadly.
"Go talk to the nice police detective," she told them.
"When she's through with you, go home! There's nothing
more we can do today. I'll be in touch. When I know
anything, you'll know it, too."

Grumbles and groans followed from within and without. People began to mill around the door to the production office, where Bernie Youngquist was still conducting
preliminary interviews, trying to get the facts down while
they were still fresh in everyone's minds. The people who
had already been dismissed by Bernie began to file out of
the warehouse, and Jackie fought her way upstream toward her chair, where Jake was tethered. He whuffed at
her and wagged his tail, dancing in place like he had to
visit the nearest tree, which he probably did.

"Has anyone seen Sondra Clark this morning?" Jackie asked Marti.

"I sure haven't," Marti replied. "Maybe she was waiting for her husband to come home, but knowing her it doesn't seem too likely." The merest shadow of a sneer crossed Marti's features. Mentions of Sondra seemed to prompt that sort of expression, and not just from Marti Bernstein, Jackie noted. "At the very least, she should have called here and asked about him, since he clearly didn't make it home last night. I wonder what's up with that?" Marti raised an eyebrow. "Do you think maybe she's the one who offed him?"

"It's up to the detectives to think," Jackie told her.

"But you *are* a detective, Jackie," Bernie insisted.

Jackie gave the assistant director a look from under lowered eyebrows, unhooked the end of Jake's lead from the chair leg, grabbed her handbag, and headed toward the warehouse doors with everyone else.

Katie was at her drawing table, holding a pencil over a blank sheet of paper, staring off into space. Jackie stopped on her way to the door and put what she hoped was a comforting hand on Katie's shoulder. She seemed to be doing a lot of that lately.

"You've got to help him, Jackie," Katie whispered.

Jackie sighed. "I don't know what I can do, Katie. He's in pretty deep."

"You're a detective, aren't you?" Katie looked up at her, and Jackie saw a stubbornness Katie didn't display often.

"No," Jackie said firmly. "No, I'm not. I'm a film instructor with a bad habit of putting my nose where it doesn't belong, and it's gotten me into trouble more than once. One of these days it's going to get me into more trouble than I know how to handle."

Now Katie's stubbornness turned to outright anger. "John's the one in trouble here, Jackie, and a little bit of trouble for you might mean a lot less for him. That's what friends are for, right?" She glared and swallowed hard, then suddenly crumpled, sobbing, onto the art table. "I'm sorry!" she wailed. "You didn't deserve that. It's just . . ."

"It's okay, Katie, I know. I'm worried, too. I just don't know what, if anything, I can do for John. But I won't turn my back on him, okay? I promise." She bent down and pulled a wet lock of hair from Katie's cheek, and marveled at how strong this young woman was, and yet still so fragile. John had a real ally in Katie, and Jackie wondered whether he knew it.

Jake whuffed again, and nosed the back of Jackie's leg. Jackie looked around and found a roll of paper towels under the table. She tore a couple off and handed them to Katie.

"Listen, I've got to go, but I'll call you later," she told Katie, who sat up and nodded, wiping her face, her breath still coming in little gasps. "Will you be all right?"

Katie nodded again, and managed a smile. "Forgive me for being a big baby?"

"You're not a baby, Katie, you're a good friend. John's lucky to have a friend like you."

Katie rolled her eyes at that, and dabbed at her nose with the wadded paper towel. "If only he knew it," she said, fresh tears starting to well up in her dark blue eyes. "Or cared, for that matter."

"Don't torture yourself. Go home and get some rest. And think about anything you can remember that might help John's case. Anything at all. I'll call you tonight." Jackie gave her a quick one-armed hug from behind, and let Jake drag her out the door and into Marcella Jacobs and Werner Benz, her long-suffering photographer.

"Jackie, we've got to stop meeting like this," said Werner, untangling himself from Jake's lead.

"No, it's perfect you're here," said Marcella. "I was

scanning the police frequencies and I could tell there was something going on over here."

"I thought your taste ran more to soft rock," said Jackie. She really didn't want to discuss all this with Marcella—it was too painful. She took the end of Jake's lead from Werner. "Jake and I have to go find a tree."

"Come on, Jackie—this could be my big break with the crime desk. Help me out here!"

"Cameron Clark was murdered last night. John's been arrested. Those are the high points, if you could really call them that."

"So he *was* sleeping with what'sername!"

"Sondra. And I really don't know." Jackie realized that the only hope she had for a balanced story was if she actually granted Marcella a few minutes to hear the details from her. "Listen, Marcella, there are still a few people in the warehouse there who'll probably talk to you, but Werner might as well go home; there aren't any dead bodies in there. If I find out you've been badgering Katie Nolan, I'll hunt you down and kill you. She's been through enough today. And don't run off and write anything until you've talked to me, too. I'm going to take Jake for a walk."

"Meet me at Suzette's in an hour?" Marcella asked.

"Yeah, I guess. That'll give me time to take Jake home first."

Jackie walked away from the warehouse, with Jake pulling steadily at the lead. It wasn't yet noon, but she was totally exhausted. A conversation with Marcella in her manic reporter mode had a tendency to take the stuffing out of her on her best day, and this was decidedly not that. She'd have to find the energy somewhere to sit down to a lunch she didn't have the appetite for and try to rein in Marcella's sensationalism enough that if her story did see print, it wouldn't hurt John too badly.

• • •

The apartment was dead silent except for Charlie's purring and the occasional dream growl from Jake. Jackie puttered around the living room, trying to stay busy so she could avoid thinking about those issues that were vying for attention at the back of her brain: how much she missed her men, Peter and Tom (the solitude was nice, but any kind of distraction would be preferable at this point); and the fact that John McBride—admittedly her favorite student from three years of teaching film—was in jail for a murder she couldn't possibly imagine him committing.

Katie couldn't imagine it either, but then, she was in love with the guy. She'd really done a job on Jackie today, though. Not that Jackie was even entertaining the thought of becoming involved once again in a murder case, but there had to be *something* she could do for poor John McBride. Assuming he was innocent. She'd promised Katie she'd do *something*.

And if John *was* innocent, then who had done the deed? Jackie found herself going over the facts in spite of herself, as she had so many times before. Kurt Manowski was certainly no friend of Cameron Clark; their history was rocky, and Cameron had practically come right out and threatened Kurt's job the day before he was killed. Kurt needed the work, all right—his career had been going nowhere for several years now—but badly enough to kill for it? And what good would it do him to kill the producer, frame the director, and shut down the film, possibly for good?

Other than Kurt, though, the only name Jackie could come up with was Sondra, who was obviously unhappy with her marriage and its effect (or lack thereof) on her career aspirations. Sondra was ambitious, yes, and manipulative, but she hadn't shown any signs so far of being a sociopath, and ruling that out, Cameron's holding her back didn't make a very good motive for cold-blooded murder, nor would a dead husband get her any closer to Hollywood than her live one had.

If not for the fact that the killer had allegedly used John McBride's truck as his instrument, Jackie thought it seemed likely that whoever hated Clark enough to off him wasn't even connected to John's film. But there was the truck, and that seemed to make a pretty strong connection. So if it wasn't John, it had to be someone who knew John. Someone who could have taken his truck and his keys, killed a man, and returned the truck to where it had been parked.

Maybe there was a connection she was missing. If she could talk to some of Clark's friends on the faculty, or back in Hollywood, maybe she could dig up—

"Hold it right there, Walsh," she said, startling Jake and Charlie awake. Charlie glared at her for a moment, then stretched and yawned and curled back up again. Jake, on the other hand, raised his head up, thumping his tail on the Oriental rug and looking at her, his big head cocked to one side. Even *he* seemed to be waiting for her to do something.

"Stop staring at me like that. There's nothing I *can* do." Jake whuffed once—reproachfully, Jackie thought—then put his head back down on his paws and joined Charlie back in dreamland.

Jackie plopped down on the sofa, picked up a popular science magazine, and forced herself to read an article on Pluto. Peter had discovered astronomy this past year, and used his savings account to buy a backyard telescope. Pluto was his favorite planet, mainly because it shared a name with a certain cartoon dog, and Peter thought that was cool. He'd told Jackie that he thought all the planets should have names like Mickey, Goofy, Daffy, Bugs . . . Jackie had told him to become an astronomer and discover a new planet of his own, and he could name it anything he liked.

He wasn't going to like this, Jackie thought. It turned out that Pluto was being demoted from very small planet to very large comet. How insulting, Jackie thought. But she remembered her astronomy instructor's difficulty explaining why Pluto behaved differently from other planets; strike one, it was made entirely of ice; strike two, it followed an erratic orbit that took it out of the solar system, then back in again. Strike three was the discovery of a bunch of icy comet-type bodies in a neighborhood not far from Pluto's. Astronomy instructors and scientists alike were probably relieved at the discovery of these similar, poorly behaved bodies in space, and the determination that Pluto was actually the largest of this new class of objects rather than the smallest planet in a class by itself. Peter would be crestfallen.

The phone tore through the silence and Jackie jumped hard, tearing a page out of her magazine and knocking a stack of books off the coffee table with her foot. She took a deep breath to still the pounding in her chest, and went to the phone.

"Jackie, it's Katie. I just remembered something." She sounded scared, and a little excited. "About John's truck."

"Hi, Katie." Jackie took a seat at the dining table and pulled her hair back from her forehead, still panting a bit. "What is it?"

"Well, remember how I said John wasn't home last night? And how he came home early this morning, right before we left for the warehouse?"

"Yeah, sure. He was gone all night, right?" Probably with Sondra, Jackie thought.

"See, that's just it. I don't know now. I got back here this afternoon—Daphne dropped me off—and I saw the garbage can out on the sidewalk—today was trash day—and I was carrying it back into the carport when I remembered—"

"Slow down, Katie. What did you remember?"

"Sorry, Jackie. I remembered that I heard John's truck last night."

"So you think he got home earlier than you originally thought?" Jackie took the phone into the kitchen and found a roll of tape in the junk drawer. She grabbed the tape, took the phone out into the living room, and sat once again on the couch.

"No. I mean, I *don't* think so. See, when I took the can out last night, John's truck was still here, but he wasn't. He'd come home to shower and left again right after. Someone picked him up, but I didn't see who. I heard a car honk, but I was doing some new sketches for the waterfront set, and I was distracted. By the time I heard the car pull off and looked out the window, there was no one there."

Jackie propped the phone under her chin and tried to piece the torn half of the page back into the magazine. "So he was out all night, and the truck wasn't." The pieces fought with her as she attempted to join them with a length of transparent tape.

"Not exactly," Katie said. "Someone must have come and gotten the truck late last night."

Jackie swore as the tape stuck where she didn't want it to. She tried to pull it up and only succeeded in doing more damage to the article text. When she tuned in to what Katie had said, she stopped in mid-stick.

"Someone? Someone who, Katie?" Jackie tore her finger loose from the adhesive and shoved the magazine aside. She was listening now.

"I'm not sûre. I remember I heard the truck start up. It woke me up, actually, since the carport's right under my bedroom window. I wondered why John was leaving at that hour of the night. For that matter, I was certain I hadn't heard him come in."

"You were asleep, right?" Jackie pointed out. "You wouldn't necessarily have heard anything."

Katie laughed. "That's where you're wrong. I'm a pretty light sleeper, and I've kind of got myself programmed to the sound of his . . ." She paused, and laughed again. "Well, anyway, it's possible he came in and I didn't hear him, but let's just say it's highly unlikely."

"Interesting, but it won't get John out of jail. Not unless he's got an alibi for where he was last night, and who he was with. Has he called?"

"No." Katie sounded disappointed, probably as much at the thought of his being out with Sondra as anything. "I guess I wouldn't be the person he'd call if they only allowed him one." Her voice was heavy with disappointment. "Listen, I'm sorry I gave you such a hard time earlier. I understand your hands are tied. I just feel so helpless, and if there's anything any of us can do to help, well then I just think we should, you know?"

In other words, Jackie thought, I understand you doing nothing if there's nothing you can do, but there is something you can do, isn't there, so no, I don't understand, not really. Jackie decided to take Katie's words at face value, anyway. Maybe she was being hypersensitive. "I just hope he has a good alibi, Katie, and then he can help himself right into your lovin' arms."

"Yeah, right." Katie laughed, and they said good-bye, and Jackie hung up feeling discouraged. She wished Tom would call again so she could cry on his shoulder, or at least into his ear.

The phone rang again, but it wasn't Tom, it was Frances calling from sunny Florida.

"Hi, Mom." Jackie tried to disguise the suffering in her voice. No such luck.

"What's wrong, Jackie? Is Peter all right?"

"He's fine. He's in California, remember? Visiting Mickey and Minnie." Jackie imagined the three of them laughing it up on a beach somewhere, and wished with

all her heart she'd skipped this whole horrid movie thing
and gone with them.

"I remember, dear. I'm not senile." Frances giggled.
"Just a little silly." She giggled again.

"Mom, are you drinking?" Frances sounded like a teenager. A love-struck teenager. Jackie caught herself grinning.

"Heavens, no, not at this hour. I'm just having the time
of my life, that's all. The weather is *beautiful!*"

"Well, I wish I was there." Anywhere.

"Now, you really will tell me what's wrong, Jacqueline.
What are you doing home, anyway? I don't even know
why I called this early—aren't you making a movie?"

Jackie took a deep breath and sighed. Then she took
another. "Mom, the movie's been canceled, or postponed,
at the very least."

"Why on earth?" Jackie heard a man's voice in the
background, and Frances covered the mouthpiece and said
something unintelligible. "I thought it only had a couple
of weeks to go."

"It did. We ran into some trouble. Or rather, someone
ran into the producer." Jackie stifled a giggle. The tension
was getting to her. "Not Andy, he's sick. His replacement,
Cameron Clark."

"Who's he? Wait, I've heard that name . . ."

"Yeah, he used to be somebody. Now he's nobody.
Literally."

"What does that mean? Someone ran into him, you
said? Oh, Jackie, you don't mean . . ."

"Of course that's what I mean, Mom. See, it turns out
I'm under some ancient curse." Jackie was getting really
tired of the subject, of the whole situation, but Frances
certainly wasn't going to let her off the hook now. "Everything I touch turns to—"

"Now, Jackie, I'm not going to listen to that. You didn't
kill him, did you?"

Jackie said nothing.

"That was a rhetorical question, dear daughter. Was it murder?"

"It looks that way, and John McBride's been arrested."

Frances gasped. "Your star student? That poor boy! He didn't do it, did he? You're going to take the case, aren't you?"

"Mom!" Jackie wailed, and managed to sound like a teenager herself. "Get off it, would you? Take the case, my *buttocks*! There isn't any case! Well, there is, but it's Evan Stillman's case, and he's a professional. I'm just a schmuck who got lucky a couple of times."

"And a couple of times before that, and a couple of times before that . . . Face it, Jacqueline, you're good at this. And you enjoy it, or you wouldn't keep doing it. Oh, I wish I was there, this is so exciting!"

"Not from where John McBride's sitting."

"I know, Jackie, that's why you've got to help him." The man's voice was back speaking quietly but earnestly in the background, and Frances giggled again. "I've got to go, daughter. Be careful."

"I'll mind my own business, is what I'll do," Jackie assured her. "Have a good time, Mom." The line was already dead.

Why is it so distasteful to imagine one's mother in a romantic situation? Jackie was happy for Frances—it had been years since she'd let herself be courted, even in a minor way, and it sounded like this time she'd been swept off her feet. But the image of her mother and some strange man together on the other end of that phone line, giggling and who knew what else . . . Had Frances been calling from Bara's place, or had she and—what was his name?—Mr. Mallon, that was it. Had she and Mr. Mallon gone on holiday, just the two of them? And why did the idea bother her so much?

Jackie shuddered, and put all thoughts of her mother

and Florida out of her mind. She picked up the ruined magazine, took it to the kitchen, and tossed it into a recycle container, making a mental note to pick up a new copy at the newsstand tonight or tomorrow.

For now, she was going up to her room for a well-deserved nap. She headed for the stairs. Jake, then Charlie, as if reading her thoughts, got up and followed her up the stairs. Maybe some sleep would put a different face on the matter, Jackie thought wearily. Maybe her mind would come up with something she hadn't put together yet. Maybe she just needed to escape for an hour or so, and if that was the only reason, she'd gladly accept it.

CHAPTER 10

Jackie woke up from a dream in which she'd run into Cameron Clark at the supermarket and politely reminded him that he was dead. He'd seemed not to understand, and had asked her advice on produce in season.

Awake now, but still groggy and disoriented, she climbed out of bed and ran a brush through her hair. It was nearly three o'clock, and she'd promised Bernie she'd be at the police department. She hoped she'd still have time to visit John at the jail. He was probably feeling pretty alone right now. Did he even have a lawyer, or had he been forced to settle for a public defender during questioning?

As usual, Jake could tell that she was preparing to leave, and he brought her his lead. "Sorry Jake, you're staying home." It was way too hot to leave him in the car, even with the windows down. "Take care of Charlie, and if anyone calls, take a message." She grabbed her keys and handbag and headed out.

Hot, hot, hot. The car seat and steering wheel were hot enough to grill a New York steak. Jackie started the engine and turned on the air-conditioning, then got out and waited for it to cool things down to tolerable. It was easily ten degrees cooler outside the car. While she waited, she pulled a tube of forty-weight sunscreen out of her bag and smeared it on her nose and cheeks. She fished out her sunglasses and put them on, and put SPF 15 gloss on her lips. The same magazine that had given her the bad news about Pluto had, in the last issue, given her the worse news about the upswing of skin cancer cases in the U.S. She was going to have to find a happier publication to read.

Opening the car door again, she was greeted with a rush of cool air that made her skin sing. She checked the rearview mirror and decided she was as presentable as she was going to get, considering she'd only been awake ten minutes tops. She put the car in gear and headed for the Palmer Jail, by way of the Palmer Police Department, by way of the corner espresso stand, where she ordered a sixteen-ounce latte and a poppy-seed bagel.

Bernie had asked her to drop by, and Jackie knew she'd have to answer a few questions from Bernie and Evan. It occurred to her that while she was doing it she might just find out something useful, or at least hopeful to take with her when she went to visit John. She sipped the last of her latte and stared around her at the drab impersonality of the Palmer Police Department's lobby, and hoped she'd come away with anything to make John feel better. Evan wasn't likely to offer her any professional courtesy, Jackie thought, not—she hastened to remind herself—that she had any coming.

Evan Stillman gestured at her from the other side of a low railing that separated the waiting area from the offices. "Let's have some coffee while we do this," he offered as they entered his office and he indicated the guest chair near his desk.

"I just had a latte," Jackie responded, holding up the cardboard container like a shield between her and the horror of Evan Stillman's coffee.

Evan shrugged and poured a portion of thick black liquid into a chipped white mug. He sat down wearily in his ancient leather chair and swiveled it around to face her. "You still think your pal John McBride is innocent, don't you?"

"Is that a trick question? Of course I do. Do you have something to say that might change my mind?"

"Other than his truck being the murder weapon?" Evan offered, raising an eyebrow.

"Prove he was driving it when the murder happened," Jackie told him, "and you might just convince me."

"I'm not going to discuss this case with you, Jackie," Evan said, "except to say that your boy John McBride isn't going to see the streets of Palmer, Ohio, for a long stretch. Maybe never."

"Have you got a motive?"

"Only that he was sleeping with the victim's wife," Evan said sarcastically, then shook his head and swore. "Dammit, Jackie, I said I'm not going to talk about it."

"Evan, I'm not after privileged information," Jackie told him, in what she hoped was a reassuring tone, "but John's a friend, and from what I know of him, it just doesn't fit. I'd like to think there's another explanation."

"Well, if there is, don't let me catch you trying to find it," Evan told her. He sighed heavily. "I don't want to butt heads with you, Jackie," he said. "But we always seem to do that. I've got someplace I've got to be right now, so I'm going to have Bernie interview you. You're not a suspect, anyway, and I don't have anything to prove by getting all over your case."

"Thanks, Evan," Jackie offered. She wanted to comment that his medication seemed to be working today, but she managed to keep the remark from getting out, or even smiling. That's what being an adult is supposed to be about, she told herself—a modicum of self-control. Even if it kills you.

Evan picked up the phone on his desk and punched in three numbers. "Detective Youngquist, I've got Jacquelyn Walsh here. I'd like you to do the interview if that's all right. I've got to get over to Glenwood on that robbery case. Great. Thanks."

He got up from his desk and walked her back outside to the waiting room. "Bernie'll send for you in a minute," he told her. "And she can't talk to you about the case either, so don't try to pull anything with her."

Jackie shook her head, and crossed her heart solemnly. "On my honor."

"Right." He glared at her for a moment, then turned and went back to his office. Jackie stuck her tongue out at him behind his back, and the watch captain snorted into her coffee. She wiped her mouth with a napkin, and stifled a smile.

Jackie glanced at the ancient magazines laid out on the end tables of the reception area. Now she knew what happened to magazines when they got too old even to be in dentists' offices. Someone donated them to the police department. If she were willing to look through them, she could probably find something that would be worth millions to a collector.

"Detective Youngquist would like to see you now, Ms. Walsh," the captain said, gesturing to an interrogation room behind her. "You can wait in there."

Business, not pleasure. She'd been hoping Bernie would come out and say hello first, but perhaps the circumstances didn't warrant being greeted like a friend. Jackie knew Bernie would want to find out what she knew about Cameron and John and Sondra, which wasn't much. She only hoped she could tell the truth without getting John in any deeper.

The interrogation room was gray paint and gray metal, with gray wood trim around the two-way mirror. Jackie wondered whether movie sets were based on real life, or the other way around. She sat in the cold steel chair and hugged her handbag. The air-conditioning kept the temperature in these rooms chilly all year, a tactic to keep people off guard, she assumed, certain that the overuse of air-conditioning couldn't possibly be attributed to the city of Palmer's generosity. The overall effect of the place was that of a . . . well, an interrogation room, she supposed. It wasn't supposed to be cheery, and it succeeded at that admirably.

Bernie kept her waiting fifteen minutes or so—another cop trick. Jackie found herself feeling resentful. She and Bernie were friends after all; was it really necessary to treat her like a perp? But when it came to an investigation, Bernie was a professional, and Jackie had to admit she had no right to expect special treatment based on any personal relationship.

"Hi, Jackie," Bernie said, cheerfully enough, as she entered the room, carrying a legal tablet, a small spiral notebook, and a cassette recorder. "Brrr, it's cold in here, isn't it? Do you want some coffee?" The second chair scraped on the bare floor as Bernie seated herself across from Jackie and set the recorder down between them.

"No thanks, I just had a latte." Department coffee was only slightly less awful than Evan's personal blend. She'd have to remember to grab an espresso anytime she might be threatened with police department coffee, she thought.

"Great, then we'll just get this over with." Bernie flipped through the little notebook until she came to a page of handwritten notes, riffled through the legal pad until she found a clean sheet, dated the top, and looked up. "Sorry we have to do this, Jackie. I know John McBride's a friend of yours."

Jackie saw genuine sympathy in Bernie's blue eyes, and found herself relaxing a bit. She smiled.

"Thanks, Bernie. I know you're just doing your job. No hard feelings," she said, and was relieved to find that there

actually weren't. The fact that there was no one else in
the room with them made it all the more likely that someone was watching on the other side of the two-way mirror—possibly even Evan Stillman. Jackie tried not to take
any of it personally. Dealing with the police in one way
or another was actually getting to be a habit in her life,
if not an especially pleasant one.

Bernie switched on the recorder and said a few intro-
ductory things, and they began. Jackie gave Bernie a run-
down of the shoot's history, of how Cameron Clark had
come to be involved, and told her that while Cameron had
been difficult to work with—to put it mildly—he hadn't
as far as she could tell given anyone a good reason to kill
him.

"Tell me about McBride and Sondra. Clark," Bernie
said, not looking up from her notes.

Jackie sighed. "She wants to be an actress, but her husband refused to move back to L.A. She hung around the
movie set a lot, and John gave her a small part. A dozen
lines. She batted her eyes at him, practically drooled every
time he got close, but he patently ignored her. He told me
he had no interest in her."

"And you believed him?"

"Yes, I did. John's only interest recently seems to have
been in his movie. Sondra's not the only cute young thing
who's had her eye on John, and believe me, he hasn't
noticed a one of them." Not even Katie, Jackie thought,
but didn't volunteer it.

"Mrs. Clark tells us that she last saw her husband at
approximately seven P.M. as he left home enraged, following her confession that she and John McBride had been
having an affair. When did you last see Clark?"

Jackie took a deep breath. *Here goes.* "At Prince Charlie's last night."

"The bar on Kentucky Street?"

"Yes."

"What time?"

"About nine."

"Did you speak to him?"

"Yes."

Bernie raised an eyebrow. Jackie new she was being obtuse, but she had to be careful here. As careful as she could be, anyway. It was hard to go wrong with one-word replies.

Bernie played along. "Please tell me, word for word, to the best of your recollection, what words were exchanged between Cameron Clark and yourself." She crossed her hands in front of her and waited.

Jackie looked up at the ceiling and did her best to recall the exact conversation the night before. Had it only been last night? This day was getting longer all the time, and she wished it could have been over about fifteen minutes ago. She spoke carefully, trying to be honest but hoping her words weren't putting a noose around John McBride's neck. Bernie nodded encouragement or asked for clarification from time to time as Jackie went back over her unpleasant encounter with the inebriated and angry Cameron.

"The deceased told you he'd actually seen McBride's shirt in his house?"

"Behind the bedroom door. But would John be stupid enough to leave it there? Would Sondra be careless enough to put it there if she found it somewhere else? And Cameron was so angry when he said he was going to have it out with John. Do you think if John actually did kill him it could have been self-defense?"

Jackie stopped. Bernie was looking at her, pen paused over her tablet, one golden eyebrow cocked. "Um . . . not considering the murder weapon, no, it doesn't seem likely. Let's skip the speculation for the moment and just go back to what Mr. Clark said to you last night at Prince Charlie's." Her eyes darted to the mirror, and Jackie was more certain than ever that they were being observed, or at least that Bernie thought they were.

At last Jackie had answered all Bernie's questions, even the ones she'd rather not have answered. "Thank you for coming, Jackie," Bernie said. "Evan or I will be in touch if there's anything further we need from you."

After Bernie left the room, Jackie gathered up her handbag and went back through the public areas of the police department and out into the hot summer afternoon. Even in his air-conditioned cell, she thought, John was feeling the heat more than she was. She looked at her watch—still time to get in a visit with him. Had she been hoping there wouldn't be? She didn't have any hopeful news for him, that was for sure.

CHAPTER 11

Jackie waited on a hard wooden bench on the far side of the visiting room, which was decorated with every bit as much charm as the interrogation room she had just come from. The paint on the walls was a dark gray blue on the lower half, and a lighter gray blue above, and whoever had painted it hadn't been overly attached to the notion of straight lines, so that the division between the two colors waved like a calm blue-gray ocean. It wanted only a few grayish fish to complete the illusion.

In the center of the room was a row of conversation areas, something like open phone booths, with battered black standing ashtrays between the booths, and ancient black telephone handsets on either side of a sheet of Plexiglas. Beyond was another door that led to the jail. That door opened finally, and John came through, a uniformed guard right behind him. The guard gestured to an empty booth and Jackie got up and met John on her side of it.

John looked pale and frightened behind the window that separated them. He wore jailhouse blues stenciled with CITY JAIL on the breast pocket and down the sides of the trousers. Just a little more humiliation to add to what he'd already been through. He managed a smile, but it gave way within two seconds to an expression of enduring misery.

Jackie and John picked up their handsets. "How are you doing?" she asked him, hearing her own voice amplified tinnily in her ear through the telephone connection.

"Jackie, I'm in jail. You figure out how I'm doing." John put his free hand over his eyes for a moment. "God, I'm sorry. I had have no right to take any of this out on you." He looked up at her again. "Let's start over. How am I? Not great. How are you?"

"Worried about you, mainly, " Jackie told him. "Evan Stillman is convinced you killed Cameron."

John looked at her for a moment. "Are you waiting for me to say I didn't?" he asked.

"I don't want to feel like I have to," said Jackie, "but they said your truck—"

"My truck was the murder weapon. I know. I'm not denying that, I guess. I mean, they have all that evidence, don't they? But I wasn't driving it when it was used to run Cameron down. You've got to believe me on that, Jackie."

"Then who was?"

"I have absolutely no idea."

"John, I called your house that night—just a couple of hours before Cameron . . . died. You weren't home when I called. Did you spend the night away from home?"

"The police have already questioned me," John told her. "Several times, actually. They seem to be hoping I'll slip up and change my story. My parents' lawyer questioned me. He seems to think I'm not leveling with him, either. And the lawyer's sending an investigator over from Columbus, and *he's* going to question me. If there's anything I don't need from my friends, it's more questions."

"I am your friend, John, but I also had to tell Bernie Youngquist that I'd talked to Cameron only a few hours before he was murdered. And the subject of the conversation was you."

"Me?"

"And Sondra."

"Jesus, that again? I already told you I wasn't interested in Sondra, and I've told the cops I'm not interested in her, and if Cameron had asked me, I'd have told him the same thing. What is it with everyone asking me about Sondra?"

"I guess Evan and Bernie haven't shared this with you yet, but I'm sure they will. Sondra told Cameron that you and she were having an affair."

"A what? That's the stupidest thing I ever heard! Where did you hear that?"

"From Cameron. I ran into him just before he was killed."

"Yeah, you told me you saw him at Prince Charlie's last night, but we never got to finish the conversation."

Jackie nodded. "He was getting drunk and he was getting ready to go looking for you. He said he'd found a shirt of yours hanging on the back of the bedroom door of their house. When he confronted Sondra with it, she confessed to sleeping with you."

"He found a shirt? I'm sorry, Jackie, that's just not possible. The last time I was in Cameron's house was the night he agreed to produce the picture. And I sure didn't leave any of my clothes there then."

"What about Sondra's confession?"

"Who knows?" said John. "I imagine you've already figured out that Sondra has her own agenda where Cameron's concerned. If not, you'd be the only person in town who hasn't. Maybe she thought she could shake him up a little."

"That's what I thought, too," Jackie told him. "Until he brought up the part about the shirt."

"I don't know what to tell you about that. Oh, wait." John stared at the ceiling for a moment. "I took a shirt off on the set one day—when was that?—and I went around the rest of the day in a T-shirt. I think I hung the shirt over a chair or something. When I went looking for it at the end of the day, it wasn't there. I thought maybe someone from wardrobe picked it up, but I never saw it again."

"And that was after Cameron came on the shoot? You're absolutely sure?"

"I'm sure. Cameron's days on the set hold a special place in my memory, believe me. Anyhow, that could be the story behind the shirt, couldn't it? I mean I still don't know why she'd do it, but Sondra could have taken it, couldn't she? And put it on the bedroom door for Cameron to find?"

"She could have, but it would be nearly impossible to prove unless someone saw her do it." Jackie thought for a moment. "There's this, though—if she was only saying she was involved with you for Cameron's benefit, and with Cameron dead and no reason to continue the fiction, she may end up changing her story anyway."

"Yeah, she might," said John, "but it's the story the cops want to believe, so how likely are they to believe Sondra if she starts denying it later?"

"Not very, probably."

"And if I wasn't sleeping with Sondra, what motivation do they think I'd have for killing Cameron?" John continued.

Jackie thought about it. "He was ruining your movie."

John laughed bitterly. "Yeah, well, it's worse than ruined now that he's dead, isn't it? That's no motivation. No, the cops are going to stick with the theory they've got no matter what Sondra says, until they find the real murderer."

"John, I really don't think they're looking for anyone else," Jackie told him.

"Well, they have to! I didn't kill him!"

Jackie sighed. She was more than half-afraid this kid was going to sit back and let his utter faith in the justice system completely destroy him if she didn't do something. At the very least, maybe she could dig up an alternative theory and slip it to Bernie, who could find a way to make Evan consider it and expand his investigation. The way things looked now, he was done investigating.

"You said your lawyer hired a detective. Maybe he'll turn up something."

"I'd feel a lot better if it was you trying to turn up something," John told her. "You know, like you have before. Like you did last winter when you found that dead body in the alley."

Jackie opened her mouth to offer an objection, but John saw it coming, and didn't give her the opportunity.

"Face it, Jackie—you know a lot more about everyone involved in this than some stranger from Columbus. And people who know you are going to be more willing to talk to you about it than they ever would be to him."

Jackie was getting arguments for her participation in this case from all sides now. "John, you know I'm not a professional at this," she protested.

"What do I care about professional?" John objected. "I *don't* care. You've had a lot of experience at it, and I'd feel a whole lot better if I knew you were out there trying to help. And I could pay you. Not right away, but—"

"I don't want money!" Jackie exclaimed. "If I did this it would be because I care about you, not because you were paying me!"

"That's just what I'm talking about, Jackie. This out-of-town guy is doing it because my lawyer is paying him. He doesn't care about me personally—to him I'm billable hours. I'm just one of a dozen cases he's probably working on!" John took a deep breath and brushed his hair back with trembling fingers. "I know I don't have any right to ask you to help," he said, his voice breaking slightly, "but it would mean a lot to me if you would."

"Okay, okay, I might be able to do something," said Jackie. She was sunk anyway—she might as well admit it. "But I'll need all the information I can get from you to get started. Where were you last night?"

John met Jackie's eyes with a calm, steady gaze. "I'd rather not say," he told her.

Jackie found it hard to believe she'd heard him say that. "You'd what?" she burst out. "John, you've been accused you of murder! You have to be able to prove you were somewhere else at the time Cameron was killed! You can prove that, can't you?"

"Not without causing someone else a lot of grief," said John.

"Going to prison for the rest of your life—or worse—is about the most grief I can imagine," Jackie told him. "Whatever you're trying to spare this other person, it can't be worse than that."

"It would be pretty bad," said John. "And I won't put them through it if I don't have to. And I don't have to. Because I didn't do it, and the police have got to figure that out sooner or later."

Jackie wished with all her heart that she could reach through half an inch of scratched-up Plexiglas and shake John McBride to within an inch of his life. "Do they?" she asked him, perilously close to crying herself now. "Do you think innocent people never go to prison? Do you think an innocent person was never executed in this state? If you do, then you're a lot more of an optimist than I am." Tears stung behind her eyes. She blinked them back.

John shook his head, smiling sadly. "Look, I know you're trying to help, and I really do appreciate it—I could never possibly tell you how much. I don't know very many people who would go out on a limb for me like this." He ran both hands through his hair in a gesture of pure mental exhaustion.

"Katie would. If I decided not to look into it myself, I have a feeling she'd be investigating this thing on her own. She's really scared for you."

"What would I do without Katie?" John wondered aloud.

"She's pretty special, all right," Jackie agreed, and decided to leave it at that for the time being. "Anyway, think about letting me in on your alibi, even if you won't tell the police. The more I know, the more good I can do you."

"I just can't, Jackie. I'm sorry. Someday I"ll be able to tell you why." John nodded at the guard, and turned back to the window. "Thanks for coming. Keep in touch, okay?"

"Is there anything I can bring you?" she asked him.

"Just some good news. My folks have everything else handled. Thanks, Jackie. You're a real friend."

He got up and let the guard lead him out of the room.

Jackie watched John walk away and fought back tears. Yeah, she was a real friend all right. Now here was someone who depended on that friendship, and was she capable of helping him? She'd been lucky so far in her unofficial investigations, but did that mean she'd get lucky this time? What if she nosed around in everyone's business and asked questions no one wanted to answer like she always seemed to do in these cases, and what if this time she didn't turn up anything that would help John? She couldn't remember a time when so much rested on her.

But there was always the detective from Columbus. At least he was a pro, and whatever Jackie couldn't find out, he doubtless would. That was some comfort, at least.

She got up and let herself out of the visiting room and walked down the cheerless halls of the jail building, following the signs that led her to the reception area. At the gate, she unclipped her laminated plastic visitor's pass, handed it to a guard, and stepped through a metal detector like the one she'd stepped through on her way in. Other visitors were waiting to go through the process in reverse: a sad-looking woman with two children in tow, and a bone-thin man in a white suit and hat. They sat at opposite ends of a row of chairs near the door and watched as Jackie emptied her pockets and stepped through the little white archway.

A bored guard on the other side of the metal detector said, "Name?"

"Jacquelyn Walsh."

The guard reached into a bin, handed her the handbag she'd surrendered on entering, and nodded her out. Jackie put the strap of the bag over her shoulder and walked toward the door, preparing herself for giving up the city's air-conditioning for the baking heat of the street outside.

"Excuse me, but did I hear your name right? Did you say you were Jackie Walsh?"

It was the thin man in the white suit. He looked expectantly at her with pale eyes in an even paler face. Jackie was pretty sure she'd remember if she'd ever laid eyes on him before. "Yes, I am . . ." she answered cautiously.

The man removed his hat and put it under one arm before proffering his hand. "I'm Piers Ackroyd, of Ackroyd and Jeffreys Investigations in Columbus. I understand you're a friend of John McBride."

Jackie held out her hand, and Piers Ackroyd shook it in a manner so businesslike and precise she had no doubt he'd learned it in handshaking school. Perhaps a night class. He didn't look like he got out much in the daytime.

"News gets around fast, Mr. Ackroyd. I thought you hadn't talked to John yet."

"Well, I was retained by Mr. McBride's attorney, and it seems you're famous enough locally that he was somewhat familiar with your habit of getting into the middle of criminal cases in Palmer."

"I see. What, exactly, did he tell you about me?"

"I'm afraid that's privileged information, Ms. Walsh. I would just like to say, though, that I sincerely hope you won't be getting into the middle of this one."

It hadn't taken Jackie this long to figure out she didn't much like Piers Ackroyd, but even if that realization had been slower in coming, she knew she'd have arrived at it by now. "*Do* you?" she asked, bristling more than a little, but trying hard not to let on.

"I do," Ackroyd confirmed with a firm nod of his pale head. "My job is going to be difficult enough, given the preponderance of evidence against Mr. McBride, without having an amateur muddying up the waters. Has Mr. McBride asked you to take a hand in this matter, as it were?"

"I'm afraid that's privileged information, Mr. Ackroyd," Jackie said with more than a little satisfaction. "Now I really do have to go. Perhaps we'll meet again."

Piers Ackroyd looked annoyed, though the expression wasn't all that different from the others she'd seen so far. "Perhaps we will," he said shortly, then turned away and sat back down in his seat as Jackie went out the front door and into the afternoon heat.

CHAPTER 12

Jackie pulled her car over just before the bridge and parked it on the side of the road, then walked to where the road narrowed over Little Canyon Creek. This was the place, Evan had told the cast and crew this morning, where Cameron Clark had died last night not long after she had talked to him. She'd seen murder scenes before, of course, but it never got over being strange and creepy, all the more so if the deceased were someone she knew. She definitely wasn't cut out for this kind of work.

A fresh scrape was evident in the dark, aging concrete of the bridge railing on the left-hand side, and skid marks were evident on the pavement a short distance away in the direction the truck had come.

Jackie leaned over the low railing and looked down. There was a narrow defile beneath the bridge, and rocks and wild berry canes, and a sparkling creek running through the middle of everything, burbling loudly as it splashed over the smooth rocks. There was nothing about the peaceful slice of nature below her to indicate that twelve hours previously there'd been a body lying down there—the body of someone she'd known. Nothing except the yellow-and-black ribbons of crime-scene tape that had been strung from the bridge railing to the far side of the berry patch and back up the other side again.

She could see where some of the berry canes had been broken, the foliage crushed, but in a few days even that evidence would be hard to find. She tried to imagine what Cameron must have looked like lying down there like a large broken doll, then was immediately sorry when she succeeded.

She heard a car engine approaching the bridge and turned around quickly, all too aware of her vulnerability— standing in the place where Cameron Clark must have been standing last night when a car bore down on him. She had a sudden image of herself flying through the air to land on the rocks at the bottom of Little Canyon. It wasn't a pleasant one.

A small white Toyota pulled up behind Jackie's Blazer and Bernie Youngquist stepped out. "I wondered if you'd be here," Bernie said when she had approached near enough to be heard over the rush of the creek below.

"That was a pretty good guess," Jackie told her. "Why here, of all places?"

"Well, I know you and Cameron Clark weren't exactly best friends," said Bernie, looking down at the creek, "but Evan told me he'd given you a couple of details about the scene this morning. Needless to say I didn't mention the possibility to him, but it occurred to me that given your tendency to investigate, you might want to take a look at it for yourself."

"Oh, I'm not investigating anything," Jackie assured her. She hoped she looked a great deal more innocent to Bernie than she actually felt saying that.

Bernie laughed. "Oh, give me a break, Walsh. I know you better than that, and you know I do. A friend of yours has been accused of killing someone, and you don't believe he did it. What did I think you were going to do? Go home and feel bad? Not a chance. Not you." Jackie expected to see a measure of Evan's disapproval in Bernie's eyes, but what she did see there looked a lot like admiration.

"Bernie, you can't ever tell Evan about this. If he thought I was interfering in any way with the real investigation, he'd . . . Well, I'm not sure what, but something, that's for sure."

"Yeah, he would." Bernie chuckled. "Something. But who says you're interfering? You know how Evan thinks. He's got his perp. As far as he's concerned, there is no 'real' investigation anymore. Mind you, I don't think he'd agree, just on principle, since the case isn't closed yet. As far as I'm concerned, though, there's no reason you shouldn't be looking into Cameron's death if you think you stand a chance of clearing John McBride." She paused, looked at Jackie. "Do you?"

"Do I what?"

"Stand a chance of clearing him?"

"I wish I knew. Why do you ask?"

"Because I'm not nearly as sure as Evan is that he killed Cameron."

"But you don't . . ."

"No, I don't have any evidence to the contrary, of course. But Evan is a 'by the book' kind of cop, and I'm the other kind, I guess. I go on intuition a lot more than Evan does, and my intuition is no slouch. Evan has all the evidence that says John's the murderer, but I just don't happen to think he killed anyone, that's all. I've brushed up against more killers than I ever wanted to in my time, and I don't think this kid's one of them."

"Then you'll help me?"

Bernie held up a hand like a glamorous crossing guard. "Whoa, girl," she said, one corner of her mouth unable to suppress the beginnings of a smile. "Let's get a few things straight. I won't hinder you. I won't rat you out to Evan, and I'll answer any questions I can without compromising

Evan's case. I guess what I'm saying is, yes, I'll help, but only in very limited ways."

"You're an angel," Jackie declared.

"Hardly," said Bernie, and the half smile became a grin. "Try goddess."

"So take me over the major points of this scene," Jackie told her. No sense beating around the bush now. She was feeling that familiar elation—that sense Jake must feel when he caught a scent on the breeze—of being on the trail of something. "I want to know just what happened."

Bernie walked back over toward the bridge railing, and Jackie followed. "Here's the point of impact," Bernie said, pointing at a spot on the bridge just beyond which was a deep scrape, gleaming with metal fragments. "Back there you can see skid marks." She indicated the skid marks on the road several yards from the bridge that Jackie had noted earlier.

"Does that mean that the driver tried to stop when he saw Cameron?" Jackie asked her.

"No," said Bernie. "Though I might have thought so myself before I knew the difference. The thing about these particular skid marks is that they're the kind that occur when a driver speeds up suddenly—not the kind that comes from someone trying to stop."

Jackie eyed the long set of marks on the road's surface, imagining the heavy steel pickup truck hurtling toward her with murderous intent. She shuddered slightly. She still couldn't picture John behind the wheel, but whoever had run Cameron Clark down like roadkill last night hadn't done it timidly.

"The driver put the truck in low gear and really laid on the gas when they got to that point," Bernie continued. "Stomped it right to the floor and spun the tires. By that time they were already over on the wrong side of the road, as you can see." She sighed quietly. "As you might imagine, that looks bad for John if the prosecution can actually place him in the car, even circumstantially. It'd be tough to argue that he hit Cameron by accident when the evidence shows he crossed over into the oncoming lane and then floored the truck. There's no sign at all that whoever was driving tried to avoid the collision."

"So the only hope for John is to prove he wasn't the person driving."

"Exactly. And you know Bill Ellenshaw's going to take this all the way."

"The new prosecutor?"

"Yep. He thinks he can get a murder-one conviction, and let me tell you, he doesn't half mind that his name's going to be mentioned in the L.A. papers. The guy's competent, I guess, but what a publicity hound!"

"In Hollywood, we called them media sluts," said Jackie. She turned back toward the scene of the crime with a sigh much deeper than Bernie's had been. She'd seen Bill Ellenshaw hamming it up for the TV cameras, and she knew that Bernie was right. This was the kind of case that could make his reputation from one end of the country to the other, and from what Jackie knew about these things, he wasn't about to go soft on it, or make John a deal to get a conviction on a lesser charge.

Jackie stood where Bernie had indicated earlier, facing in the same direction Cameron had probably been. "So Cameron was walking along the bridge here, and he had his back to the oncoming truck?"

"That's what they determined from the injuries," Bernie said. "You said yourself he was intoxicated, so he probably wasn't too alert. I don't know that he didn't hear it and try to outrun it, but the coroner thinks it pretty much took him by surprise."

"Now here you can see that the driver scraped the bumper of the truck up against the railing," said Bernie, walking farther up the bridge and pointing to the cement railing at knee height on her left. "The victim wasn't crushed against the railing, so that must have happened as he was going over the side, leaving his shoes behind on the pavement."

"His shoes?"

"All laced up and everything. Physics in action."

"You mean inertia?"

"Yep. The body's at motion, the shoes are at rest. It happens quite frequently in the case of sudden collisions with pedestrians. It's one way of knowing the exact point of impact."

Jackie looked back at the long black skid marks on the pavement, then at the deep scrape on the bridge railing. "This was pretty cold-blooded, wasn't it?" It was less a question than a statement—one that reflected the steady tightening in her stomach ever since Bernie had started describing Cameron Clark's death.

"Yeah, it was. And as if this weren't convincing enough, the murderer left the scene and washed the truck."

"How about prints?"

"The steering wheel and gear stick had John's prints on them, of course, since he drove the truck to work that morning. The other interior surfaces were clean—cleaner than they would have been if someone hadn't wiped them down. There are a couple of prints from the dash that haven't yet been identified. Passenger side, though, so don't get your hopes up."

"So far nothing is getting my hopes up," said Jackie. "So did the truck kill him, or the fall?"

"Well, the fall might have by itself, the way he landed, but the injuries caused by the impact with the truck— shattered spine, neck broken just at the base of the skull from being snapped back—those are sufficient to have caused death, and that's what counts. Bill Ellenshaw's not going to back down on the first-degree-murder charge if he can help it. This is the biggest case to hit Palmer in a long time, and the first really big one since he was elected, and he wants his name in lights."

"Of course John's lawyer might be a match for Ellenshaw. Especially if there's no direct physical evidence linking John to the scene."

"It's not over until the jury foreman sings," Bernie agreed. "But you probably don't want to leave it to that, if I know you. The arraignment's tomorrow morning, and if I had a quarter I wouldn't bet a nickel of it on the chance the judge will set bail."

"If John isn't back out on the street before this goes to trial, his movie goes down the toilet," said Jackie. "What we have to do is stop it from going that far."

"What *you* have to do," Bernie reminded her. "I have to keep my job and my professional integrity. So don't go asking me for something I can't give you."

"How will I know what that is if I don't ask?"

"Ask, then," Bernie said with a shrug. "Just be prepared to hear me say no."

"Okay. Would you be willing to tell me anything about what you learned when you questioned Sondra Clark?"

"No."

Jackie nodded. "I think I see how it works, now."

"Good. You're a quick study, Walsh. I will tell you something I saw, though. There's no way to keep it a secret, I suppose."

"What's that?" Jackie asked.

"She's got a shiner under her left eye that no amount of makeup could ever cover."

"You think Cameron . . ."

"That's what Evan thinks." Bernie gave Jackie a wave and walked back toward her car. "Call me about lunch in a couple of days if I don't call you first."

"It's a deal," Jackie called after her. As Bernie pulled away toward downtown, Jackie looked up the road toward Cameron Clark's house, located out of sight around several bends and a lot of trees in a newly built suburb of Palmer. What could it hurt to drive by and see if Sondra was home? Absolutely nothing is what, she assured herself.

She got back into the Blazer and drove in the direction of the Clark residence. Cameron hadn't been that far from home when he had his run-in with fate and a '61 Chevy pickup, she thought to herself, and now he was never going to get there. Who had seen to that?

CHAPTER 13

"I really can't talk to you," Sondra Clark said, turning away and leaving the front door open. She was wearing tight white jeans and a flowered shirt knotted above her midriff, delicate white leather high-heeled sandals—an outfit that suited Los Angeles better than it did Palmer, Ohio. Her hair and makeup were their usual careful perfection, but no amount of makeup could cover up the bright, fresh bruise on her left cheekbone.

"I've got to pack," Sondra said as she turned away and walked back into the living room. "I'm going back to Chicago to be with my mother and father until the funeral on Tuesday." She stopped in her tracks and clenched her fists, looking up at the ceiling. "God, I can't wait to get out of this miserable town!"

Jackie took the open door to be an invitation and followed Sondra into the relentlessly pale living room she'd last seen the night the four of them drank a lemonade toast to the success of *Under the Dog Star*. It had been less than a week ago. A long damned week for everyone concerned.

A suitcase and garment bag were open on the long white sofa, and a pile of shoes cluttered the floor nearby.

Bottles and jars and brushes and tubes overflowed from an overnight case on the coffee table. Sondra disappeared into the bedroom without saying anything else to Jackie. Jackie waited, glancing around at the expensive but ever-so-slightly-tacky surroundings. The house seemed to have been decorated by someone whose idea of elegance was garnered from watching movies about movie stars. Come to think of it, that probably fit Sondra Clark to a tee.

Sondra re-emerged with a double armload of clothes on hangers and proceeded to stuff them into the garment bag. "What happened to your face?" Jackie asked, touching her own face and almost feeling that painful swelling. The skin on Sondra's cheekbone was broken in a tiny zigzag line. Whatever had hit her had hit her hard.

Sondra's fingers went to the injured cheek and hovered just above the broken skin. "I got clumsy," she said, in a tone that left no room for any suspicion that the subject could be any of Jackie's business. She bent down and continued poking loose bits of fabric into the corners of the garment bag.

"Are you sure it's all right for you to be leaving town?" Jackie inquired.

Sondra straightened up from her clothes stuffing and looked over her shoulder at Jackie. "I'm not a suspect," she told her. "Nobody thinks I killed my husband."

Not quite nobody, Jackie thought. She probably shouldn't have expected Sondra to be beside herself with grief for Cameron—after all, no one else was—but it seemed more than a bit odd to her that the brand-new widow's overwhelming emotion right now seemed to be impatience to leave Palmer. Jackie began to entertain—not without a certain amount of satisfaction—the idea that Sondra may have been the one who put out her husband's lights.

"Where's my list?" Sondra asked no one in particular. She fished in her jeans pocket and withdrew a crumpled sheet of paper. "Okay. Pack clothes, turn on porch lights, leave some lights burning, check doors, check stove . . . I get so nervous when I go on a trip. I'm always afraid I'm going to forget something important. Usually I do." She hurried into the kitchen. Jackie followed. Sondra jiggled all the knobs on the stove and seemed satisfied with their positions.

"So you've already spoken to the police?" Jackie asked.

"That big guy. The one you mentioned. Efrem something. He gave me his card. It's over there on the counter."

"That'd be Evan Stillman."

"That's the one. He asked me so many questions about my relationship with Cameron I wondered if he was moonlighting as a marriage counselor. Except that Cameron's dead, so there isn't any more relationship. Poor Cameron," she said, but without much conviction. But then possibly she hadn't spent as much time contemplating the vision of Cameron's broken corpse as Jackie had. Sondra turned on a light outside the sliding-glass door that led from the backyard to the kitchen, closed the door, and walked back into the living room with Jackie close behind her.

"He said it would be fine for me to go visit with my mother and father until the funeral, but I had to give him their address and phone number, he said, in case he needs to get ahold of me for some reason. I can't imagine what reason he'd have, frankly. Have *you* talked to them?"

"I had an interview with Detective Youngquist a little while ago. They don't think I did it, either." Sondra snorted, an unattractive sound coming from one so glamorous.

Jackie had decided long since that Sondra wasn't too bright—not exactly a difficult conclusion to arrive at—and maybe if she took the offensive just a bit, it would never occur to Sondra to question her right to ask any of these things in the first place. "Did Detective Stillman ask you about your affair with John?" Jackie asked, as matter-of-factly as she could manage.

Sondra tried a hostile look, then abandoned it. "I guess everyone must have guessed by now, anyway," she said. "John and I have been an item since my first day on the set. He spent the night here when Cameron went to Chicago to buy new film stock, and the night I said I was out of town? We spent that night at a motel. I'm not in love with him or anything, but it was just one of those things, you know?" She wrestled the hangers onto the hook at the top of the bag and snapped it shut.

"I'm not sure I do, but I'll take your word for it. And how did Cameron take it when you told him?"

"I didn't tell him. He found one of John's shirts in our bedroom and confronted me with it. But he didn't take it well, since you ask. There was a terrible scene. Lots of yelling and screaming. What would you expect?"

"Is that where you got the bruise?"

"I told you, I got clumsy. I bumped it on something. A door."

Right. The bruise on Sondra's cheek looked to Jackie as though it had been made by a fist—a right fist, probably, given that it was her left cheekbone that had taken the damage, and probably wearing a nice heavy ring that would account for the broken skin over the cheekbone. It didn't seem too far a stretch, all things considered, to attribute that fist to Cameron Clark.

Sondra zipped up the garment bag and went back into the bedroom. When she came out again she was almost hidden behind a huge pile of clothes, shoes, and toiletries, which she proceeded to dump into the suitcase and mash down with one hand while pulling on the zipper with the other.

"Need any help with that?" Jackie asked.

"Yeah, do the zipper while I get the clothes out of the way," Sondra requested. "I've got a taxi coming in five minutes, and I don't want to miss my plane."

"What motel?"

"Excuse me?"

"Do you remember which motel you and John went to?"

Sondra straightened up and placed her hands on her hips. "My, aren't we the curious one!"

"A friend of mine is in jail. Tomorrow he'll be arraigned, probably on first-degree murder. Then he'll go on trial for his freedom, or just possibly his life."

"I'm sorry," said Sondra, but she didn't seem particularly sorry to Jackie. "No, I don't remember which motel. One of those cheap ones out on the interstate." She waved her hand in the general direction of the highway in question.

"I should think you'd care what happened to John," Jackie suggested, "if you and he were as intimate as you claim."

"I already told you I'm not in love with him," Sondra intoned with more than a hint of impatience. "I barely know him."

Jackie crossed her arms in front of her chest. "Frankly, Sondra," she said, "I don't believe John was sleeping with you. I don't know why I don't—you're beautiful, and I'm sure men go crazy for you right and left, but I don't think John was one of them. Maybe you got Cameron to believe it, and it sure looks like the police believe it, but you haven't convinced me."

"I don't care if you believe me or not," Sondra said adamantly. "It's true. John's crazy about me. Cameron suspected it even before he found the shirt. That's really the reason he was being such a big jerk to everyone, but I didn't want to bring it up at the time."

"Aren't you worried that John might actually have killed your husband? That's what the police think."

Sondra sighed deeply and rolled her eyes heavenward.

Then she proceeded to explain to Jackie as if she were a small and not terribly bright child. "No, I don't think he killed Cameron. He couldn't have. He was with me all night. And that's what the police *know,* because I told them when I talked to them today."

Jackie's heart sank. An alibi from Sondra was worse than no alibi at all, given that it was John's whereabouts at the time of her husband's murder. "I don't believe you," she told Sondra.

"I already said I don't care."

Well, this was going nowhere. "Let's get back to the shirt for a minute."

Sondra looked at her watch. "Half a minute," she said, picking up her luggage and carrying it to a spot near the front door.

"If you were seeing someone behind your husband's back, why would you leave an article of his clothing where your husband could find it?" Jackie called after her.

"Well, I didn't do it deliberately," said Sondra in a tone of complete exasperation as she set down her luggage. "I guess I just forgot it was there."

Jackie shook her head. If the shirt had been hanging on the door, as Cameron had told her, then someone had gone to the trouble of hanging it there. A man who would rendezvous with a married woman in her own home would be unlikely to hang his shirt neatly on a hook behind the door of a room she shared with her husband, and Jackie was pretty sure that if she were the one entertaining an illicit lover in such a shared bedroom, she wouldn't go around picking up his discarded clothing and hanging it where Cameron was almost sure to notice it sooner or later. And bright or not, she didn't believe for a moment that Sondra would either. "I just forgot" just didn't wash somehow.

A car horn honked outside. "That's my taxi," said Sondra. "Oh, my God, I forgot my jacket. Tell him to wait!" She ran upstairs in a clatter of high heels.

Jackie opened the door and stepped out onto the porch. The taxi driver leaned over and held out his hands in a questioning gesture. "She'll be right out," Jackie called. She glanced back the way Sondra had gone. Why wasn't the impatient widow at least putting on a pretense of grieving for the dear departed? she wondered. Was it more suspicious or less so that Sondra seemed almost entirely unaffected by the death of her husband? Jackie wished she knew.

Sondra was back down the stairs in a flash wearing the missing jacket, a little white bolero thing to match the jeans. She switched on a floor lamp next to the sofa, picked up both pieces of luggage, put them back down to turn the lock the on the front doorknob, then picked them up again.

"I really am sorry about John," she told Jackie, "but there's nothing I can do about it." She turned her house key in the deadbolt lock, trotted onto the sidewalk, opened the taxi door, and flung the suitcase and garment bag into the backseat.

"Yes, there is," Jackie called after Sondra as she closed the cab door. "You could tell the truth!"

CHAPTER 14

The message light on the answering machine was blinking again, and Jackie fought with the impulse to throw a dish towel over it. Instead she punched the button and listened to her messages as she read the latest postcard from Peter in California. Jake came through the pet door with Charlie close behind, and lay down next to her feet.

"Jackie, let's get together and talk." That was Ral Perrin. "I didn't get a chance to tell you what Matt Darwin had to say about Kurt and Cameron. I think in light of what happened today, we ought to discuss it." Jackie sighed. She had hoped to get away from the subject of dead producers for a few hours, but it would appear that wasn't going to be possible. "Mercy and I are having dinner at Miranda's at six—" Jackie consulted her watch. It was five forty-eight, and she was starved. "—and we hoped you could join us. See you then, I hope."

So something was finally starting to brew between Ral and Mercy. Jackie had known it would eventually, if Mercy had anything to say about it.

"Jackie, this is Lorraine Voss." Jackie's eyebrows rose in surprise. Not every day she had a message from the former star of *Eyes of the City*. Not *any* day up until now.

"I'm really at loose ends with the shoot on hold and everything," Lorraine was saying, "and I was wondering if you wanted to get together tomorrow for lunch or something. I promise we won't say a single word about Cameron Clark, because if your day was anything like mine, that's all anyone wants you to talk about."

"You've got *that* right," Jackie muttered to the answering machine.

"So I'll call you in the morning—not too early—and we'll come up with someplace to go. If you want to, that is. If you're free and all. Bye for now."

Jackie made a mental note to keep some time free for Lorraine, though she had no idea what they'd talk about if not the murder of their producer; it wasn't as if they had a great deal in common. Maybe they could reminisce about L.A., though Jackie didn't actually remember those days all that fondly.

"Hi, babe." Jackie smiled at the sound of Tom Cusack's voice coming out of the little speaker on the machine. "Sorry I didn't catch you at home. We're on our way up to San Francisco and points north. We should be in the city late tonight, and I'll give you another call when we get checked into a hotel. I thought the kids would enjoy doing the whole tourist thing tomorrow—cable cars, Fisherman's Wharf, Alcatraz, and all that. Then we'll go up to San Rafael and stay with my brother and his wife for a day or two. Anyhow, I'll talk to you tonight. Love you. Bye."

Jackie's eyes teared up. After what she'd been through today, she really wanted to feel Tom's arms around her, hear him saying everything would be all right even if neither of them actually knew that for sure. From the sound of his message he hadn't yet heard of Cameron's murder, didn't have the slightest idea what she was going through.

"Oh, well," she reminded herself with some difficulty.

"I can't feel too sorry for myself. I'm not the one who's dead, and I'm not the one who's in jail. I guess I only *think* I've got problems." She saved Tom's message in case she needed to hear his voice again before he called, and grabbed her handbag up from the sideboard. "Jake, Charlie, I'm going out to dinner. You're not invited. I'll leave the pet door unlocked, and you can let yourselves in and out until I get back."

Jake raised his head, ears perking up at the sound of the word "dinner."

"Oh, gosh, I've got to feed you guys, haven't I?" said Jackie. She hurried into the kitchen and poured them each a dish of food. At the sound of the food hitting the dishes, the big shepherd and the small ginger cat trotted in and waited for her to finish—Jake patiently, and Charlie less so. She gave them each a pat as they settled into their meal.

"See you tonight, boys," she said as she headed for the front door. "Don't do anything I wouldn't do while I'm gone." The restful evening at home she'd been hoping for was shot, but she figured it was all to the good. It was time to get a juicy meal and some juicy gossip.

"I got this straight from Matt Darwin," Ral said, "and you know he isn't inclined to exaggerate."

"Not as well as you do," Jackie reminded Ral, "but I'll take your word for it for now."

Ral nodded as he took a bite of his "heat loaf," Miranda's answer to meat loaf. There was no meat involved, but the thick slice of whole-grain loaf was studded with bits of fresh green chilis, smothered in roasted jalapeños, and drowned in a zesty Mexican sauce. It was probably the spiciest dish you could get in this corner of the Midwest, and in the absence of authentic Mexican food between here and Texas, Ral ate it every chance he could get. He hadn't eaten anything resembling real Mexican food, Jackie imagined, since he left Los Angeles and the movie industry behind for a quiet couple of years teaching cinematography at Rodgers University. His eyes lit up like a Christmas tree. "This is just too damned good." He sighed as he sawed off another bite.

Mercy had opted for the Portobello mushroom wrap with three cheeses, and Jackie—when she finally arrived, fifteen minutes late—had wisely followed her example. When the meal arrived, they had tucked in earnestly, too busy enjoying Miranda's cooking to get into yet another conversation about the late Cameron Clark. Finally, though, their plates were empty, small talk had been exhausted, and the waitress had come around with the after-dinner coffee. Ral opened up the conversation they had come here to have:

"Jackie, do you remember when Kurt Manowski got the professional-hitman part in that action movie of Jim Nesmith's a couple of years back? I think it was called *Killer's Heart.*"

"No, that was Jack Wynn," Jackie corrected him. I know because Peter rents that video about once a month. It's one of his current favorites. Wynn did a hell of a job in that, I thought. It's not that easy to make an audience believe a sympathetic killer." She poured cream into her coffee until it turned a very light brown.

"Oh, yeah, I saw that one," Mercy chimed in. "It was Jack Wynn, all right. Pass me that cream pitcher, Jackie."

"Okay, you guys pass Pop Culture 101," Ral admitted. "It was Jack Wynn in the part of the hit man when it was released, but what you two probably don't know, and I didn't either until I talked to Matt, was that Nesmith originally shot four weeks' worth of footage with Kurt Manowski in that part."

"Four weeks?" Mercy sounded amazed. "From what I know, it'd be pretty expensive to replace four weeks' worth of principal photography. And I'm guessing that film didn't exactly have an enormous budget."

"Well, they didn't replace every shot, of course," said Ral, "but they did go back and do pickups with Wynn, and reedit everything up to that point."

"Why, exactly?" Jackie asked him. "Why did they decide they had to replace Kurt? He's a good actor, and I'd imagine he was perfect for the part. Was it the drinking thing again?"

"That was the official word from the producer," Ral said, "but Matt says Kurt had cleaned up his act a whole bunch to get that part. After nearly thirty years of working his way up from bit parts to third- or fourth-billed heavies, it would have been his first lead in a feature, and it probably would have meant a whole new career for him. Matt says the word around town is that Kurt put everything he had into making good on that shoot, but the producer had it in for him, and got him fired."

"Didn't Kurt beat up Wynn in some bar after that?" Mercy asked. "It was in all the trades, and even the *L.A. Times* carried it on the front page."

"That's what happened all right," said Ral. "The short version, anyhow. He was charged with aggravated assault, but the judge seemed to think there were mitigating circumstances, and from what I know of Jack Wynn's reputation, there probably were. He reduced the charge to assault and battery, and let Kurt off with probation if he'd check himself into a clinic. So he did, but after he got out he was back to smaller parts again. Lead roles for a guy who looks that mean don't come along very often, I guess."

"I guess not," Jackie agreed.

"And besides that, the word was out on the street that Kurt was trouble," Ral added. "A lot of producers just wouldn't touch him after that."

"There's been more than one career derailed by 'the word,'" Mercy noted.

"So," said Ral, leaning forward as if to let them in on a juicy secret, "would you like to hazard three guesses as to the name of the producer of *Killer's Heart*?"

Jackie and Mercy looked at one another and nodded. "Would we need more than one?" Jackie asked him.

"Nope."

Jackie sat back against the padded back of the restaurant booth. "You'd think I would have noticed his name, I've watched that movie so many times. So that's why Kurt hated Cameron. Why did Cameron hate Kurt?"

"That much I don't know," Ral admitted.

"It would seen like it had to go back to before they worked together on *Killer's Heart,* if Matt's story stands up," Jackie said, thinking aloud. "I mean if the story's true, Cameron already had it in for Kurt before he fired him from the project. But as the producer, wouldn't he have had to hire him in the first place? Or at least have a say in it? I wonder what that's all about."

Ral shook his head. "Matt didn't say."

"Would you talk to him some more for me?" Jackie asked. "I'd like to get every possible detail. If there's any likelihood that Kurt Manowski is our killer, I'd like to take it to Evan and see if he'd get the prosecutor to consider it."

"You could talk to him yourself if you wanted," said Ral. "Matt still remembers you from your television-writing days. He told me that he once directed an episode of that cop series while you were scripting it. He says before he got that gig, the only thing he'd ever directed was beer commercials."

"The series was *Cop Lady,*" Jackie reminded Ral. "Yeah, I remember the episode Matt directed. And I remember running into him from time to time around town in those days. And strangest of all, I remember those commercials of his. Weird, but I guess they sold the beer. He was an odd kind of guy, but I liked him."

"He seems to remember you fondly, too."

"In that case," said Jackie, "go ahead and give me his phone number. I'll call him tomorrow."

"Maybe if you're lucky you can dig up something that will make Evan stop looking at John and start looking at Kurt," said Mercy.

"Maybe if we're *really* lucky," said Ral, "we can get John out of jail before his cast and crew scatter to the four winds, and get this movie made."

"To getting John out of jail!" said Jackie, raising her drink above the table. Ral and Mercy joined glasses with Jackie in a toast. "To getting John out of jail, and to getting our movie made!"

CHAPTER 15

Jackie pulled away from Miranda's and looked at the clock on the Blazer's dashboard. It was half-past eight, and given the time difference in California, she didn't expect Tom to call for a while yet. She wasn't looking forward to telling him about the latest developments since their conversation last night. Was it only last night? How different everything had become since this morning. It felt like weeks. At any rate, she had to talk to Tom, and she had to be honest with him. He wasn't going to like learning that she was looking into Cameron's murder, and as bad as she felt about that, she didn't feel bad enough to back off—not if it meant weaseling out on John.

And she had to talk to her mother, she supposed. Frances would want all the dirt on Palmer's latest murder, and Jackie knew she'd have to suffer through a certain amount of gloating when she confessed that yes, she was actually investigating, sort of. But the person Jackie really wanted to talk with right now was Kurt Manowski.

Or did she? She had to admit she found him intimidating, but then so did a lot of people. Like the rest of them, she'd been conditioned by years of movie viewing. From playing young thugs at the beginning of his acting career, Kurt had moved on to play middle-aged thugs, armed robbers, major criminals, and strong-arm men. She couldn't recall once seeing him in any role where an audience was actually supposed to like him. If Cameron hadn't fired him from *Killer's Heart,* how differently his career might be going now. And if she had seen him in that part, how differently, she wondered, might she be thinking about him now?

There was something about Kurt's face and bearing that seemed to hint at menace, though she had to admit to herself that he had never acted unfriendly to her on the set. Still, the thought of running into him in a dark alley was not a welcome one. Right now he was one of her two top candidates for the job of cold-blooded murderer, and having witnessed that last confrontation between him and the late producer of *Under the Dog Star,* she didn't have a lot of doubts about his feelings for the deceased. The question was, was he capable of going from feeling to action? Could his hatred of Cameron have been strong enough to make him murder the man with John's truck? And was he cold enough to then hang the rap on John? Because whoever had stolen John's truck, then washed it and returned it to his house, had done so to pin the crime on someone else. The last thing Jackie wanted was to arouse Kurt's suspicions about her unofficial investigation, but she very much did want to watch his face when she raised the subject of Cameron Clark.

Although Kurt never touched alcohol these days, she knew she could probably find him at the Crow Bar at some time in the evening unless his usual habit of hanging out with his buddies from the set had been abandoned in the wake of Cameron's death. Knowing this, Jackie turned away from her usual route home and turned down Indiana Street. Would it seem just too strange, she wondered, for her to walk in and invite herself to sit with them, since she'd never done it while Cameron was alive? She guessed she'd just have to play it by ear.

Up ahead she could see the flashing neon sign depicting a crow wearing a waistcoat and a top hat, with a walking stick under one arm. One flash, and the crow tipped the hat off his head with the tip of one wing and winked his eye. Another, and it was back on again. Jackie slowed down as she neared the bar and eyed the parking situation. Not good. Just as she was getting ready to drive around the block, she saw a nearby car turn on its lights and pull away from a perfectly good parking spot. Then the driver of the car turned his head, and she recognized Kurt's profile. Well, there went her chance of getting him into a conversation, she thought, not without a grain of relief.

As Kurt pulled away, Jackie had a sudden thought. Why not just follow him unobtrusively to wherever he was going? If it turned out to be a public place, she could arrange to bump into him and initiate that conversation after all. If he was going home, she'd call it a night and try her luck again tomorrow.

Kurt's car—a rented late-model compact—drove at a reasonable speed through the streets of downtown Palmer, and turned onto East Wisconsin Street, which quickly left the city proper behind, changing into a gently winding two-lane road as it approached the ravine that separated the city from its newest suburbs. With a jolt, Jackie realized that Kurt was heading for the scene of the crime. His crime? She wished she knew—it might help her decide whether or not she wanted to follow.

She did follow, dropping back to where she could barely see his taillights so that she'd be less likely to arouse his suspicion. The car drove over the fateful bridge without slowing down, and up the slight hill beyond to where the trees thinned out and the houses began. Jackie began to get a very strange feeling as Kurt retraced her route of the day before and turned onto Cameron and

Sondra's street. She made a right turn into the street just before their house and parked the car several houses from the corner.

For a few moments Jackie sat in the driver's seat of her Blazer and considered whether she wanted to get out. She looked down at her clothes, and was relieved to see they were all dark—she'd be less obtrusive that way, she was sure. Taking a deep breath to calm the hungry butterflies that seemed to be chewing their way through her stomach, she opened the door and stepped down into the street, then walked to the corner and looked in the direction Kurt had gone. His car was parked two or three doors down on the same side as Cameron and Sondra's house, and she couldn't see anyone sitting in it. Jackie took another long, slow breath and turned the corner.

Why is it, she wondered, that when you're walking down a street where you have no business being, you'd be willing to swear in a court of law that every single neighborhood resident is peering at you from behind their curtains? She hazarded a glance at the house she was passing; the curtains were undisturbed, as her rational mind knew they would be.

She looked over her shoulder. Nothing there. Of *course* there was nothing there. But when you feel like a criminal, there's always something there in your imagination. Jackie gave thanks that she was not a criminal. There were lots easier ways to make a living, and she was grateful to have found one.

She was approaching the car she had followed here— Kurt Manowski's car. It suddenly occurred to her that Kurt might not have gone into the house at all, that he might be slumped down in the driver's seat waiting for her to come walking by, that he might even be crouched down in the passenger seat, hand poised on the door handle, waiting for her to get close enough to reach out and—

"Oh, stop it!" she whispered to her racing imagination.

She came abreast of the car and looked inside. It was empty. Her knees shook as she walked past, and her heart thumped painfully. There were also easier ways to make a living than following murder suspects around, she reminded herself. Why was it, then, that she always seemed to find herself doing it? If she really liked her quiet life as a college film instructor, why didn't she just do her job and go home and watch television like everyone else?

There was a light burning downstairs in the living room of the Clark house, and one somewhere upstairs. Jackie remembered Sondra switching on a lamp before she ran to her cab, but she had no idea if Sondra had left a light on upstairs, or whether this light might have been turned on by someone who was inside now. She stepped up onto the porch and cautiously tried the doorknob, but it didn't give. Stifling the urge to turn and run back down the sidewalk, she stepped down onto the lawn and crept around the side of the house.

The side gate opened without a sound, and Jackie felt gratitude again—this time that Cameron and Sondra had never seen fit to acquire a dog. She closed the gate behind her and looked at the house. What was wrong? Then she remembered. No porch light. Sondra had turned a porch light on outside the sliding-glass doors to the kitchen just before she left this afternoon. Either it had burned out since this afternoon, or Kurt had switched it off to make his coming and going less conspicuous, and that meant that her movements were less noticeable as well. Thanks, Kurt, she thought.

As she suspected, the sliding door wasn't locked. Sondra had probably forgotten it in her hurry to get the hell out of Palmer. Gingerly, she applied pressure to the handle, and the door obliged her by sliding gently open enough for her to slip through. She closed it behind her, then opened it again, thinking it might be best to have a quick exit available.

Now what? Jackie realized she'd feel a lot less conspicuous in a completely darkened house, but the light from the living room made her uncomfortably visible here in the kitchen. A lot of good these dark clothes were doing her now. She listened for noises from other rooms, but there was nothing going on that was any louder than the pounding of her heart. Cautiously, she walked out of the kitchen and into the hallway that connected the downstairs rooms. A stairway led up to the bedrooms, and as she got closer she was certain she could hear something now— the sound of rustling paper and the sliding of a drawer— from somewhere above.

Jackie put a foot on the bottom stair, then stopped before she transferred her weight to it. Stairs, in her experience, always creaked. There was no way to sneak up a set of stairs if the person you were trying to sneak in on was paying any attention at all. As long as Kurt was upstairs, she was going to have to stay downstairs. And that sort of took all the purpose out of it. Maybe it would be best to leave now and avoid the embarassment—or worse—of being discovered.

She turned away from the stairway just as she heard the sound of heavy steps approaching the stairs from above. She ran into the kitchen just before hearing footsteps coming down the stairs—which creaked—and squeezed out through the doorway she had left herself. Scanning quickly, she saw that the walk back to the side gate was too long and unprotected. She needed cover, and she needed it now. She dove under a row of dark juniper bushes just to her right, and lay very still.

Footsteps across the kitchen, then a pause, probably at or near the door. Had he remembered that he'd shut it behind him? He stepped out onto the cement porch and slid the door shut again. She didn't hear him locking it, which could mean that he planned to come back. By looking to her left without moving her head, Jackie was able to see part of a pair of black shoes walking by her. Close by her. The shoes stopped just in front of her face as their owner stood there, probably scanning the yard. She could hear his breathing, a bit labored, just above her. Jackie tried not to breathe at all, but that wasn't exactly practical. She let out the breath she'd been holding, very slowly, and fought the urge to gasp as she took in some air.

The feet turned, paused again, then moved away, slowly. Jackie waited for the sound of the side gate latch clicking shut, which followed within a few seconds. Kurt hadn't been in the house very long, she observed. Did that mean he had found whatever he came looking for? And what would that be? Evidence that would link him to the crime, or to Cameron? But why here, of all places? Her mind raced around in circles for what seemed like forever, but was probably less than half a minute. What brought her back was the sound of a car starting up somewhere down the street and pulling away. Kurt's car? She could only hope.

Jackie crawled out from under the bush and got to her feet slowly, brushing dirt and dried juniper bits from her clothing. Thankfully, Kurt had neglected to turn the porch light back on. She looked back toward the gate to make sure he was really gone, hesitated on the porch for just a moment, then opened the sliding-glass doors and let herself back inside. This time she walked up the steps and found herself in a hallway, dimly lit by the light coming from a sliver of doorway ahead. She opened the door and found a large bedroom lit by a small lamp on a dresser, with a vanity area beyond that led to a bathroom.

Jackie stood just inside the door and looked around. This room, like the living room, reflected Sondra's decorating habits. It was overwhelmingly white, with lots of metal and glass. The mirrored walk-in closet doors were standing open, and a trail of clothes and hangers led from it like a trail of giant bread crumbs. A polished steel

dresser topped by a mirror occupied a nearby wall. Jackie
pitied the movers whose job it had been to haul it up those
stairs.

A couple of dresser drawers were standing open with
lacy things spilling out of them and little piles of more
lacy things on the floor below. A tall heap of clothes occupied the center of the queen-size bed. From the hurry
Sondra had been in on her way to the airport, all of this
mess could have been made by her. Unless Kurt was looking for something Sondra may have stashed in her lingerie
drawer, he probably hadn't been responsible for the
room's present state of disarray.

A tall cherrywood chest with brass handles stood along
the opposite wall from Sondra's dresser, looking totally
out of place in the gleaming white room, and not seeming
to have been rifled, either. She opened a drawer and saw
neatly folded dress shirts. A second drawer held little bun-
dles of socks, folded identically, and inserted into little
diamond-shaped organizing containers that each held one
pair. A third held several pairs of men's pajamas, also
folded with precision, the tops on top—neatly buttoned—
and the bottoms on the bottom. They looked entirely
undisturbed, especially in contrast to the rest of the room.
So if not here, where had Kurt been looking?

She walked back into the hall and opened another door,
revealing a carefully made-up guest room in pastels.
Jackie was practically allergic to pastels, and had been
even when she'd had a home in the suburbs not entirely
unlike this one. She could almost feel a rash breaking out
on her body when she looked at the minty greens and
yellows and pinks. She forced herself to go inside and
look around, but the drawers contained only clean linens
and towels, and the closet only sealed packing boxes.
There was nothing under the neatly made-up bed but a
few juvenile dust bunnies.

The next door led to a bathroom, and the door next to

that to a linen closet, but the final one opened onto what seemed to be a study—Cameron's, by the look of it: leather and dark wood and framed pictures of actors with personalized inscriptions, and what looked to be a terrific movie souvenir collection. A banker's lamp with a glass shade cast a soft green light on everything.

There was nothing pastel in sight, and nothing white aside from paper. It must have been Cameron's sanctum sanctorum—his shelter from Sondra's obsession with pale. The leather-topped oak desk held a few piles of papers, a much-thumbed-through copy of the script to *Under the Dog Star,* and a clipboard of schedule sheets. It didn't look disturbed, particularly. True, it was considerably more cluttered than the living room or the guest room, but it didn't appear to have been ransacked. Jackie stepped inside and took a closer look.

Going through Cameron's drawers gave her a very strange feeling. She was reminded of watching over Peter's shoulder one evening as he was seated at the computer, absorbed in an on-line role-playing game. Every time he killed a monster, he double-clicked on the image of it lying on the ground, and took whatever gold, weapons, or whatever it had been carrying. "What are you doing?" she had asked him. "Looting corpses," he'd replied with a wicked grin. That's how Jackie felt as she opened Cameron's desk drawers to survey their contents—like she was looting a corpse.

No treasure here, though. Lots of student papers and production paperwork from the movie, and some Hollywood memorabilia. The top drawer wasn't locked, but it held nothing more interesting than pens, rubber bands, and paper clips. What could Kurt have been looking for in here, and did he come downstairs so quickly because he had found it, or because he had given up?

She closed the last drawer and straightened up. Turning around slowly, she surveyed the room, trying to take in the general feel of it as well as the details. Every available shelf and every flat surface held at least one movie prop— an antique telephone, a reproduction of a flintlock pistol, a couple of breakaway glass whiskey bottles with old-fashioned labels, a jar of fake rubber army ants, half a dozen miniature monster models, their latex skins beginning to peel and crack. Lots more stuff, too—enough to keep a movie nut like her amused for hours.

Jackie wished she had the time and the inclination to take a good long look at all of it, but she just wanted to get out of there. She'd followed Kurt and damned near gotten caught. She'd gritted her teeth and come inside again for a look around, but now she'd looked around and hadn't found anything. She just really wanted to get out and get home.

As she was guiltily wiping her fingerprints from the brass doorknob on the way out, her gaze stopped on a small wooden table between the printer stand and a book-case that was completely bare. She hadn't really noticed it before, but she had to wonder why, as crowded as everything else was, there would be nothing at all on this one table.

She walked back into the study and looked closer. A light coating of dust had settled on the table since it had been dusted last, and Jackie noticed that there was slightly more around the edges, less in the center, and none at all in the four square spaces where four feet, each perhaps an inch across, had rested on the table. So Kurt *had* found something up here. But what? She tried to imagine what would have sat there, with a footprint about a foot square, and been intriguing enough to Kurt Manowski to make him take it with him. A safe?

She hurried downstairs and outside, where she shut the door behind her. There was no way to lock it from the outside, she realized, and that was the real reason why Kurt hadn't locked it, not that he planned to return. If he had Cameron's safe, he probably figured he had what he needed. She was sorry she couldn't lock the door, though, and hoped no real burglars would discover the house while Sondra was away.

Kurt's car was nowhere in sight, not that she'd thought it would be. She walked down the darkened street to her Blazer and climbed inside with an almost palpable sense of relief. She didn't feel good about having gone poking around in Cameron and Sondra's home, but she'd have felt a lot worse if she'd been caught!

CHAPTER 16

Matt Darwin wasn't at his phone all morning, and after Jackie had called three times she remembered that according to anyone who'd ever known him, Matt wasn't usually at much of anything before noon besides sleeping. She decided to let her message speak for itself. He'd call her back when he got it, she was sure.

Not for the first time, Jackie wished she'd succumbed to temptation and bought herself that sexy little cellular phone she'd seen at ElectroVision when she'd gone to get Tom a new car stereo for his birthday in May. All this going back and forth to pick up messages from such an archaic device as an answering machine—not even a digital one at that—made her feel like a character in a period film.

Even Tom, who didn't seem to care one way or the other about gadgets, had a pager so Joseph could reach him in an emergency if he was away from the kennel, and Marcella Jacobs had both a voicemail service and one of those little boxes that showed you who was calling. Jackie felt awfully behind the times. She made a vow to catch up one of these days.

The doorbell rang. Jake looked up from his place on the rug at the front door, then at Jackie.

"I know, I know," she told him as she walked across the living room of her town house. "It's not your job to answer the door. Some days I wish it was, though." She peeked through the little hole at eye level and saw a fish-eye view of Katie Nolan standing on the front porch with tears running down her face.

"Katie, come in." Jackie opened the door wide and Katie stumbled forward into her arms.

"Jackie, I just came from the courthouse. They indicted John on a charge of first-degree murder, and the judge denied his bail!" Katie sobbed against Jackie's shoulder.

Jackie felt awful, but she wasn't particularly surprised. She knew John's lawyer would probably try to get the charge reduced, but between Evan's certainty and the district attorney's eagerness to try this case in the living rooms of America, there was no chance they'd make any kind of deal. And if the DA would, John McBride wouldn't. He knew he was innocent and he was relying on the rightness of things to free him.

Also, although it wasn't as much of a foregone conclusion as most people thought from watching television, the fact was that judges almost never granted bail on a first-degree-murder charge; there was too much likelihood of the defendant taking advantage of his temporary freedom by trying to disappear. When someone's life is on the line, there are powerful temptations not to meekly show up in court. So it pretty much had to come to this, given the circumstances, but Katie hadn't thought that through, and now she was very nearly hysterical.

"I want you to come into the kitchen, and I'm going to make you some herb tea and we'll talk. John's been indicted, not convicted. We still have a lot to hope for."

She led Katie by the arm to her vintage dinette set, sat her down in one of the chairs, and handed her a box of tissues from a nearby countertop. "Here," she said. "You need these." She poured water into a teapot and started a fire under it while Katie blew her nose and wiped her eyes.

"Thanks, Jackie." Katie sniffled. "I didn't even know I was coming here until I pulled up in front of your house. I just don't know what to do."

"I'll tell you what you have to do," said Jackie, searching through her cupboards for packages of herbs. "You have to be strong for John. He's going to need someone to be there for him and connect him with the outside world. Not just his mother and father, but someone like you."

She found the herbs she was looking for—valerian and chamomile—her mother's tried-and-true recipe for emotional upset. The combination tasted a bit like sugared sweatsocks, but some honey should help to disguise that. She found one of those little squeezable plastic bears and added it to a tea tray along with two cups and a bag of Barry's Gold Blend for herself.

"I know John doesn't care about me," said Katie, "but, Jackie, I love him so much!" She started crying again, more quietly this time.

"You don't know anything," Jackie reminded her, bringing over the tea tray and sitting opposite Katie. "What you think doesn't necessarily have any bearing on reality, and you don't have any idea what John thinks."

"No, but look at his last girlfriend."

"That tall blond number? Clarice something?"

"Clarissa Vogel. She's everything I'm not—beautiful, sexy—"

"But John broke up with her, didn't he?"

"He did, but he's been sneaking out to see her on the side. Her current boyfriend works nights."

The teakettle screeched, and Jackie got up to make the tea. "That doesn't sound like John to me," she said. "Why would he sneak around to see her? Why wouldn't they just get back together again?" She handed Katie her cup and sat back down. "Put the saucer over that and let it steep at least ten minutes," she told her.

"I guess he's sneaking because her boyfriend's a big, mean animal," Katie said, placing the saucer on top of the cup and wrinkling her nose at the smell. "And I guess they're not getting back together because that's not what John wants. He told me he's been going over there and talking to her at night, trying to help her get up the courage to leave this guy."

"He's abusive, this boyfriend?"

"He broke Clarissa's nose in a fight, then walked out and left her bleeding on the floor. She called John and he took her to the hospital, and of course she lied about what happened so the bruiser wouldn't get in trouble with the law."

"Sounds like a great relationship so far," said Jackie, stirring honey into her tea.

"John told me she made him promise not to beat the crap out of what'sisname, but it was killing him to keep it. He wanted to kill the guy." Katie looked up, wide-eyed, when she realized what she'd said. "But John would never—"

Jackie put a hand over Katie's. "Of course he wouldn't. He couldn't. That was just the way men talk when they're being protective. It was just talk."

"It's just that he's so softhearted," Katie told her. "I know that's a good thing, but sometimes he goes too far, and Clarissa's a perfect example."

Jackie stared off into space while the steam from her teacup rose up to cloud her vision. "John told me he was protecting someone," Jackie said. "He said he was with someone who'd be caused a lot of grief if that were known. Do you suppose he meant Clarissa? Could she be his alibi?"

"You don't think he was with Sondra?" Katie asked.

"No, I don't, though she told me to my face that he was. John denies it, of course."

"But that would be an alibi, wouldn't it?"

"Yeah, if he actually was with her. Or is she the one he's trying to protect?"

"Why would Sondra need protection from anyone?"

"Somebody was hurting her, too, and I think it was probably Cameron. I saw her yesterday on her way out of town, and she had a big old nasty bruise right here." She pointed to her left cheekbone. "The night Cameron was killed, Sondra had told him that she and John were sleeping together."

"I knew it!" said Katie, bursting into fresh tears.

"No, I don't think she was telling the truth," Jackie rushed to assure her. "She told me the same thing, and I think she was lying through her teeth. But she had one of John's shirts, and it was hanging on the back of the bedroom door, and Cameron found it there."

"John lost a shirt on the set," said Katie, looking up from her tattered tissue. "He asked me if I knew where it was. Neither one of us ever found it."

"Well, I think Sondra stole it and took it home to provoke something with Cameron. I think she provoked herself right into a black eye. She was probably trying to get Cameron the hell out of Palmer, Ohio, by lying about John and her. Of course she's Sondra. Who knows what she was thinking."

"Or *if*," Katie snorted. "Thanks, Jackie." She plucked a fresh tissue from the box and blew her nose. "I feel a little better. And you're right—John needs me not to be making him feel worse by getting all hysterical. I should go visit him."

"Yes, you should."

The phone rang. Matt Darwin at last, she thought. "Hello?"

"Hi. It's Lorraine. I meant to call earlier, but I slept in this morning. I think yesterday kind of took it out of me."

"Me, too," said Jackie with feeling.

"So, how about that lunch?" Lorraine asked.

"Name a place."

"What do I know about Palmer?" Lorraine asked. "I get breakfast and lunch within two blocks of the set, and drink my dinner at the Michigan Grill."

"In that case, I'll name a place," said Jackie. "Why don't you meet me in front of the main entrance to Farmers' and Growers' Market at noon?"

"I don't think I know where that is," Lorraine told her.

"Aren't you staying at the St. Luke Apartments over on Tenth" Jackie asked.

"That's right. Number twelve."

"I'll just come over and get you, then. I know it's pretty hot out, but do you mind walking?"

"It's not something I'm exactly accustomed to," Lorraine replied with a dry chuckle, "but I think I can survive."

"I'll bring Jake," Jackie said. "He's got lots of friends in the market."

"See you around noon, then," Lorraine agreed. "Bye."

"Come on, Jake!" Jackie called when she hung up the phone. "We're going for a walk!"

Jake scrambled up from his place on the rug, upsetting Charlie, who had been fast asleep on the Shepherd's flank. Charlie tumbled to the floor and looked up grumpily, then lay back down in the warm place Jake had left and curled up as if nothing at all had happened. Jake walked into the kitchen and took his heavy leather lead down from a hook near the back door, then came back into the living room carrying it in his mouth.

"Good boy, Jake." Jackie gave her dog a pat and a good scratch between the ears, and was rewarded with a broad doggie smile. She clipped the lead onto Jake's collar and

called good-bye to the cat on her way out the door, but
Charlie was curled up in a tight orange ball, oblivious to
the world.

"Come on in," Lorraine said, "I'm just about ready to go."
She gestured with a hairbrush she was holding in one
hand. "Just making myself presentable for beautiful downtown Palmer."

"Okay if Jake comes in? His manners are impeccable,"
Jackie promised.

"Not a problem to me. Make yourselves at home," Lorraine said. "I won't be more than a minute."

Jackie and Jake walked into the living room of the
small but neat apartment that Andy Fry had rented for
Lorraine when she first came to town, a few days before
principal shooting had begun on *Under the Dog Star*. Lorraine excused herself and walked into a small bedroom,
shutting the door behind her.

Both the out-of-town stars of John's movie lived here
at the St. Luke, Jackie reminded herself, though she had
no idea which of the apartments was Kurt Manowski's,
and she didn't recall seeing his car parked outside when
she got here. It was perhaps a quarter of a mile from here
to the set, and John had arranged rental cars for both Lorraine and Kurt—not luxury cars, by any means, but reli-
able transportation.

The apartments had been rented furnished, and there
was little in this one to suggest it was more than a temporary place for someone passing through—the carpet,
drapes, and furniture were a bit tired looking but clean,
and the freshly painted walls were bare except for a large
print depicting a Pacific Ocean sunset that hung over the
sofa. It was the same kind you usually saw in shopping-
mall craft shows, one very much like another, so often as
to make you despise seascapes, she thought. The one exception to all the impersonality in the room seemed to be

a cluster of gold photo frames arranged on a brightly colored scarf laid over the mantel of the tiny gas fireplace. Jackie walked over for a better look.

Three of the frames held pictures of individual children, blond and good-looking—what appeared to be twin boys about ten years old and a girl perhaps two or three years younger. The fourth and largest frame held a group shot of the same three children and Lorraine, posed professionally but casually, seated on a huge leather sofa.

Lorraine came back out of the bedroom. "My kids," she said, gesturing at the photographs.

"They didn't come with you?"

"They're around a lot when I film closer to home, but it wasn't exactly in the budget on this production," said Lorraine with half a smile. "They're staying with my husband in Malibu until I get back. My ex-husband, I should say."

Jackie couldn't help but notice the slight but unmistakable drop in Lorraine's voice when she said the word "ex-husband." Not a happy situation, then, not that divorces could usually be characterized as happy, despite the happiness she herself had felt to finally obtain her own. Probably best not to get into it—it certainly was none of her business, and she'd had entirely too much contact the day before with things that were none of her business.

Lorraine looked for a long moment at the picture of the four of them, her face strained and sad. Then she seemed to come out of it. "I'm ready for our walk when you are," she said.

The sprawling Farmers' and Growers' Market building took up a one-by-three block chunk of what was known as Palmer's Market District. It was unashamedly old-fashioned, with a large painted and gilded sign, completely devoid of neon, over the main entrance, proclaiming its name amid artfully placed piles of flowers, carrots, cabbages, and the like. Inside, the first floor was almost entirely devoted to produce and flowers, and the second and third floors were given over to shops and restaurants. "Let's eat first," Jackie suggested, "and I can do my vegetable shopping on our way out."

They walked up a wide wooden staircase that led to the upper floors. The stairs were worn down in the middle by millions of footsteps over the last ninety-some years. It gave her a pleasant sense of the passage of time, much as she always got when she came here, and she tried to get here once a week to shop for vegetables and fresh flowers, if nothing else. "We're going all the way to the third floor," Jackie told Lorraine. "The view's great from up there."

"Yeah, if I don't give myself a heart attack, I'm sure I'll enjoy it," Lorraine quipped.

On the third floor they walked past the picturesque diner that John had arranged to film in after hours one night next week for an upcoming scene in the movie. The place had been carefully designed to look like it existed in the 1940s, with dark red upholstery on the booths and stools, lots of gleaming chrome and steel, and a genuinely old Wurlitzer jukebox. It would have been a perfect set for John's movie, but now that all-nighter might never happen. Lorraine had promised they wouldn't discuss Cameron Clark, and Jackie hoped they'd stick to that. If she brought up the movie it was going to be impossible to stay off the subject, so she forewent pointing out the diner as they passed. She'd done all the thinking about murdered producers she wanted to do, at least for a few hours, and she had no doubt Lorraine felt the same.

A few doors farther down, past Gillian Zane's cozy bookshop—A Reader's Market—and a vintage clothing store—Rags and Riches—was Il Matto, a modest little Italian place that Jackie loved. The food was good, the service unobtrusive, and there was a nice view of the gently rolling countryside beyond Palmer from the tables nearest the windows. It should be perfect for a bit of low-pressure socializing.

"I've been dying since I came to this place," Lorraine admitted over bowls of thick minestrone and tiny loaves of bread, "but whether out of loneliness or just boredom, I couldn't say."

"It's not for everyone," Jackie admitted. "And it's certainly not as stimulating an environment as Los Angeles. But it wasn't too tough a decision for me to come back." She indicated their view of the city and the landscape beyond.

"Of course not," said Lorraine. "It's very pretty here, in a small-town sort of way. And you had a son to raise."

"Oh, but I didn't mean . . ."

"No, it's all right." Lorraine dismissed any suggestion of offense with a wave of her hand. "I chose to raise my children in L.A. because I had to work there. My husband—as was—produces a very successful television series, and we could afford the best schools, and to live in the best neighborhoods." She shrugged. "I'll admit it's not perfect, but what town is?"

"None I've seen," said Jackie sadly. She remembered her attempt to find perfection in the suburbs, and how badly that had turned out. She was definitely not the suburban type, she knew now, though it had taken her entirely too many years to figure that out.

"And besides, what else would I do for a living if I didn't act?" Lorraine wondered aloud. "I've been at this for so long, I'm really not qualified for anything else. I never really had another job, unless you count waiting tables to help pay my way through college. But you want to know a secret? What I always wanted to be was a detective."

"Is that why you took the part in *Eyes of the City?*"

"Get real. I took the part because it paid so damned

much money. The fact that it was a detective show was pure gravy. But I really got a kick out of getting to do all that mysterious stuff every week, even if it wasn't really me. Know what I mean?"

"Absolutely."

"I even made a couple of suggestions to John to try some of the little tricks I used to use on the show, you know?"

"Yes, he mentioned he was going to incorporate some things from *Eyes of the City* at your suggestion. He seemed to think they'd fit right in."

Lorraine sighed. "I'm worried about John. You don't suppose he'll be in jail for long?"

"He might have to stay until he goes to trial—the judge refused bail. That's usually the case when the charge is first-degree murder."

"You don't think he actually did it, do you?"

"No, I don't. But the police do."

"But won't they have to let him go when it becomes evident that he didn't kill Cameron?"

"That might not come out until the trial," Jackie told Lorraine. What she didn't want to say was that it might not come out at all. It was entirely possible that John might be convicted of Cameron's murder on the strength of circumstantial evidence, but that was a discussion that was just too depressing to have with Lorraine. "Unless the detectives uncover something else before then." She also thought it might be best to avoid mentioning that the detective in charge of the case wasn't likely to spend any time looking for evidence in John's favor.

"So what are you going to do now that the shoot's on hold?" Jackie asked Lorraine. "I know John doesn't expect you to wait around Palmer forever for him to be able to put things together again."

"I've talked with Kurt about it," Lorraine said. "We've decided we can both afford to stick it out until the end of the month. The rent on the apartments is already paid, and our contracts had us here for that long, anyhow. We're hoping they'll just let him go and we can get the movie made. If they don't, though . . ."

"I understand. Your work is in L.A. You have to get back there and rustle some up. Of course you've got that part you were going for . . ."

"Yeah, but that project's not even out of preproduction yet. They won't be shooting for another couple of months. It's Kurt I worry about. You know how hard it is for him to get work nowadays. Or I presume you do, anyhow."

"Well, I don't exactly keep on top of industry gossip anymore, but I know Kurt had some difficulties."

Lorraine laughed without humor. "That's a polite way of putting it." She picked up her wineglass, drained it, and signaled the waiter for another. "I guess you're something of a detective yourself," she said to Jackie. "I mean John wrote *Under the Dog Star* about your adventures, didn't he?"

"Not exactly. And I'm not exactly a detective. It's kind of hard to explain, but it all started when I first met Jake."

"Your dog?"

Jake, whose lead was tied to a wood-and-iron bench outside Il Matto's door, and who had been napping happily in the hallway outside, perked up his huge black ears as he always did at the sound of his name.

"Yep. It's really all his fault I got involved in an unsolved murder, and the rest just sort of happened."

Lorraine gave Jackie a wry half smile. "There was a handsome police detective involved, if I'm not mistaken."

Jackie could feel herself blushing. "There was. His name is Michael McGowan. Now I've got the label of 'detective,' and he's writing a new cop show down in L.A."

"That new dramatic series that's premiering in the fall with Bart Hogan?"

"Yep, that's Michael's show," said Jackie. "He's happy as a clam down there."

"And you two aren't an item anymore?"

Jackie shook her head. "Not for a long time now. I'm seeing a dog trainer by the name of Tom Cusack."

"Any regrets?"

"About me and Michael? Lots, actually, but that water's gone past the bridge long since."

"And you wouldn't be tempted if he showed up back in Palmer? Or if you found yourself in L.A.?"

A waiter arrived with their main course, and Jackie wasn't required to answer that question right away.

"Michael was an important person in my life once upon a time," Jackie told Lorraine after their waiter had retreated to the kitchen, "but what I've got with Tom is right now, and it's too special to risk."

"Is this shaping up to be a permanent relationship?"

"The words 'permanent relationship' still give me a chill, even nearly four years after my divorce. But yeah, it seems like that's what it's on its way to becoming, all right."

"Mark is my second husband," said Lorraine, gazing out the window and pouring herself another glass of wine. "I was married for the first time when I was barely out of my teens, and it was a real lesson in what kind of guy not to choose. I thought I'd learned a lot about people in general and men in particular before I got married the second time, but I was still miserable most of the time. Maybe it was just me."

"Well, I think we're all responsible for a lot of our own misery, comes to that," said Jackie.

"I guess I'd have to grant you that," agreed Lorraine. "I wasn't bitter about the marriage, or about Jeffrey, or about much of anything until he started threatening . . ."

"Threatening what?"

"This is too heavy a conversation to have over spaghetti

aglio olio," said Lorraine with a wry half smile. "Some other time, maybe. Or maybe not even then."

"Whatever you say. Let's keep it to safe subjects, then. We've been doing a pretty good job so far. Let's hear more about your detective aspirations."

"Oh, it was never very serious, just sort of an adolescent fantasy of mine. Back when I was in college in Pasadena, I used to follow the crime stories in the newspapers and see how the police arrived at their conclusions. I once bought a book about how people manage to disappear and construct new identities, and then another one about how good detectives can find them. I wrote notes in all the margins."

"Sounds like a strange but interesting hobby," said Jackie with a smile.

"It was that. What I always wanted to do, but never had the guts, was to follow somebody."

"Anybody in particular?"

"Oh, you know, just pick someone leaving a parking lot and follow them and try not to be seen. Just for fun. Have you ever tailed anyone?"

"Not that I can recall," Jackie lied.

"On television, of course, people notice right away if someone's following them, provided it's necessary to the plot. But I don't think most people ever consider the possibility that someone might actually be tailing them. I know I don't."

"True. But most people don't commit crimes any more important than the pilfering of office supplies."

"True. Anyhow that was my fantasy. Not quite a strong enough one to change my major from theater to police science, though."

They were getting closer to that subject they'd agreed to stay away from, Jackie noted to herself. Did she dare broach the forbidden subject of Cameron Clark?

Lorraine decided the matter. "Enough about crime. I

had to talk about crime all day yesterday, to the police and everyone I laid eyes on. I ended up going home and closing the blinds and pretending I wasn't there. I just wish all this were over." She delivered this without her usual "couldn't care less" attitude, so it was clear to Jackie that she really meant it. Jackie wished it were over, too. But first, she wished John would get out of jail and whoever killed Cameron Clark with his pickup truck would be there in his place.

CHAPTER 17

"I'll take two of those crookneck squash, half a pound of snow peas, and a pound of spinach," Jackie told Paulie Signorelli as she stood in front of his produce stand and assembled the ingredients for a stir-fry. She had already picked out baby carrots, zucchini, and broccoli to add to the brown rice she'd picked up at another shop.

"Are you going to eat all that food?" Lorraine asked incredulously.

"I guess I'm used to buying in larger quantities when Peter and Tom and Grania and my mother are here," Jackie admitted. "We all have dinner together a couple of times a week. But I suppose I can cook up a really big meal and freeze what's left over. It's not like I have a lot else to do right now."

"I never learned to cook," said Lorraine. "I guess I was always too busy with something else."

"I'm not that good at it myself," Jackie assured her, "but Peter's learned to eat whatever I put in front of him, pretty much."

Paulie added up Jackie's total with a pencil and notepad, and she paid him for the vegetables. "Can Jake have a biscuit?" he asked her.

"If you're determined to spoil him, there's nothing I can do to stop you," Jackie told him.

Paulie reached into a paper bag behind the boxes and stacks of fresh fruit and vegetables under the "Signorelli Brothers" sign. He pulled out a dog biscuit, and held it slightly above Jake's head. Jake opened his mouth and Paulie dropped the biscuit inside. Jake made short work of it.

"Say thank you, Jake," Jackie instructed him.

Jake gave two short barks, and Paulie laughed at the trick like he always did. "See you next week, Ms. Walsh. See ya, Jake."

"Bye, Paulie." Jackie moved on down the aisle between the vendors, and Jake followed. From here they usually went to Mrs. Chan's flower stand, and Mrs. Chan was always good for another dog treat. Jake was a favorite with a lot of folks in the market, Jackie knew, and with dog treats so easy to come by, market day was always a favorite with Jake.

"Peter's your son, right?" Lorraine asked as they walked along toward the flower vendors, weaving among hundreds of other determined shoppers.

"That's right. He just turned fourteen."

"You're very lucky to have him," said Lorraine.

Jackie turned to face the actress, surprised at the emotion in her voice. "I know I am," she said. She was afraid to say anything more. It was evident that Lorraine was very close to tears. Evidently, even though she had three beautiful children of her own, Lorraine's family situation was far from happy right now.

They stopped at Mrs. Chan's, where Jackie knew she could always find the freshest flowers in Palmer. She picked out two bouquets while Jake received his snack and a pat on the head from Mrs. Chan. "I'll take both of these," she told the flower vendor. Mrs. Chan wrapped the bouquets in plastic bags and cones of newsprint. After paying, Jackie handed one of the wrapped bouquets to Lorraine. "Maybe this will help make that temporary apartment of yours feel a little bit more like home," she told her.

Lorraine took the bouquet, tears standing in her eyes. "Thanks, Jackie," she said. "They'll make the place beautiful."

They walked on past dozens of stalls selling produce, flowers, honey, preserves, and farm-fresh eggs. Then they entered the crafts pavilion and made their way past jewelry makers, quiltmakers, woodcarvers, and purveyors of tie-died T-shirts before they came to the end of the market's ground floor and a big open door leading out into the summer sunshine. Lorraine reached into her handbag, pulled out a pair of sunglasses, and put them on.

"So have you had your turn being grilled by the Palmer police yet?" Lorraine inquired.

"Yes, thankfully," said Jackie.

"What do they think?"

"Besides that John ran Cameron down in cold blood with his truck?" Jackie asked.

Lorraine flinched.

"I'm sorry," Jackie offered. "I didn't mean to snap at you. It's just that I believe John when he says he didn't do it. And I went to visit him in jail today."

"How is he?"

"Utterly miserable and utterly uncooperative."

"Huh?"

"I know he has an alibi for that night," Jackie told her, "but he won't tell me what it is. He's protecting someone."

"That's very like him, I think," Lorraine said. "He's very softhearted, isn't he?"

"To a fault, I'd be forced to say right now." Jackie sighed. "He's taking his life into his hands."

"But surely you don't think they'll convict him if he didn't do it. You don't, do you?"

"I hope not," was all Jackie could offer on that note.

"So who do you think did it?" Lorraine wanted to know.

"Sondra could have," Jackie offered.

"Anyone else?"

"Cameron had a long and bitter history with Kurt," said Jackie.

"Cameron had long and bitter histories with a lot of people," said Lorraine.

"But not all of them were in Palmer, Ohio, night before last," Jackie reminded her. "And Kurt has a history of violence."

"I suppose he does. Still, I've never thought him capable of killing anyone."

"How well do you know him?"

"Oh, we've worked together from time to time since I got into the business. He had a recurring bad-guy role on *Eyes of the City*."

"Oh, I remember! Nestor Verona, right?"

"Very good! Yeah, I go back a way with Kurt," said Lorraine. "We're not friends, exactly, and we don't stay in touch or anything, but we do seem to keep turning up on the same projects. Like this one, for instance."

"And you don't think he could have done it?"

"I can't really say that I know he couldn't have," Lorraine said thoughtfully. "He just never seemed the type, in spite of his looks. Of course I wasn't there when he almost killed Jack Wynn."

"Well, whoever did it now has Piers Ackroyd to contend with," Jackie said.

"Who the hell is Piers Ackroyd?"

"He's a private investigator from Columbus. He's in town to find out anything he can that might help in John's defense. I'm sure he'll be talking to you."

"By your tone of voice, I gather this isn't something I should be loking forward to with joyful anticipation," Lorraine ventured.

"He's an unpleasant man," said Jackie. "But at least he's a professional investigator."

"Does that mean you won't be doing an investigation of your own?"

The fewer people around town who knew Jackie was looking into Cameron's murder, the less likely that word would get back to Evan Stillman. "This is way over my head," she told Lorraine, choosing her words carefully to avoid an outright lie. "The smart thing to do would be to let Piers Ackroyd handle it."

"Yeah, he's the professional, I guess," Lorraine agreed.

Yes, Jackie thought to herself, Ackroyd's the professional. But she knew that wouldn't stop her from doing whatever she could.

"I'm not sure I have anything material to add to what I told Ral when I talked to him the other day," said Matt Darwin when Jackie finally stopped playing phone tag and got ahold of him later that afternoon. "I wasn't there on the set, so my information is secondhand, but I got it from a lot of sources and weeded out the exaggerations, and it's still pretty awful."

"I know this is all speculation," said Jackie, "but from what you know personally of Kurt, do you think he could have killed Cameron?"

"Gee, Jackie, I wish I could say. I guess I do, anyhow. I've always kind of liked Kurt, but there's no denying he has a long history of violence."

"You mean like that thing between him and Jack Wynn?"

"Yeah. That, and a few other little mix-ups he's been in over the years. Of course Jack Wynn picked that particular fight in the first place, which is probably why Kurt got let off so light even after he put Wynn in the hospital with a fractured skull. To say he was provoked would be putting it politely."

"So he could be violent if he were provoked? Because Cameron seemed to be going out of his way to provoke him, if you ask me. And what started all this in the first place? I mean did it start back when Kurt still had that part in *Killer's Heart*?"

"I just don't know. But I know someone who may."

"Don't hold out on me, Matt."

"Do you remember an old screenwriter by the name of Neville Ice?"

"The British guy?"

"Yeah, he had a couple of Oscar nominations in the sixties and seventies."

"He sort of dropped out of sight after that. What happened? Is he still alive?"

"Not by much, if you want the truth. He's dying of lung cancer, but he's determined not to croak until he finishes a book he's been working on for ten years about some old Hollywood mystery. It's going to be his masterpiece, he says."

"He's writing a mystery?"

"Not fiction—it's a real mystery. It's all about some starlet who disappeared a long time ago. It got covered up at the time, and most people have forgotten about it, but Neville's been investigating it for a few years now. He's not well enough now to do a lot of the legwork any more, but he hopes he can still find out enough to get his book written before he gets too sick."

"And what's that got to do with Kurt Manowski and Cameron Clark?"

"Well, Neville knows a lot about Cameron—a lot more than he's ever been willing to tell me. He told me once that he thought Cameron might have a part in this story he's been writing about, but it turned out to be a sidetrack that went nowhere. Before he found that out, though, he uncovered some pretty unsavory stuff about him."

"Do you think he'd agree to talk to me if I called?" Jackie asked Matt.

"He might if you could actually talk to him," Matt told her, "but you'd have to get through his wife and his sister to get to talk to him in the first place, and I'm not sure that'd be possible. They're very protective of the old guy. They screen all his phone calls, and there aren't more than half a dozen people in the world who can actually get through to him in person anymore."

"Do you happen to be one of them?"

"Aw, I never call Neville. Too much bother running the Ice Women's gauntlet for a phone conversation. But I go by and see him about twice a week, and they don't even try to keep me out, 'cause me and Neville are such old friends. Too bad you don't live in L.A. anymore, Jackie."

Jackie had been thinking the same thing. "When are you going to see him again?" she asked.

"Uh, let's see—that'd be the day after tomorrow. We've got a date to play poker in the afternoon."

"Do you suppose you could ask him some questions for me?"

"About Cameron Clark? I guess I could, but you're the one who knows what happened out there, not me. It could take days to pass questions and answers back and forth through me. I get the feeling time is important, here, and no one knows how much of it Neville's got left."

"You're right, of course." Jackie was getting an idea, and she didn't particularly like it. "What if I were there? Could you get me in to see him?"

"No problem. If you're with me, you're okay. Neville loves to talk to people, and he doesn't get much of a chance these days. A lot of his old Hollywood buddies have kind of fallen away since he got sick. And if you don't mind my saying so, it'd probably do him a world of good to see a good-looking woman after being shut up in that house with his wife and sister for most of the past year. Those women are terrifying."

"I never mind being called good-looking, Matt," Jackie said. "I'll be on the first plane I can get out of here tomorrow." She wondered where that sudden decision had come from, but she knew she wasn't going to change it now that it had arrived.

"Do you need me to meet you at the airport?"

"I don't think so," she said. "I've got an old friend down there."

"You're going to Los Angeles?" Tom's voice was nothing short of incredulous over the telephone connection. "Why, Jackie?"

"There's a man down there that I have to talk to. He knows the whole story of what happened between Cameron Clark and Kurt Manowski. I can't reach him by phone; I have to talk to him in person."

"Kurt Manowski the actor?"

"Yeah, he and Cameron had a long and bitter history before fate and appendicitis threw them together on this shoot."

"And you think Manowski may have killed Clark?"

"I don't know, Tom. I just know I don't think John did." It seemed best not to mention the fact that she had seen Kurt at Cameron's house the night before, and that he had possibly taken something from the house. To go into that subject she'd have to admit that she was following around someone she thought might be a murderer, and that she had illegally entered Cameron's house herself. She'd tell Tom all about it eventually, when it was distant enough that they would both have a good laugh about it. She wished heartily that day were here already.

"Michael McGowan's still in L.A., isn't he?"

"Yes, but you know that's not why I'm going down there."

"Yeah, I guess I do. I'm sorry." Tom paused. "Will you see him while you're there?"

"Yes, Tom, I'm planning on seeing him. We're friends now. In fact, I've talked to him already. He's going to be picking me up at the airport." Jackie waited for Tom's response, which took a moment to come.

"Okay." He sighed. "I'm sorry, Jackie. I'm sorry I can't seem to just accept that like a mature human being."

Jackie knew why Tom was concerned about Michael, and it warmed her heart a bit. "Who's mature when it comes to love?" she asked him.

"Good point. I love you, babe."

"I love you, too, Tom."

"And you'll be careful?"

"Excruciatingly careful."

"Should I cut the trip short and come down there?"

"I can't imagine what good that would do; you and the kids have already been to L.A. I'm just going to spend some time talking to this friend of a guy I used to know in Hollywood, catch a plane back home, and wait for you guys to come back."

"Are you taking Jake?"

"No, I'm leaving him and Charlie both at the kennel with Joseph. I'm only going to have a conversation with an aging screenwriter. I shouldn't need a trained police service dog for that."

"I guess not. Peter wants to talk to you."

"Put him on."

"Hi, Mom! You've got another case, huh?"

Jackie sighed. "Sort of, Peter. I'm just talking to a few people who might be able to get an ex-student of mine out of jail."

"Aw, don't make it sound so dull, Mom," Peter protested. "I think it's cool."

"Of course you do, dear." Jackie flinched when she heard herself sounding so much like her mother. "Are you still having fun?"

"Yeah, California's pretty cool. Tomorrow Tom's brother Pat is going to take us up to the lava beds in Modoc to see the place where Captain Jack held off the U.S. Cavalry. I've got a book about it and everything."

"That sounds lots cooler than me interviewing people about a dead movie producer."

"A matter of opinion, Mom," Peter maintained. "Anyhow I gotta go. We'll call you again after you get to L.A. Love you."

"Love *you*, darling son," she said. "Talk to you soon."

"You be careful down there," Tom said after Peter handed him the phone.

"I already said I would," Jackie protested.

"Yeah, but I know you," Tom countered. "Just do it."

Unlike Tom, Frances Costello almost never admonished her daughter to be careful. If Jackie were more careful, after all, her mother would miss out on an awful lot of adventure in her life. "I just wish I could go with you." She sighed. "Are you sure you can't wait until I can get back home?"

Jackie allowed herself to imagine Frances helping her interview Neville Ice in Hollywood. It wasn't pretty. "Not a chance, Mother," Jackie assured her. "You'll just have to wait and hear all the juicy details from me when you get home. How's Mr. Mallon?"

"Oh, he's a dear. And what a dancer that man is! Took lessons for six years from the Arthur Murray studio in Coral Gables. He's teaching me to rumba."

"Sounds exciting," Jackie said without meaning it.

"Until you've rumba'd with Dennis Mallon, my dear," her mother assured her, "you haven't danced at all."

CHAPTER 18

The jetliner descended from its cruising altitude of thirty-five thousand feet into a thick layer of gray-brown murk that Jackie reminded herself was the stuff she'd be breathing for the next couple of days. Her lungs hurt already, just thinking about it. She didn't visit that often these days, and when she did, she usually ended up hanging on to a low-grade headache from the time she stepped out of an airplane in Los Angeles to the time she arrived back in Palmer. People who lived here got used to what they were breathing, but Palmer, Ohio, wasn't yet big enough to have a serious pollution problem, and Jackie was grateful to be accustomed to cleaner air.

She closed the buckle on her seat belt, pulled the belt tighter, and looked across the empty seat in the middle of the row and past the woman in the window seat to watch Los Angeles appear out of the layer of smog as the plane lost altitude. The sun was only a slight red glow on the western horizon, and city lights were just beginning to pop on here and there in the dusk. She and her seat mate had only exchanged a few words since the flight began five hours ago. The woman had been preoccupied with her laptop computer for most of the flight, and Jackie had been absorbed in her own thoughts. Now the woman had closed the computer and was reading the in-flight magazine.

Jackie could clearly remember when this had been her home, and she had thought she might be here forever. As a would-be writer and a writer's daughter, she'd gravitated toward Hollywood as the place to make her fortune after a string of unimportant and unrewarding postgraduate jobs in the Midwest. Some old friends of her father's had introduced her around, and she'd been able to land a job as a production assistant on a crime drama series, *Night Streets.* Since she was determined back then not to teach if it killed her, it had seemed a pretty good way to use her film degree.

She could probably have worked her way up to producing or directing someday, but what Jackie really wanted to do was write. During the second season someone finally agreed to take a look at a script she'd done on spec for the show, and when after seemingly endless rewrites it was accepted for production, her career began to move forward.

It had been exciting, Jackie remembered now, to be a minor part of the scene in Hollywood, even as a television writer, and not a very well-known one at that. It certainly paid better, even back then, than teaching film in a small private university did now. But at some point she'd decided that she wanted something more for her life, and after she met tall, dark, and handsome Cooper Walsh during a visit home to see her parents one holiday season, she thought she had found it.

Okay, she'd been wrong about that, but at least she had a bright and promising fourteen-year-old to show for it, and she could never regret that. Peter was more than reward enough for those soul-crushing years in suburbia, married to a man who didn't know the meaning of the word "faithful."

The plane's wheels met the runway with a little screech, then settled down and rolled Jackie in to the terminal gate. Back in L.A., she thought.

"Been gone long?" said the woman in the window seat, looking up from her magazine, and Jackie realized she must have been thinking out loud.

"About a million years," she answered.

"That's pretty long," said the woman with a slight smile. "So how do you feel about coming back after all that time?"

"I wish I knew," Jackie replied, still staring out the window at the buildings going past as the plane slowly taxied up to its place at the gate. "I really wish I knew."

"I'm glad you called me when you knew you were coming to town," said Michael McGowan. He glanced over at Jackie from behind the wheel of his car as he negotiated a lane change on the crowded freeway between the airport and the Hollywood hotel where she'd reserved a room for two nights.

"I'm glad you were able to meet me at the airport," Jackie told him. "I have to admit I wasn't looking forward to facing my first evening in town alone."

"You told me on the phone you were here to talk to somebody you had to see in person," said Michael. "What's that all about?"

"His name is Neville Ice. He's a friend of Matt Darwin's."

"The screenwriter? I thought he was dead."

"Dying, apparently, but not until he finishes his book."

"And is that the reason you're here? Something to do with his book?" He shook his head. "I'm sorry. I'm being nosy. It's not like I have the right—"

"No, I don't mind. Really. I don't know anything about the book, but apparently while he was researching it, Mr. Ice found out a few things about Cameron Clark."

Michael laughed and slapped the steering wheel. "Now I get it. I should have known. You're here investigating Cameron Clark's murder! I'll bet Evan Stillman's overjoyed about that."

"Evan doesn't exactly know I'm here," Jackie admitted. "And he doesn't exactly know I'm investigating, either. I'd be really grateful if you'd neglect to mention it to him."

"I can tell there's a story behind all this," Michael said. "We might as well save it for dinner. Are you hungry?"

"I guess not really," said Jackie. "I snacked on the plane."

"I know a great Mediterranean place in Santa Monica," Michael told her.

"Well, that's different." Jackie indicated the nearly solid mass of cars that surrounded them on all sides. "By the time we get to Santa Monica, I'll probably be starving!"

Michael's Mediterranean restaurant was barely larger than Jackie's living room, but the smells emanating from the kitchen were mouthwatering. Jackie realized that even though they had gotten here much sooner than she had anticipated, she actually was starving. They ordered a big platter of food to eat between them, and managed to keep the conversation to gossip and news of mutual friends until dessert—baklava accompanied by tiny cups of Turkish coffee flavored with cardamom.

"So tell me about this case of yours."

"It isn't my case—" Jackie began, but Michael held up his hand as if to ward off any further denial on her part.

"You flew out here from Ohio to talk to an old screenwriter who might have some dirt on the murder victim and your preferred suspect in Palmer's most notorious recent murder case, and you want me to believe you're not investigating?"

"No, I guess I don't want you to believe that. I *am* involved. Of course I am. Who am I fooling?"

"Evan Stillman, I hope," said Michael with a smile. "If you ever want to be on the good side of the Palmer Police Department."

"But Evan's not investigating the case anymore," Jackie protested. "He's convinced he already knows who did it. John McBride."

"And why are you convinced he's wrong?"

"Because I know John," Jackie said, "and I know he couldn't have killed someone like that."

"Not even someone like Cameron Clark?"

"Oh, did you know him, too?"

"Never met the man. But there's been a lot of talk about him the past few days since the news hit. You know that old saw about not speaking ill of the dead?"

"Yeah, I know. And I know it doesn't seem to apply to Cameron Clark."

"Not a popular guy, by a long shot. Even when his career was going places, he didn't exactly have a lot of real friends in this town. And he hasn't exactly picked up a lot of them since he died, either."

"But that doesn't mean John killed him."

"I guess not, necessarily," said Michael with a shrug. He finished his coffee, and Jackie followed suit. "You ready to go?"

"Might as well. I'm worn-out from the flight and I ought to try to get some sleep, if I can sleep after drinking coffee you could eat with a fork."

Michael left money for the tab and helped Jackie into her jacket. They stepped outside and began the walk to Michael's car, which was parked on the next block.

"What's Evan's case?" Michael wanted to know as they walked.

"John's truck was the murder weapon."

"Not good, but still circumstantial. Any hard physical evidence?"

"Well, it *was* John's truck," Jackie told him, "so he's been leaving evidence all over it for years, as you'd expect. John's prints on the wheel, of course. No evidence at the scene, apparently, except what was left by the truck itself."

"And John swears he wasn't driving, of course?"

"He says someone must have stolen the truck."

"Well, whoever did that might have left some evidence," Michael said.

"Not exactly. The truck wasn't broken into, and it wasn't hot-wired. Someone appears to have started it with the keys."

"Spare keys?"

"John's keys. And after they ran Cameron down, they washed the truck and returned it to the carport, where he found it the next day."

Michael was cleary incredulous. "Jackie, why would someone borrow a guy's car, whack somebody with it, then return it to where they found it? If it wasn't your friend John who was driving, why wouldn't they just leave the car abandoned somewhere? It sounds to me like your friend did the job on Clark, washed the car to get rid of any inconvenient bloodstains, and went home to bed. What does Evan think the motive is?"

"He thinks John and Cameron's wife were having an affair."

"Evidence?"

"Cameron found a shirt that belonged to John in their bedroom. And the wife says they'd been sleeping together."

"Well, there you go," said Michael. "It sounds pretty classic to me. A guy who's sneaking around with some other guy's wife decides to get rid of the husband. Maybe the two of them are in it together."

"You sound just like Evan!" Jackie protested.

"Well, I'm a cop, Jackie."

"Not exactly. Not anymore."

"I'll always be a cop, even if I never clock in to another police job in my life."

"And it's looking like you won't." They had arrived at Michael's car. He pushed a button on his key chain and the doors unlocked with a loud click.

Michael nodded as he opened her door. "It'd be pretty tough to go back to that kind of work after a couple of years writing scripts. The money's good, and no one ever takes a shot at you."

Jackie heard a sharp *pop!* and then Michael's hand on the back of her neck, pushing her down to the pavement. Her knees stung as the rough asphalt of the street ripped open the knees of her pants and shredded the skin underneath. Pain vied with bone-deep fear for her attention. She looked up to see Michael looking around frantically for the source of the sound and reaching into his inner-jacket pocket for a gun he no longer carried. A dark-colored car was turning the corner up ahead on two wheels. Michael stood up and helped Jackie to her feet. "You okay?"

"Yeah." Her voice was trembling. "Scraped up, but okay."

"Sorry about your knees," he said, looking down at the damage.

"Better my knees than my head," Jackie told him. She hung on to the car door for support. "Did someone in that car just take a shot at us?"

"That's my guess." Michael pointed to the building they were parked next to. Something had taken out a big chunk of plaster just over the top of his head. "The question seems to be which one of us were they shooting at?"

CHAPTER 19

"They couldn't have been shooting at me," Jackie assured him. "No one knows I'm here except Tom, Peter, Grania, and Tom's assistant, who's boarding Jake. And Mom. And her new boyfriend, I guess."

"Well, they couldn't have been shooting at me," said Michael. "I'm a screenwriter!"

Jackie brushed the worst of the dirt and gravel off her pants. Her legs were shaking. In fact she was shaking all over from the rush of adrenaline her body had provided at the sound of the shot. "No one shoots at screenwriters?" she asked, attempting some levity to counteract her terror of moments before. "Not even directors?"

"It would be something new in my writing career," Michael told her. He scanned the street in all directions, but the dark car had not returned, and the street was otherwise nearly deserted. "Listen, do you think you should go to your hotel? What if that shot was aimed at you and they know where you're staying?"

"If they know where I'm staying, why not just wait for me there instead of following me from Inglewood to Santa Monica to do the job?" Jackie wanted to know. "It seems like an awful lot of trouble. No, Michael, I just don't believe anyone's trying to kill me." She got into the passenger seat of Michael's car, trying to hold the fabric of her pants legs away from the worst of her two scraped knees. "Of course they nearly frightened me to death, but that may not have been their intention."

Michael got into the driver's seat and fastened his seat belt. "Not even if you're getting close to Cameron Clark's real murderer?"

"I thought you didn't believe there was any real murderer besides John McBride."

"Oh, that was just me thinking like a cop. I don't know who whacked the guy. What if you're actually getting close? Who do you think did it?" He started the car and made a wide circle in the deserted street, then pulled away in the direction they'd come.

"I'm torn between the victim's wife and and actor named Kurt Manowski."

"The scary-looking guy? Always plays a crook? He's in John's movie, right?" Michael glanced into the rear-view mirror.

"That's the one. He and Cameron had a hate-hate relationship going back a few years. I'm supposed to find out all the details tomorrow."

"From that old guy Matt Darwin knows?" He signaled, then turned left onto a side street.

"Yeah. Is this the way back to the freeway?"

"How do you know his friend really knows anything?" Michael asked, ignoring her question. "How do you know you didn't just fly all the way out here for nothing?" He turned again at the next corner, right this time.

"I don't, I guess. I'll just have to play it by ear. Do you actually know where we're going?"

Michael looked into the mirror again, and frowned.

"What?" Jackie wanted to know. "Do you see something?"

"Just a car that pulled away about the same time we

did. It's made every turn with us. Let's see if that's a coincidence." Michael turned again, without signaling this time, or even slowing down much.

"What are the odds it was just a random act of terrorism?" Jackie asked him, holding on to the armrest on the door to avoid being flung into Michael's lap.

"In L.A.?" Michael laughed without humor. "It happens. Still, the odds on it are pretty long. It's much more likely that was somebody you know."

"Or somebody *you* know," Jackie reminded him.

He stepped on the gas, moved over to pass three slower cars, changed lanes again, sped down several blocks with no signals or stop signs, then zipped onto a freeway on-ramp going north.

"Did you lose him?" Jackie turned around to look behind them, but there were several cars and she didn't know which of them had worried Michael.

"I think so," he said. "If there was ever anybody at all. I don't know about taking you to your hotel, though. What if whoever shot at us followed you here and knows where you're staying?"

"Where exactly were you thinking about taking me?" Jackie asked him.

"My place."

Jackie shook her head. "I don't think that would be such a good idea."

"I'd sleep on the couch if you asked me to," he offered. "I'd be a perfect gentleman unless you didn't want me to be." He looked over at her as if to gauge her reaction.

"Michael, you know I'm involved with someone else now."

"Yeah, the dog trainer. I've heard a little about him from Evan. How serious is it?"

"Pretty serious. I wouldn't want to do anything to jeopardize what I've got with Tom no matter how tempting the offer might be."

Michael smiled. "Then you admit to being tempted."

Jackie thought about lying, then thought better of it. Dishonesty on both their parts had been the ruination of a pretty good relationship. "Very tempted on one level," she admitted.

"That's good to know," he said softly.

"And it's good to know you're still interested enough to tempt me," she continued, "but I couldn't live with myself."

"Even if Tom never found out?"

"Even if he didn't know, I'd know."

"Well, that's good, I guess. I mean I might as well be philosophical about it as not, seeing as how I'm not going to have my way with you." He grinned over at her. Then the grin faded. "But dammit, Jackie, I'm still worried about you."

"Don't be," Jackie told him. "I'll be fine." Michael's caution was beginning to rub off, though, and she was certain he could hear the doubt in her voice.

"We could find you another hotel. Just pick one at random." He glanced up into the mirror again. "I think we lost our friend, or maybe there never was anybody and I'm just paranoid."

"Getting shot at has a tendency to induce a sort of useful paranoia, I think," Jackie said. "And in that spirit I'll take you up on your second suggestion. Let's just pull into a hotel and I'll check in. I can call Matt in the morning and tell him I'm not going to be at the Holiday Inn."

"First, though, we find some first-aid supplies for those knees."

They left the freeway in Hollywood and drove up Sunset until they saw an all-night drugstore. They went inside and Michael picked out a double armload of gauze, tape, and assorted disinfectants. "You look like you're preparing for major emergency surgery," Jackie told him. "It's just a couple of banged-up knees!"

"I'd rather be thorough," Michael told her.

"What do you have there?" she asked, trying to get a look at the boxes, tubes, and bottles in his arms.

"Only what's strictly necessary," he insisted, guarding his hoard of medical supplies from her gaze. "Just leave it to Dr. McGowan. If this is the only playing doctor I get to do tonight, I'm going to do a damned good job."

Michael laid his purchases down at the checkstand. "Opening a hospital?" the clerk remarked, straight-faced.

"Whose side are you on?" Michael asked him.

They got back in the car and drove until they spotted a fairly respectable-looking motel among dozens they had seen that were definitely not. Michael checked the rearview one more time and pulled in.

After Jackie had secured a room from the elderly Japanese couple who expressed a great deal of concern about her injuries in two languages, Michael carried in her suitcase and his collection of supplies. "Those pants have to go," he said, pointing at her ruined clothing.

Jackie picked up her suitcase and retreated to the bathroom. "Right back," she called out as she closed the door. When she emerged again she was wearing a light cotton nightgown and bathrobe which she belted around her waist as she came out.

"Sit down there," Michael instructed, pointing to the end of the bed and removing his jacket. Jackie sat, and he knelt in front of her and proceeded to clean the knees of dirt and grit with some disinfectant and gauze pads.

Jackie winced at the sting of the liquid against torn skin.

"Sorry," Michael said, not looking up from his task.

"Don't pay any attention to me," Jackie said, "I'm just being a big baby."

"Jacqueline Shannon Costello," Michael intoned in a manner not unlike her mother, "you are not a big baby." He stopped swabbing for a moment and looked up at her.

"You are quite simply the bravest woman I have ever known."

"Thank you, Michael," said Jackie. "That's nice of you to say after I've checked into an anonymous motel to avoid someone who's probably not following me, and probably not shooting at me, either."

Michael returned to scrubbing. "We're not taking chances with your life," he told her. "You go see Matt Darwin's friend tomorrow if you have to, but then you get yourself back to Ohio."

"Where it's safe?" Jackie asked. "Where people don't kill other people?"

Michael sighed. "I know it's not safe anywhere. That's part of the reason I went into police work in the first place. And while you're poking around in a murder case, you probably wouldn't be safe at the bottom of the Grand Canyon."

"Nope," Jackie assured him. "Rattlesnakes. Scorpions."

"It's just that I worry about you," he said, "and it's not my job to protect you anymore. Not," he went on quickly, "that I think you need someone following you around and looking out for you."

"Well, sometimes I do, apparently, and you always did a great job of it."

"And now it's that dog trainer's job," said Michael, tossing the gauze into a bedside wastebasket and opening a new package.

"That dog trainer's name is Tom Cusack," Jackie reminded him.

"How is he in a rough spot?" Michael wanted to know.

"Not bad," she told him. "Courageous, resourceful, calm in a crisis. He'll do for the job."

"Good." Michael left off scrubbing the knees, apparently satisfied, finally, that he hadn't left anything in the wounds that would cause an infection later. He unwrapped a few plastic-covered gauze pads and laid them out neatly on their wrappers on the bedspread, then opened a tube of antiseptic cream and spread it over both knees.

"What's this about your mom having a boyfriend?" he asked.

"Someone she met in Florida," Jackie told him. "A summer romance."

"Yeah, but what if it's not?"

"A romance? Trust me, it's a romance. I know the symptoms."

"No, I mean what if it's not just for the summer?"

"Mr. Dennis Mallon would be crazy to give up Florida winters for Ohio ones," Jackie assured him.

"Well, you notice I haven't been back since I got a taste of the climate in Southern California," Michael told her. "Straighten your legs so these bandages don't fall off."

Jackie obediently stuck her legs straight out, balancing the gauze pads on top of her knees while Michael opened the tape dispenser.

"I guess what I mean," said Michael, tearing off a length of tape, "is what if Frances decides to move down there?"

"Oh, look! You got the kind that won't irritate my skin!" said Jackie, pointing at the tape.

"Suitable for your delicate constitution," Michael told her. "Now answer my question."

"Oh, okay. I don't know. I've been trying not to think about it." She sighed in irritation at herself. "Of course I want my mother to be happy," she said.

"But maybe not happy a thousand miles away?"

"I guess that's not exactly fair, is it?"

"What it is, exactly," Michael assured her, "is a perfectly normal reaction to what might be a big change in your life. When it comes to what's fair, Jackie my dear, that's what you'll always do in the end." He laid down the last piece of tape and sat back to admire his handiwork. "You can put your feet down now," he told her.

Jackie did so. Michael got to his feet and put his jacket on.

"Thanks Michael," she told him. She got up and took a few stiff-legged steps around the room. "The legs still work."

"I don't think I broke anything that wasn't under warranty," he told her. "Change those bandages in the morning, and again before you go to bed tomorrow night."

Jackie looked at the heap of first aid supplies lying on the end of the bed. "And when I get back to Ohio I'll be prepared for fires, floods, earthquakes, nuclear attack . . ."

Michael leaned down and gave her a chaste kiss on the cheek. " 'Night, Jackie," he said. He smiled at her, a bit sadly, walked out of the room, got in his car, and drove away.

Jackie pulled back the curtains on the room's window and watched him pull out of the driveway and onto Sunset Boulevard, then disappear in the stream of cars. She felt strangely sad and more than a little lonely when she couldn't see his taillights anymore.

In her dream, Kurt Manowski was standing on his mark on the warehouse set, with lights blazing all around him and cameras rolling. He put his hand inside his jacket the way he had in his scene with Lorraine, only now Jackie was no longer watching from the sidelines—she was playing Lorraine's part in the movie, and Jake was nowhere in sight. "I don't want to kill you," Kurt was saying.

"That's my line!" Jackie protested. She turned to complain to the director, but the director's chair was empty. There was no one behind the camera, and no crew beyond the lights, watching the scene. The two of them were all alone. Kurt withdrew a gun from inside his jacket and fired it. The bullet went past in slow motion, just over her left shoulder, and plaster exploded from the wall behind her that hadn't been there a moment ago. Jackie saw Michael McGowan running toward them with agonizing slowness, and knew he could never reach her before Kurt fired again.

Kurt leveled the gun at Jackie's face. She dropped to her knees and cried out in pain.

And woke up. Her knees were stinging beneath Michael's carefully applied bandages, and her heart was pumping double time. She rolled over and stared at the dingy ceiling and watched headlights from Sunset Boulevard dance across it until she fell asleep again.

CHAPTER 20

"So you decided to downgrade your hotel accommodations," said Matt Darwin as Jackie opened the door of the motel room to his knock the next morning.

"Good to see you again, Matt. You haven't changed a bit." Matt Darwin didn't look a day older than the last time Jackie had seen him, during her television writing days. Unruly curls of brown hair poked out from under the tweed cap he wore in all kinds of weather, and his clothes still seemed to have been assembled from some bizarre yard sale of the rich and famous. In fact, Jackie knew, they were carefully chosen from a store a few blocks from Paramount Studios that sold old movie wardrobes.

"You either."

"Liar."

"But I'm a good liar," Matt protested. "It's a skill I've honed to a razor's edge dealing with producers and studio heads."

Jackie closed the door of the room, and she and Matt walked to the motel's office, where Jackie turned the keys back in to the concerned couple. "Your knees are better?" the old woman asked.

"Much better, thanks."

"Would you like to come in and have coffee?" the old man offered.

"No, we really have to be going. Thank you, though."

The old couple bowed and Jackie bowed back, uncertain of the etiquette involved and feeling more than a bit foolish, but what the hell? She was spending the day in Los Angeles, land of the foolish and home of the fantastic. And about a thousand times more international than anyplace in Ohio.

As they left the office, Matt pointed across the parking lot. "My latest ride," he told Jackie. It was a beautifully restored wood-sided station wagon, painted a shade of deep green they hadn't used on cars for fifty years.

"It's gorgeous!" Jackie exclaimed. "Did you do the work yourself?"

"No, I bought it from a director who was down on his luck. Now he's got five projects lined up, and I'm out of work."

"Sell it back."

"Never."

Matt opened the passenger door and waved Jackie inside. She slid onto the green-and-cream leatherette bench seat and bounced up and down a couple of times.

Matt got into the car and started the engine, then reversed out of the lot. As they passed the parking spot nearest the street, Jackie saw Michael's car parked there, and Michael asleep in the driver's seat.

"He came back!" she said.

"Who? That guy?"

"I don't believe he spent the night in the parking lot guarding me," she said. "But I guess I should have known he would."

"You have your own bodyguard?" Matt said, raising an eyebrow. "I'm impressed."

"Someone shot at me," Jackie told him. "It's a long story."

"In that case, I'll buy breakfast," said Matt, "and you can fill me in. There's a coffee shop up on Gower, and we're not expected at Neville's until almost noon."

"And you can fill me in on Neville and the Ice Women," Jackie told him.

"Well, a bit," said Matt, "but I think Neville Ice and his wicked stepsisters are best encountered like a really good film—the less you know about it going in, the more involving the experience."

Neville Ice's Beverly Hills mansion was a Spanish fantasy in white stucco and red clay roof tiles, with a fountain out front in the turnaround that looked like it had been transported from a Mexican village. There were four cars parked out front, two of them restored antiques and the other two expensive imports. Jackie and Matt walked up the terra-cotta front steps to a huge carved double door. Matt pressed a button.

"Yes?" a woman's voice came out of a little speaker to the right of the door. It didn't sound at all friendly or welcoming.

"It's Matt, Sylvia."

A moment's silence.

"Matt Darwin."

"Just a moment." The speaker went dead.

"Don't you just love Sylvia already?" said Matt. "Nobody gets in here without her say-so."

"She doesn't have three heads, does she?"

"No, she's not actually Cerberus," said Matt with an evil grin, "but I think she might be his mother."

One of the wooden doors opened a crack and a woman's face peered out. "It's just me, Sylvia," Matt said, giving the woman a little wave. I'm here for my poker game with Neville."

"And *this* is . . . ?" Sylvia wanted to know.

"This is Jackie Walsh, an old friend of mine. I've already cleared it with Neville."

"Well, come in, then."

Sylvia opened the door wider, and Jackie could see a nearly identical and even more disapproving woman behind her. This would have to be Elizabeth. Matt had told her that over the forty years Neville and Sylvia had been married, she and Neville's sister Elizabeth had grown to look alike, sort of like an old married couple. Jackie could see this was true; they dyed their hair an identical shade of dark brown and wore it in the same outdated style, dressed in the same conservative clothes and shoes, and wore the same expression of fierce determination and disapproval.

They turned their identical disapproving expressions on Jackie as Matt dutifully made introductions all around. Then, like a guard dog who has barked, sniffed, and determined you're no particular threat as long as you don't try anything funny, they seemed to relax just a bit. "Neville's on the back porch," Elizabeth said, "though I think we'll have to bring him inside if it gets much warmer."

"Well, you ladies can just leave all that to me for the rest of the afternoon," Matt told them, "and go off and get drunk or something."

Jackie was sure the two women had heard this joke before, but they stared calmly at Matt as though he had spoken in a foreign language and would realize any moment that he hadn't been understood.

"We'll just nip off to the back porch, then," Matt said. "I know the way."

Sylvia and Elizabeth made no move to follow them as they left the living room behind, but when Jackie turned to look over her shoulder, they were standing in the same spot, watching them go.

"I can see why you call them the Ice Women," said

Jackie to Matt with a mock shiver when they were out of earshot. "Why should they worry about how hot it gets outside? All they'd have to do is sit out on the porch with poor Neville and lower the temperature by fifteen degrees!"

"I think that's why they don't go outside much," Matt told her. "They'd turn L.A. into a subarctic zone in a matter of hours."

Matt led her down a long hallway lined with photographs, and pointed out some of Neville with famous film stars and other Hollywood notables of the past. The mini-history detailed by the photographs reached from the pre–World War II era almost to the present. There were even a few old pictures of Sylvia and Elizabeth, younger and almost pretty, but already souring, seemingly doomed to become the women they were today.

At the end of the hallway a glass-paneled door with wispy white curtains admitted shafts of sunlight to brighten the dark wood paneling. Matt opened the door and they stepped out onto a long, narrow porch that ran along the length of the house and around the corners on both sides. Massive wooden beams held up a red-tiled roof, and bright bougainvillea wrapped around them and grew up onto the roof tiles, dropping deep pink blossoms everywhere.

A few feet away, in a patch of sunlight, was a wheelchair pulled up close to a glass-topped table. The man in it was dressed in white trousers and a white sport coat. He turned around at the sound of their footsteps, withdrawing a deck of cards from his jacket pocket. "Matthew!" he exclaimed. "I was hoping you'd show up before long. And you've brought me a visitor!"

Jackie turned to Matt. "You told Sylvia I was expected."

"Oh, never mind that," said the man. "If you're Matthew's friend, you're welcome here, Sylvia or no." He set the deck of cards on the table. His deep blue eyes twinkled in an open, friendly face framed by white hair. "Matthew and I know how to get around my wife. He's almost as good at it as I am."

"Jackie Walsh," said Matt, "may I introduce Mr. Neville Ice. Neville, Jackie Walsh—screenwriter, professor, and detective."

"I'm very pleased to meet you, Mr. Ice. I've been an admirer of your work for many years."

Neville took her hand in a firm, dry grasp. "Thank you, that's very kind. Did Matthew say you're a detective?" His white eyebrows lifted up in an expression of surprised interest.

"Matt's exaggerating a bit, Mr. Ice," Jackie told him. "I'm a film instructor at Rodgers University in Palmer, Ohio."

"Ah, a town that's been in the news out here of late," Neville remarked.

"Yes, and it's true that I came here to ask you about something that affects a criminal investigation. I hope you don't mind."

"You must call me Neville," he said. "Life's too short for useless formalities. Of course I don't mind. You have no idea how boring life can become when you're a prisoner in your own house. Well, well! A detective!"

"I'm just helping out a friend who's been accused of a crime," said Jackie.

"A true friend indeed, then," Neville commented. "Well, sit down, sit down, both of you. There's lemonade in the pitcher here, and I'll have the ladies bring us some extra glasses."

"Oh, don't bother . . ." Jackie began, but Neville waved off her objection.

"They don't actually bite, you know," he said. "One almost gets used to them after a while." He reached behind him and pulled a cord that hung down from the porch roof near the wall. From far away inside, Jackie heard a buzzer ring. "They take quite good care of me, and I'm almost certain it's not only because they know they're going to inherit."

Footsteps approached down the hallway inside, and the door opened. "Do you need something, Neville?" asked Elizabeth.

"Some glasses for my friends, Libby dear, and make sure Arletta knows to make enough lunch for everyone, won't you? The three of us will eat out here." He glanced at Jackie and Matt to see if they agreed. Jackie nodded gratefully. A meal taken with the Ice Women would probably freeze her appetite for life.

"Yes, out here. There's a nice breeze. You don't mind vegetarian, I hope?"

"As a matter of fact, I prefer it," said Jackie.

"Excellent! Bring us our glasses, there's a good girl, Libby. We'll all have some lemonade."

While they waited for Elizabeth to return with drinking glasses, Jackie admired Neville's garden. Citrus trees and hibiscus bushes and crimson geraniums completed the perfect Southern California ambience suggested by the huge Spanish-style house. More bougainvillea and climbing red roses covered an arbor at the far end of the yard, where a white Persian cat lay watching birds with one sleepy eye. "It's like a little piece of paradise," she told him.

"It is indeed. My own piece. I used to take care of it myself," Neville told her. "It's such wonderfully brainless work to tend a garden. By which I mean that it puts one's intellectual facilities on hold and lets the more creative aspects of the subconscious out to play. At least that's how it always was for me. Nowadays I have a man in to tend to it, so it's still beautiful to look at, but I miss messing about with it." He pulled a white handkerchief from the breast pocket of his jacket and coughed into it. "So sorry," he said. "My lungs aren't what they used to be."

Elizabeth came silently with the extra glasses, and left just as quietly. Neville poured lemonade all around and handed them their glasses. "I know Americans seem to prefer iced tea," he said, "the ones south of the Canadian border, at any rate. But I never could get used to the stuff. I've lived here for some years now, but I could never get over the notion that tea is something you drink hot with milk and sugar."

"You're right about Canada," said Matt. "I was up there shooting that comedy series—the one that tanked—for eight months three years ago. It's like pulling teeth to get iced tea up there that isn't served in a can."

"Well, you see, Matthew, that's because Canadians are a bit more like us Brits," said Neville. "They put pictures of the queen on the money, and drink their tea hot with milk and sugar. They even spell properly. But they do seem to have picked up the annoying American habit of driving on the wrong side of the road.

"It's true that Matthew didn't tell me you'd be joining us today, Jackie," said Neville, turning to her, "but he knows me well enough to know how happy I'd be to meet you. Has he perhaps told you about my own very minor attempt at detection?"

"He's mentioned that you were working on a real-life mystery," said Jackie, "but he made it sound pretty major, actually."

"Well, I don't think it's important to anyone now living, with the possible exception of myself," Neville said. "Solving it won't make the world a better place, but it's been nagging at me for years, so I finally decided to do something about it."

"He also said that while you were investigating, you found out a few things about Cameron Clark."

"The late? Oh, yes. In fact I found out things I never asked to know about quite a few people, which makes it likely the book won't be published before my death." He coughed again, longer this time. Matt put a hand on his back, and Neville straightened up and tucked the handkerchief back into the pocket of his jacket. "Of course, time will probably see to that at any rate," he said. "So tell me, Jackie—what is your interest in Cameron Clark?"

"My friend is accused of his murder."

"And do you think your friend actually performed this public service?"

"No, I don't. The more I learn about Cameron the more likely it is that people were lining up and taking numbers to kill him."

"Very likely there were," Neville agreed. "Cameron had tons of charm, which he turned on and off like an electric switch. And a tendency to violence when in his cups. And other habits that make one unpopular in polite society."

"Like what?" Jackie wanted to know.

"Like blackmail."

CHAPTER 21

"Ah, here's our lunch!" said Neville as Sylvia and Elizabeth, accompanied by another woman who was probably the cook or housekeeper, wheeled out a tea tray loaded down with covered dishes.

"Goodness!" Jackie exclaimed. "Are you expecting more guests?"

Neville unfolded a napkin that Sylvia laid down in front of him and tucked it into his collar. "I never did believe that breakfast is the most important meal of the day," he told her. "Who can do justice to a meal who's just got up from bed? It's all I can do to choke down an orange juice with my coffee. Lunch, however"—he waved his hand at the dishes Sylvia and the other woman were uncovering—"is quite another matter."

With practiced and efficient motions, the three women cleared everything from the glass-topped table and set three places with silver, crystal, and plain white china. They transferred the food from the tea cart to the table and stayed just long enough to fuss over Neville until he shooed them off. "Whatever are they going to do when I'm not around?" he wondered aloud as he watched their retreating backs.

"If they're lucky they'll find some other old coot to make a fuss over, I guess," Matt told him.

"Good heavens! Do you really think so?" Neville picked up his knife and fork. "In that case I'd better stick around a bit longer and spare that poor bloke the misery! Well, let's eat, everyone, shall we? We can always satisfy our appetites for murder and blackmail after we've filled our stomachs. This is pumpkin-and-orange soup," he told them, indicating a white tureen of golden soup garnished with fresh parsley. "That's courgette salad—zucchini to you—and those are mushrooms in Madeira or my nose is no longer working. There's a spinach risotto, and last but not least, pears in Roquefort sauce."

"My God," said Jackie, arranging her napkin. "Do you eat like this every day?"

"He does, actually," said Matt.

"You'd best believe it," said Neville. "That's why I employ a woman who knows how to cook this well. If I depended on my wife and sister for sustenance, I'd have been carried off by starvation years since!"

"We'll forgo our poker game today if you don't mind, Matthew," Neville said after the cook and the Ice Women had wheeled away the lunch dishes.

"No, you two have a lot to talk about," said Matt. "I hope you don't mind if I stay and listen."

"Your discretion is, as always, appreciated," said Neville. "I still hope to complete my book before I get too ill. I only wish I were a bit stronger so that I could still get out and nose about in person. These days," he said, turning to Jackie, "I'm doing most of my detective work on the Internet. You'd be amazed the things you can find out about. More all the time."

"It's amazing, all right," Jackie agreed. "My teenage son's teaching me to find my way around."

"Yes, young people seem to be born with a grasp of

new technologies," Neville agreed. "I hired a high-school student to get me up and running earlier this year." Another coughing spell interrupted him for half a minute, and when he'd recovered he took a deep, careful breath and folded his elegant hands in his lap. "Would you like to hear a story?" he asked Jackie. "Matthew's heard it before, of course, but that's what he gets for spending one afternoon a week keeping an old man company."

"You know I never get tired of talking with you, Neville," said Matt. "Or of listening to you."

Neville smiled at his friend. "Most of the people in this story are dead now, or very nearly so. And in time it does lead straight to the door of Cameron Clark, though it's a bit of a winding road to get there."

"I'd love to hear it," said Jackie.

"Well, fifty years and more ago, when the Second World War was still being fought, there was a lovely young actress by the name of Virginia Tobin. She was an Irish lass like yourself, with a wild, independent streak that kept her from being as successful as she might have been. The contract-player system of those days was quite different from the sort of free-agent method we have now, and she never liked being told what to do, where to go, or who to be seen with. She butted heads with directors, producers, and studio heads, and she paid the price. Actresses who were far less talented, creative, and beautiful were getting opportunities that might have gone to her had she been more tractable." He shook his head and chuckled softly. "But Ginna was never what you'd call tractable."

Jackie listened as Neville told the story of how Virginia Tobin had been courted by dozens of men, among them Leo Vanetti, the youngest son of a prominent crime family that was extending its operations to the West Coast.

"Not the same Leo Vanetti who's serving twenty to life or some such in federal prison right now?" Jackie asked.

"The same," said Neville. "He went on to head the fam-

ily after all three of his older brothers died violently in
gang wars, but in those days he was just the pampered
youngest son of a powerful and dangerous man. He was
in Hollywood and using the family expense account to
attract women by the dozens. Then he met Virginia Tobin
and told all the others to go away."

"She must have been something special," Jackie commented.

"You have no idea," said Neville softly. He coughed
again and sat back in his chair for a few moments. "Well,
it's a longer story than I realized, and I'm shorter of breath
than I used to be. Also it doesn't relate directly to Cameron Clark, so I won't bore you with it after all."

"What happened to Virginia? Will you at least tell me
that much?"

"She disappeared in 1947," said Neville, his voice
breaking. "She was last seen leaving Leo Vanetti's apartment in Los Angeles, and never again to this day."

Neville cleared his throat. "A very old story and not of
interest to anyone, really."

"Except you," said Jackie. "You were in love with her."

"Except me," said Neville, attempting a smile. "And
yes." He wiped his eyes with the sleeve of his jacket, then
struggled to compose himself. Jackie and Matt remained
silent while Neville took a sip of his lemonade. "So let
me skip the intervening fifty years and get directly to what
you came here to find out. What is it you want to know
about Cameron Clark?"

"Do you know an actor named Kurt Manowski?" Jackie
asked Neville.

"Oh, my, yes! Kurt and I worked together on three
films. Or perhaps it was four. Yes, four films counting
Last Hours."

"And do you know about his feud with Cameron Clark?
Or perhaps I should say Cameron's feud with him? The
one that got Kurt fired off the set of *Killer's Heart*?"

"Oh, I think nearly everyone in the industry who pays attention knows about that. It's not every producer that will go to the trouble of firing an actor four weeks into principal photography and reshoot all his scenes with someone else. Especially when the actor in question hasn't done anything to deserve firing."

"Yes, Matt told a friend of mine that Cameron trumped up reasons to fire Kurt off that picture."

"He did indeed. He told everyone who'd listen that Kurt was drunk when he got to work and screwing up his scenes. Mind you, if you talked to anyone else on the production, Kurt was one hundred percent professional and doing his finest work. It looked to everyone who was watching at the time as though there was nothing more important to Cameron Clark than destroying Kurt Manowski's career. And he very nearly did. Of course we can't lay Kurt's aggravated-assault charge at Cameron's door, or not directly at least. But Kurt's conviction and subsequent downfall made Cameron Clark very happy, I can tell you that."

"What did Kurt do to him to make Cameron hate him so much?" Jackie wondered.

"Well, in my experience, Jackie," said Neville, "the thing that gives a person the greatest cause to hate another is not if that person wronged them, but if they themselves wronged that person."

"So Cameron did something to Kurt."

"In a way. Let me drop back a bit and fill in some details. A year or so ago, before I became too ill to drive, I started visiting Leo Vanetti in prison."

"You actually know Vanetti?"

"We have always had a few mutual friends. And of course there was my interest in the Virginia Tobin case. I arranged one visit to ask him some pointed questions, and we sort of hit it off, you might say. I returned there half a dozen times just to talk. Leo appreciated having someone to talk to who wasn't in his particular industry. You know how that goes, I'm sure."

"You became friends?"

"Oh, I know it's not fashionable in polite society to admit to liking someone like Leo Vanetti, and I didn't want to. I didn't want to like him, or respect him. Not even that. I went there thinking that he was probably the person who had murdered Ginna, or at least arranged her murder. But I left that day knowing he'd loved her as much as I had, and that he hadn't any more idea than I what had happened to her all those years ago. It gave us something very strange in common, didn't it? Two old men still pining after the same vanished love."

"So how does all this tie in with Cameron?" Jackie asked. "And where does blackmail fit into the picture?"

"Well, Leo and I talked of many things in our visits. He knew nearly as many people in the film industry as I do. And at some point he encountered Cameron Clark. Cameron was always living beyond his means," said Neville. "You may have heard the old joke where the bloke says, 'Once I had a million dollars. Half a million I spent on wine, women, and song, and the rest I wasted.' " Neville chuckled. "Well, Cameron Clark was always spending more money on women than he made. Or at least he liked to pick women who would spend it for him."

"That sounds like the Cameron I knew, all right," Jackie agreed.

"People in the industry used to speculate where he made all the money his women spent," said Neville. "He even married a couple of them, and they got even more from him in divorce settlements! Well, I don't know the answer to that, exactly, but according to Leo Vanetti, Cameron did develop a little hobby on the side that he thought might keep him from going completely over the edge of financial ruin."

"He blackmailed people?"

"Let's say he tried," said Neville. "He really wasn't very good at it, you see, or perhaps it would be closer to the truth to say that he was every bit as adept at picking blackmail victims as he was at picking wives."

"And you heard all this from Leo Vanetti?"

"Over a period of time. It's possible I don't know the names of all Cameron's victims, but he didn't get much out of any of the ones I do know about. Let's see, he began perhaps ten years ago with a young actress who did a few porn films, and then came into an inheritance from her late father. Ingeborg something, or Ingmar. No, that's a man's name, isn't it? Anyway, she thought to improve her lot with this bit of money, since she no longer had to take off her clothes to pay the rent, but no sooner had she changed her name and gotten a part in a real feature than down swooped Cameron Clark and demanded money in return for not revealing her former occupation."

"And did she pay?"

"Not a red cent, according to Leo's source. She gave up acting and went home to Minnesota or whatever frozen hell she'd come here from."

"He didn't pursue the matter? What about her family—they still didn't know, did they?"

"Her only family was her mother. The young woman and her mother confronted Cameron and told him there was no more reason to extort money from them, since everything was known. His first attempt at blackmail had netted him nothing."

"What then?"

"Well, apparently he thought he'd hit on a pretty good idea—taking advantage of young actresses. There was another by the name of Sally Manning, who'd had an affair with a married producer. She got pregnant, got dumped, got an abortion. But she came from a strict and very old-fashioned family, and it was very important to her to keep all this a secret. Few things stay a secret long in this town, and she became Cameron's next target."

"And did this one pay?"

"She did. What she thought was a onetime payment to keep Cameron Clark's mouth shut. Then Cameron found another expensive girlfriend, and asked for more money. Miss Manning was already skating on thin emotional ice, and this extra strain was more than she could take. She killed herself."

"Oh, my God," Jackie breathed.

"And she left a note for her brother explaining everything. They'd been close, and she knew he'd understand." He patted Jackie's arm. "Don't worry, my dear, we're getting closer to Cameron Clark all the time. Why, we're practically breathing down his neck this very minute."

"Don't worry about me, Neville," Jackie told him. "I'm enjoying the story tremendously."

"Well, I hope I can get a publisher to have that same opinion when I finish the book," said Neville. "If I do finish it, that is. There are still so many unanswered questions, and time is not exactly on my side." He turned to Matt. "Now we're getting in to territory unknown even to you, Matthew, or parts of it, at least."

"Anything you say is confidential, Neville," said Matt.

"I'm pretty sure you'll recognize the confidential bits when we get there," Neville told him. He sipped at his lemonade and took a few deep breaths with his eyes closed.

"Are you sure you wouldn't rather we came back tomorrow for the rest?" Matt asked him. "You look exhausted."

"Nonsense," said Neville, opening his eyes again. "This is only marginally more tiring than a rousing game of nickel-ante poker. And I usually lose, anyway. So, where were we?"

"Sally Manning killed herself," Jackie reminded him.

"Ah, yes. Well, soon after Sally's death, James Nesmith, the director—are you familiar with him?"

"Only with his work," said Jackie.

"A very good man. Well, James was putting together a package for a movie he'd written called *Killer's Heart*. He didn't yet have a producer for the project, but he had some good actors lined up. And he made a very unusual decision regarding the lead role. He offered it to Kurt Manowski."

Jackie felt a chill go up her spine despite the warm afternoon temperature.

"When he got a studio to sign on, they insisted the film be produced by Cameron Clark. His films had been making respectable money, most of them, for some years, and he'd just had a critical success as well. Cameron, in turn, was eager for the job of producing *Killer's Heart*, though he did favor giving the lead role to Jack Wynn rather than Kurt. He pushed his agenda, and James pushed back, and in the end Kurt kept the lead role. But on the day shooting began, according to someone who was there, there was a private conversation between the two. No screaming or throwing chairs about, but Cameron came out of it shaken. And it was the beginning of a war."

"Does anyone know what was said?"

"Private, as I said, and unfortunately or otherwise, no one overheard it. Of course no one knew then or now, outside of a few friends of Leo Vanetti's, that Cameron had been the one to hound Sally Manning to her death, but although it wasn't highly publicized to movie fans, it was not exactly a secret that poor Sally had been Kurt Manowski's younger sister."

Jackie gasped. "Then he must have told Cameron that he knew!"

"And knowing that Kurt knew drove Cameron a bit mad, I think, or so I've come to believe as I've pieced all this together. He must have been waiting for the other shoe to drop. After all, if he had something on someone, he'd be extorting them, wouldn't he? Apparently that wasn't Kurt's style, and at any rate he could hardly have exposed Cameron without making his sister's past a public matter."

"And he wanted to spare their family."

"That's my guess," said Neville.

Jackie sat back and shook her head. "Ral Perrin already told me about the feud between Kurt and Cameron. But I had no idea Kurt blamed Cameron for the death of his sister."

Neville looked at her intently. "May I hazard a guess that Kurt Manowski is a suspect in Cameron's murder?"

"Not as far as the police are concerned, no," said Jackie.

"Yes, they have the young director in their sights, don't they?"

"And in jail." Jackie sighed. "He's been indicted."

"So Cameron goes on spreading misery even after he's dead," said Matt. "That's typical."

"And let me guess," said Neville to Jackie. "You'd like to take this story to the Palmer, Ohio, police and get them to look more closely at Kurt Manowski."

"In a word, yes."

"Well, I can scarcely blame you for that. And you have my blessing to do so, if you need or want it, but I'd hate to believe Kurt was the one to dispose of Cameron in such a callous manner."

"You've got to admit he had motive," Jackie reminded him.

"More than enough for some," Neville agreed cautiously.

"I don't know," said Matt. "Why wouldn't Kurt have offed Cameron a long time ago? When did all that happen? Four years ago? Five?"

"Around then," Neville said. "But sometimes it takes

time for hate to grow that large and overpowering. Murder is a serious decision. If it were not, we'd all be merrily eliminating people who irritated us on a daily basis."

"I just want all the facts to be known," said Jackie. "I'm not trying to railroad Kurt, but I don't want the police and the DA to overlook anything in their rush to convict John."

"Perfectly understandable," Neville said, patting her hand.

"So was that the end of Cameron's brilliant blackmail career?" Matt asked Neville.

"Oh, no," Neville exclaimed. "Stopping at that point would have been intelligent. No, he found another unfortunate mark, and that was the one who brought him to Leo Vanetti's attention, and led to his eventual downfall."

"Another young actress?"

"You perceive a pattern?" Neville asked, smiling. "Yes, Cameron wasn't likely to pick on anyone who looked like they could pick back. In the case of the young lady from Minnesota, he'd underestimated her sheer guts. In Sally Manning's case, he pushed too hard and killed his cash cow. Those mistakes were nothing to Cameron, however, compared to the one he was about to make.

"Cameron's next extortion victim was a young woman I'll call Mary. Good generic name, that, and I can't mention her real one for reasons which will become evident. So here's Mary arriving in Hollywood and expecting to become famous overnight simply because she's blond and beautiful and has a body to die for, and who knows— maybe she can even act."

"There are only a few million like that in this town," Matt commented.

"Exactly," Neville agreed. "So she didn't become famous and she ran out of money and went to work as a waitress and was too ashamed to call her parents in New Jersey and tell them she was a failure. She very quickly fell into the clutches of one of those opportunistic men who like to make their living from young women down on their luck."

"They're called pimps, Neville," Matt commented.

"Such an ugly word. Well, she met up with this pimp, then"—this with a nod to Matt—"who convinced her that she could easily supplement her meager income by working for him part-time, just until her big break came along, you know. A sort of 'escort service.' Strictly high-class call-girl business—no walking the streets.

"So Mary goes to work escorting visiting businessmen and the like, and after a year of saving her pennies and looking for acting jobs during the day, she finally lands one. On a Cameron Clark production, as luck would have it. And Cameron recognizes Mary from having hired her to date a banker from back east he was kissing up to while trying to get a project financed. He didn't say anything at first, and she apparently didn't recognize him, so he befriended the girl. He learned that she was the product of a strict Catholic family—one of her brothers was a priest—and her mother was very ill. He had found his next victim."

"So what was the catch?"

"Only that her poor sick mother was Leo Vanetti's cousin, something Cameron could have discovered himself with a little research. Our Mary calls up cousin Leo and tells him a man is blackmailing her. She swears him to silence, then tells him what she's been doing for the past year, and how her mother can never find out, and is there anything he can do to help?"

"And there was, I take it."

"Family is very important to Leo," said Neville. "He had a trusted subordinate on a plane to the West Coast that afternoon, and the day after that Cameron Clark was kidnapped on his morning jog at the local high-school track, blindfolded, and taken to a warehouse in San Pedro.

There he was convinced, by whatever means Vanetti's men found necessary or perhaps even enjoyable, to leave Los Angeles and never show his face here again, or for that matter anywhere in the state of California."

"So they made a believer out of him," said Matt.

"You should envision Bruce Willis's last scene in *Billy Bathgate*," said Neville, "only I'm sure Cameron was never so noble. I am given to understand that he was pissing himself inside five minutes. They made him beg for his life for quite a long time."

"I can see it like it was right in front of me," said Matt, holding his hands up like a viewfinder. "What a scene that would have made!"

"A nice bit of Mafia theater," Neville agreed. "Doubtless they cadged a lot of it from the movies. Leo was inclined to be generous with Cameron, since his cousin's daughter had come to no harm, and no actual money had changed hands. He thought later that he might have gone too easy on him, but a deal's a deal, the way Leo sees it, and Cameron escaped with his life."

"For about nine months," Jackie said. "He blew into town like a Hollywood big deal, accepted a job teaching film production at Rodgers, and married a wannabe starlet from Chicago. There was always a lot of speculation about what he was doing in Ohio in the first place."

"Now you know," said Neville. "He had no choice but to be anywhere but Los Angeles, and Rodgers University had a teaching position open. And given Cameron's tendencies to take money that wasn't his wherever he went, you might find that the answer to your quest lies back in your own backyard. Who had Cameron chosen to provide his extra income in Palmer, Ohio?"

"You can bet I'll be trying to find out," Jackie told him.

Neville coughed into his handkerchief and sighed. "And now I fear I must go inside and rest. I usually don't nap on the days Matthew comes by, but then I don't usually talk this much, either."

Matt got up and positioned himself behind Neville's chair. Jackie went in front of them and opened the glass-paneled door to the house, and the three of them proceeded down the hall of photographs to the door to Neville's room.

"I'll take it from here, Matthew," said Neville. "I'm sure Sylvia or Elizabeth will be swooping down on me any minute now if I need any help getting into bed. Will I see you next week, then?"

"If I'm still out of work you will," said Matt.

"Well, we can always hope for that," said Neville, chuckling. "Jackie my dear, it's been a pleasure." He took her hand in his. "I hope you'll come to see me again if you're in Los Angeles. I'll put your name on the list so the bouncers don't heave you out."

"The pleasure was mine, Neville," Jackie told him. "And I do hope I can come back and visit again someday."

"And I hope I'm here to receive you when you do. Cheers, then." He turned the chair around and wheeled it through the bedroom doorway. The Ice Women were nowhere in sight, so Jackie and Matt let themselves out.

"So are you glad you came to L.A.?" Matt asked when they were back in his car and driving away from the big Spanish mansion.

"I wouldn't have missed meeting Neville for the world," Jackie told him. "Altogether I guess I'd say that except for being shot at, it was a highly successful visit."

"And since the shot missed you . . ." Matt began.

"Yes, given that," said Jackie, "I guess I'd have to say my visit was a success all around."

CHAPTER 22

Palmer, Ohio, seemed like a welcome dose of everyday reality after two days in Los Angeles, and Jackie's spirits were lifting as she drove away from the airport toward the kennel where Jake and Charlie were waiting for her. She had something to tell Bernie and Evan that might make them reopen the investigation, and that was all she'd really dared hope for. As for people shooting at her, she had managed to convince herself that it had been nothing more than a terrifying coincidence—a reminder of why she preferred life in reasonably quiet Palmer to life in Los Angeles any day of the week.

Matt Darwin had given her a ride to the airport, and she had flown out that afternoon after visiting with Neville Ice. Her head had been full of his stories as she dozed on the gently rumbling plane, catching up on the sleep she'd been robbed of the night before by anxiety and nightmares.

It was nearly ten P.M. by the clock on the Blazer's dashboard as she turned off the highway into the long, sloping driveway of Cusack Kennels. There were lights on in the farmhouse that Tom and Grania shared with Joseph. Jackie had called from the airplane and asked him to expect her, unwilling to leave her dog and cat another night when she could have the pleasure of their company at home. Driving to the top of the driveway, she could see Bernie Youngquist's white Toyota parked next to the house. Good, Jackie thought. She didn't have to wait until tomorrow to fill Bernie in on what she'd found out in California.

Jackie climbed down from the Blazer and walked up to the house. Joseph had the front door open before she could ring the bell. "We figured you'd be here about now," he said, motioning her inside. "We already put on a pot of tea."

"What a wonderful idea," Jackie said with real feeling.

"I'll just go into the kitchen and get the cups and stuff," said Joseph. "Make yourself at home."

"Hi, Jackie." Bernie had one leg thrown over the end of the old frizee sofa, reading a magazine. She was casually dressed in a pair of bleached blue jeans and a work shirt knotted over a black tank top, but on her the outfit looked like a full-page designer ad in *Vanity Fair*.

"Hi, Bernie," said Jackie. "Miss me?"

"You didn't exactly advertise that you were going anywhere," Bernie told her with a wry smile. "If I hadn't seen Jake and Charlie when I came to visit yesterday, I'd never have known you were gone."

Jackie sank down into one of the two big, deep easy chairs that flanked the fireplace and put her feet up on a fringed ottoman. "It didn't seem like the sort of thing I ought to spread around," she said.

"So you were detecting, huh?"

"Yep. How 'bout you?"

"Oh, it was a quiet couple of days in Palmer. I don't think we're allowed more than one murder a week."

Joseph came in with a tray holding a teapot, china cups, sugar and cream, and a plate of shortbread biscuits. He set it down on the coffee table and took a seat beside Bernie on the sofa.

"How was L.A.?" he asked, pouring tea into the teacups.

"Warm, interesting, a bit dangerous." Jackie shrugged. "Pretty much like always. I do have a few things to tell you, but they can wait until we have our tea."

"I have a few things to tell you, too," said Bernie. "But tea comes first. Milk and sugar?"

"Please."

"Biscuit?" Joseph inquired.

Jackie gazed at the rich shortbreads stacked up on the plate. "I really shouldn't . . ." she protested.

"They're whole-meal," Joseph told her.

"Well, that makes all the difference, then," said Jackie with a grateful smile. She put two of the biscuits on her saucer, stirred her tea, and sat back in the chair. "I can't tell you how good it feels to finally relax," she said. She took a sip of her tea. Perfect.

A loud beeping sound erupted from somewhere in the vicinity of the sofa, and Bernie reached into the pocket of her jeans and retrieved her pager. "It's Evan," she said, glancing at the display. "I'd better call him." She reached into a black leather jacket she had thrown over the back of the sofa, pulled out a little phone, and keyed Evan's speed-dial code. "You rang, boss?" she said into the phone, then, "Oh. Uh-huh. Never heard of him. I'll be there in fifteen. Bye."

She turned off the phone and looked at Joseph and Jackie. "That's what I get for being smug about murders in Palmer," she told them. "We've apparently just had another one. Somebody shot some guy named Piers Ackroyd, if you can believe that."

"I can, actually," said Jackie when she could get the words out.

"You know the guy?"

"We met once, at the jail."

"Why don't you just come on back to town with me?" said Bernie. "We can talk on the way, and I'll bring you back here tonight."

"I'll wait up," Joseph offered, "and you can pick up Jake and Charlie."

"Let's just let the three of you sleep," said Jackie. "I'll follow Bernie in my car and leave the boys here until tomorrow morning."

"Well, I do have a puppy class first thing in the morning," Joseph admitted.

"I'll come over as soon as I'm reasonably awake," Jackie promised.

"No hurry," Joseph assured her with a grin. "It's not like Tom's going to charge you for an extra day."

The parking lot of the Ohio Motor Inn looked like a police conference attended by officers with poor parking skills. Cars were angled this way and that, lights spinning. The central part of the motel was wreathed in yards and yards of black-and-yellow police tape. Evan Stillman's unmarked dark gray sedan was in the big middle of all of the others, and Evan's silhouette could be clearly seen in the headlights, huddling with a lot of other silhouettes Jackie assumed to be officers and evidence techs.

Bernie parked as carelessly as the rest, angling her little car between Evan's and one of the blue-and-white PPD cars. Jackie, good citizen that she was, parked neatly between the white lines, a safe distance from any police vehicles. Bernie got out of her car and ducked under the flimsy barrier of plastic tape to join Evan, and Jackie was right behind her.

Evan said nothing when he saw Jackie, but even in this light she could see him roll his eyes. "Thanks for showing up so quickly, Youngquist," he said to Bernie. "What we've got is a male Caucasian in his early-to-mid fifties, nude, with a hole in his head you could watch TV through. The ID says he lives in Columbus. We've called the Columbus PD, and they're looking for any next of kin."

"He was a private detective," Jackie told him.

"Cripes, Walsh, you're good!" Evan exclaimed, turning to Jackie. "I think I'll just go home now and let you take over. You haven't even seen the guy yet and you already know what he does for a living! How the hell do you know he's a private detective? There wasn't any license among the effects."

"She knew the guy," Bernie told him.

Evan turned a pained look on Jackie, the kind she'd never quite gotten used to. "You knew the victim," he said, and didn't bother making it a question.

"We weren't exactly buddies," said Jackie. "He's the PI John McBride's lawyer brought in from Columbus to turn up some evidence for the defense. We met exactly once. I didn't like him."

"You didn't like Cameron Clark, either," Evan reminded her. "Would you like to just confess to both these murders right now and save Detective Youngquist and me a whole lot of work?"

"You're joking, right? Right?"

Evan sighed deeply, like a man in great pain. "What else do you know about him?"

"He told me the name of his company, but I don't know if I can remember it. He didn't give me a card. Let me think. Ackroyd and somebody. Ackroyd and Jefferson? Ackroyd and Jeffreys! That was it. In Columbus."

"Thanks," said Evan, writing it down in his notebook. "Now get the hell out of here, okay?"

"I'll be responsible for her," said Bernie.

Evan shook his head wearily. "Stay out of the way," he told Jackie.

Jackie resisted the urge she often felt to salute when on

the receiving end of a command from Evan. "I will," she assured him.

"Come on," Bernie said. "Let's go have a look at Mr. Piers Ackroyd."

"No, that's okay," Jackie assured her. "You go right ahead."

"I'm responsible for you, remember. You can either come along where I can see you're not getting into any trouble, or go home and miss all the fun."

"You call this fun?"

"My mother thought I ought to go to secretarial school," said Bernie. "So yeah, compared to running an office, this is fun." She took off at a brisk clip for the fatal motel room, whose door was standing open while uniformed and plainclothes personnel walked in and out. Jackie scrambled to catch up.

"Stay on this side of the doorway," Bernie called back over her shoulder. "If someone's going to screw up evidence, it should be one of ours, not a civilian." She stepped into the room, pulled on a pair of latex gloves from a box offered by a tech, and proceeded to examine the late Piers Ackroyd.

Jackie stopped just outside the doorway of the motel room, but even from there she could smell the blood, and the slight scent of gunpowder that accompanied it. Inside, a man's body lay facedown across a rumpled bed whose sheets would never be white again no matter what kind of laundry miracle product was put on the job. There were blots and spatters of blood on the walls, and a puddle of blood on the floor under his head.

A flash startled her, and a painful black spot took over most of her field of vision, then shrank in on itself. An evidence tech with a camera—the same one who'd been with Evan at the warehouse that fatal Friday morning when John had been arrested—was standing on the far side of the bed getting a shot of the corpse. She lined up another shot, and this time Jackie looked away before the flash.

Jackie had seen more than her share of dead bodies—all victims of violence. She'd come pretty close to victim status herself more than once, and had experienced some amazing and very lucky escapes. She'd stood face-to-face on several occasions with people who killed. More than most people she knew, she had a firsthand knowledge of the kinds of things people are capable of when driven far enough.

Sometimes it was an outside force that propelled someone far enough over the edge to take a life, and sometimes it was just wanting something bad enough that it didn't much matter who got in the way. The end result was the same no matter what the circumstances that led up to it; someone alive and capable of thought and feeling and interaction with others was reduced to a piece of meat no different in any meaningful way from the stuff they sold by the pound at the butcher's counter. Piers Ackroyd may have been an officious, irritating little man, but all he was now was a dead one.

After a few minutes Bernie came out and disposed of the gloves in a plastic trash bag outside the room, which was emblazoned with a prominent orange-and-black biohazard emblem. "We're going to be a while here, and you don't really have to stick around," she told Jackie. "I was just yanking Evan's chain a little. After all, you are sort of involved."

"More than I want to be. What are the chances that Ackroyd's dead because he was investigating John's case?"

"Like you are?" Bernie shook her head. "I wish I knew. When we know who killed him, we'll also know if there's any connection, probably. Do you feel like you need police protection? I'm not sure they'd grant it under the circumstances, but I could stay at your place tonight if it'd make you feel better."

"Oh, I don't think that's necessary," Jackie told her. "I mean even if there is some sort of connection, Ackroyd was probably going all over town telling people he was investigating Cameron's murder. The only person I've told around here is you."

"Well, I'm not going to kill you," Bernie said, looking at her watch. "I've got reports to write up, and I'd like to get a few hours' sleep tonight. Oh!" she exclaimed. "I remembered what I was going to tell you, only not in front of Joseph."

"What's that?"

"When the evidence folks did the undercarriage of John McBride's truck, they found some fibers from the victim's trousers up around one of the tie rods. There was blood on them."

"Even after a car wash?" Jackie asked.

"The cheap auto washes don't even do the undercarriage. They just wash the top and sides. Anyway, that kind of clinches the truck as the murder weapon. It's pretty indisputable."

"But not who was driving the truck."

"There's no evidence that anyone besides John McBride had driven the truck in quite a while. Sorry it couldn't be better news, but I thought you'd want to hear it anyway."

"I don't think I wanted to, but I guess I needed to. Thanks, Bernie. I appreciate you keeping me posted. Good night."

"G'night." Bernie stifled a yawn.

"Call me if you find out anything you think I ought to know about this," said Jackie, pointing in the direction of the bloody motel room.

"I will," Bernie promised. "Right now it's looking a lot more like he was done in by a jealous girlfriend than anything else. The evidence magicians will doubtless tell us the whole sordid story in the morning."

CHAPTER 23

"Jackie, you've got to find another hobby for all our sakes," said Cosmo Gordon, Palmer's Chief Medical Examiner, cutting into his Crêpes Aubergine. "Leave the police work to the police." They were sitting in Suzette's— Cosmo's favorite lunching spot ever since he decided that real men actually do eat crêpes. Jackie had suggested this place for lunch to soften Cosmo up for the favor she was planning to ask. Now that she had, he was refusing her.

"How often have you told me that, Cosmo," she reminded him, "only to find out in the end that I was right?" Jackie picked at her spinach-and-Camembert crêpe. After visiting John in jail this morning—the day after the private investigator his lawyer had put on his case turned up dead in a motel room—her appetite wasn't up to it.

Cosmo frowned. "You're not always right, you know."

"No, but you have to admit that I have a different angle on things than the police."

"You certainly do." He chuckled. "Tell it to Evan Stillman."

"I'd rather *you* did," said Jackie. "He'd listen to you where he never would to me. That's why I just want to run a few things past you. For instance, Sondra Clark . . ."

"He listens to me because I'm the chief medical examiner," Cosmo explained, interrupting her. "I examine the evidence and give a medical opinion on it."

"Okay, this is more of a theory than evidence, and I'd have taken it to Bernie, but Evan sent her to Columbus to ask around about Piers Ackroyd."

"The fellow who was shot to death last night? My, Jackie, you do get around. How do you know anything at all about the late Mr. Ackroyd?"

"That's not important . . ." Jackie began, but before she could finish the sentence, Marcella Jacobs's head popped up over the divider behind Cosmo's back.

"You knew the man who was murdered last night? I should have known!" Marcella came around the divider and gave Cosmo a kiss on the cheek. "Hi, Cosmo dear," she greeted him. "And how can you say it's not important? Jackie, you never cease to amaze me!"

Cosmo beamed. "Marcella! What a great surprise! How are you?"

"You should know, you devil," said Marcella as she sat down in one of the empty chairs. "I was at your place all night."

Cosmo blushed becomingly.

"So tell me all about you and the murdered man," Marcella said to Jackie.

"Which one?" Jackie inquired. "If you ask Evan Stillman, I know everyone who gets murdered in Palmer."

"Well, you know more of them than most," Marcella pointed out, accurately enough.

This was going nowhere. Cosmo didn't want to hear anything she had to say, and Jackie wasn't in the mood to dish with Marcella. "I've really got to be going, so I'll leave you two lovebirds alone," she said, getting up from the table.

"Oh, come on, Jackie," Marcella said. "I can play footsie with Cosmo anytime. Sit back down and fill me in.

Did you see my series—'Sex, Cinema, and Death in Palmer, Ohio'? It ran Saturday and Sunday. Page one. The crime-desk editor is very impressed."

"I was out of town," Jackie explained, "but I'm sure the papers are at home somewhere. Listen, I really do have to go. I promised Jake I'd take him for a romp in the park." She put some money on the table for her crêpe.

"Oh, I'm picking this one up, Jackie," said Cosmo, handing back her money. "It's the least I can do for being so uncooperative."

Inwardly Jackie agreed, though she would never hurt Cosmo's feelings by saying it out loud. "Thanks, Cosmo," she said. "Next one's on me."

She waved good-bye to her two friends and started for the door.

"Out of town?" she heard Marcella call after her. "Where?" She pretended not to hear.

"Evan, I know you don't want to discuss the case with me," Jackie began. Jake's trip to the park had been postponed just a bit. As long as she was downtown and had to go right past the police department, and as long as Cosmo Gordon wasn't going to intercede for her with Evan, she might as well bite the bullet and face him herself. It wouldn't be the first time.

"Coffee?" Evan asked. Before she could say no, he poured a cup of inky-black liquid into a thick white mug and handed it to her. "Do you take milk with that?"

"It wouldn't help," Jackie said, accepting the mug with a mixture of dread and resignation.

"So which of the murder cases you're involved in this week don't I want to discuss with you, Jackie?" Evan asked with exaggerated mock sincerity as he sat down in his ancient leather reclining chair.

Jackie stifled a sigh. "Either one. But don't play dumb.

I'm sure Bernie's already told you I went to Los Angeles."

Evan's eyebrows went up two notches. He leaned forward in his chair. "It didn't come up. But now that it has, what the hell were you doing in Los Angeles?"

Jackie bristled, in spite of having expected this reaction. "Am I required to file travel plans now?"

"No," said Evan, "but you wouldn't be telling me this if it didn't have something to do with a certain murdered movie producer, would you?"

Jackie nodded. "Good point. That must be why you're a detective and I'm not. I did go to L.A. to talk with someone about Cameron Clark. A man named Neville Ice."

Evan leaned back again. The chair creaked and popped like a pair of bad knees. "Never heard of him."

"That's okay, he told me he never heard of you either."

"So what did you find out from this Ice guy?" Evan wanted to know. Jackie had to admit that he sounded less bored and more interested than he had a moment ago. Maybe he'd actually have to pay attention to her.

"A reason Kurt Manowski had to kill Cameron Clark."

"So Manowski's your suspect?"

"I have a theory about Sondra Clark, too, if you want to hear it," Jackie offered.

"One suspect at a time," said Evan. "I already heard about how Clark fired Manowski from some movie a couple of years back. From what I understand, if every out-of-work actor in Hollywood picked off the last producer who canned him, there'd be nobody left to produce anything."

"But there are significant details to the story you haven't heard," Jackie told him, "and I think when you've heard them, you'll agree that Manowski makes a swell suspect."

Evan looked at his watch. "I don't have to be anywhere

for half an hour," he told her. "I'm all yours."

"What a lucky girl I am," said Jackie. And before he could react to that, she began to tell him the story she'd heard only the day before from Neville Ice. To his credit, Evan listened attentively until she was through, and if he wasn't interested, he didn't let on.

"So if Manowski was going to kill Clark for driving his sister to suicide, why wouldn't he have done it at the time? Why wait—what, two years? Three? Why not just put his lights out in the heat of the moment?"

"Come on, Evan. You've seen enough murders to know that sometimes the camel's back breaks when you apply the straw, and sometimes it doesn't. Sometimes it takes years to snap. So what do you say?"

"About what? You want me to tell you that I'm going to talk to Manowski. Would that make you happy?"

"Delirious."

"I shouldn't do it, then. But I will. When Bernie gets back from Columbus after lunch, we'll go look him up at his apartment or that bar he plays poker at with your ex–movie crew every night."

"Thanks, Evan. You're a pal."

"I'm not doing it because I'm a pal," he told her. "I'm doing it because you have a point, and I want to make sure it's not a good one before I start ignoring it."

"Good enough. I'll take it." Jackie got up from Evan's guest chair and picked up her untouched cup of coffee.

"Something wrong with your coffee?" Evan asked.

"Nope," she told him, and bravely drank half the cup before putting it back down on his desk. She managed not to shudder. God, the sacrifices she had to make sometimes.

"So what's your other theory?" Evan asked.

"Sondra Clark."

"I thought you had something to tell me I don't already know."

"You mean you think she killed Cameron?" Jackie was incredulous. "Then why did you arrest John?"

"I didn't say I thought she killed him alone," said Evan. "It's pretty obvious they were in collusion on the deal, but we had all the evidence we need to convict McBride, and next to nothing on the Clark woman."

"That's why you're keeping her on such a long leash," said Jackie. "You're hoping she'll screw up."

"Hell, yes. She's not smart enough to realize how obvious a suspect she is. Did you see that shiner she was wearing around the morning after her husband was flattened?"

"I did, actually. And Cameron did seem to be the most likely person to have given it to her."

"And I never saw a grieving widow so disinclined to even pretend to grieve," said Evan. "So for me the question becomes did she call up her boyfried after her husband left and get him riled up enough to kill him, or were they already planning the whole thing, and this was just gravy?"

"Why is it so impossible to believe she might have killed him herself?"

"Well, first of all, a '61 Chevy pickup is a pretty macho weapon, don't you think?"

"Not really. I don't know which gender is more likely to run people down with cars, statistically."

"Me neither, but if she was driving, it's because she got the keys from McBride."

"Wait a minute! What did you say?"

"I said she got the keys from McBride. Either that, or—"

"You're absolutely right! She got the keys when she got the shirt!"

"Jackie, are you back to that stolen-shirt theory again?" Evan demanded.

"Hear me out, Evan. John came to the set every morning in a T-shirt with a plaid flannel shirt over it. Then when it got hot he'd take off the flannel and throw it somewhere. He remembers that he never found one of those shirts."

"Yeah, I know that story," said Evan. "It's damned convenient he never found it, seeing as it turned up in the Clark woman's bedroom."

"There's more," Jackie told him. "John always kept his car keys in his shirt pocket. That's why he was searching so hard for that missing shirt—he thought his car keys were in it. Later he found the keys somewhere else." She leaned forward to make her last point. "So just supposing Sondra were sneaky enough to pick up John's shirt, planning to use it later to provoke her husband. She feels something in the pocket. Keys! Knowing John's not going to go looking for them until the end of the day, she takes off when everyone breaks for lunch and has the keys duplicated."

"Why? You think she's already planning on borrowing his truck to run down her husband later?"

"Probably not. That would be thinking too far ahead for Sondra. But she had a thing for John. Maybe she wanted to let herself into his house one night. Maybe she just wanted to fantasize that she could if she wanted to. Hell, I don't know what she was thinking," said Jackie, sinking back in her chair. "But the shirt and the keys are a connection. I know they are."

"You also know she and McBride weren't fooling around, but she says they were."

"And he says they weren't."

"And the jury will decide," said Evan.

"I'd like for this not to drag on that long," said Jackie.

"Yeah, that's what your Mr. Ackroyd was hoping for, too, I imagine. Before some greedy hooker plugged him."

"You're sure his death didn't have anything to do with his investigation?"

"His death had to do with flashing a wad of cash around in a very bad part of town," said Evan. "Lots of people saw it. Witnesses say he picked up a blonde in the Fantasy Lounge. Evidently he took her back to his room—she was even nice enough to leave some hairs in the sink—and she decided that she wanted the whole bankroll. End of story. So you don't have to worry that poking your cute little Irish nose where it doesn't belong is going to get you a .38-caliber slug through the head."

"You think my nose is cute?" Jackie asked.

"I think you poke it around too much."

"Yeah, that's probably true, but I can tell you really like me," Jackie told him.

"Whatever gave you that idea?" Evan inquired with a frown.

"Because you just spent the last fifteen minutes discussing the case with me."

Evan put one hand over his eyes and rubbed his temples like a man with a severe headache. "Get out of here before I arrest you for killing me," he told her.

Jackie got up and put down the mug of coffee. "Thanks for everything, Evan," she said. "See you around."

"I always do," he replied wearily.

CHAPTER 24

The morning of Cameron Clark's funeral was bright and sunny and heading toward hot—quite the opposite of the sort of weather funerals were supposed to feature, if one got one's view of reality from movies. Jackie wouldn't have minded sometimes if life wanted to be a bit more like cinema. Afer all, life in the movies made sense— good guys prospered for the most part, and bad guys got punished. If something happened to somebody in a screenplay, they had to deserve it, and the audience had to believe they'd deserved it. Basic story ethics.

Had Cameron Clark deserved to die? Jackie wondered to herself as she went through her closet looking for something properly dark yet not too hot to wear to a late-June funeral. "He certainly wasn't a good person," she told herself aloud, "and blackmail's a dangerous occupation. There should be hazard pay or something. Where's that short-sleeved black dress?" She'd gone through all her hangers three times, and the one thing she needed was nowhere in sight.

Jake looked up at her from the end of her bed as if to say she shouldn't blame him. "Right," she told him. "Dogs have enough sense to bury things that are important to them so they can always find them again when they need to. Why didn't I just bury the damned dress?"

She slipped into jeans and a T-shirt and stepped into a pair of shoes. She still had more than two hours to buy herself another dress, get home, and get ready to leave again. No problem. "You stay here, Jake," she told her dog. "Men and male dogs are absolutely no use when you're shopping."

Since fall clothes were already on the racks despite the temperature being in the nineties most days, it didn't take Jackie long to find the dress she wanted—a deep eggplant-colored knit with a nice drape to the skirt and short sleeves so she wouldn't roast standing out in the cemetery. It was dark enough not to stand out in a crowd of mourners and attractive enough to wear a lot of other places, too. A bargain at under sixty dollars.

Jackie consulted her watch and decided there was time to hit the video store on her way home. Maybe she could find a new martial-arts film for Peter and something new for herself, too. A romantic comedy to watch with Tom seemed a good choice, or maybe she should just skip the comedy and go straight for the romance. She looked up and down the shelves for something to jump out at her and ask to be taken home.

What jumped out at her was a shelf full of pictures of Lorraine Voss. A dozen stacks of tapes showed pictures of a slightly younger Lorraine in the foreground, looking over her shoulder at a dark human form coming toward her from the shadows. *Eyes of the City,* Jackie read off the shelf banner. *Two episodes on each cassette.* She picked one up and scanned the contents.

"I think that was my favorite episode," said a man's voice from behind her. He pointed to the tape Jackie was holding, which read "To Kill a Rat" and "High Crimes."

" 'To Kill a Rat,' I mean. It was nominated for an Emmy for best dramatic episode."

"No kidding?" Jackie sped through the back blurb on the episode. "Sounds good; thanks for the recommendation."

"I came in the other day and bought just that one tape," said the man, loading up his arms with videotapes, "and now I'm going to get them all. She's staying here in town, you know, making a movie. I do her hair. Not on the set, of course, but she comes to my shop to get her hair colored."

"Going gray, huh?"

"Going blond, if I don't keep up with it," said the man. He walked off, smiling, with a stack of tapes he could barely see over.

"Think I'll just settle for one today," said Jackie. She tucked the tape under her arm and gave herself five more minutes to buy everything she was going to buy and get home. It wouldn't do not to look her best at Cameron Clark's send-off.

All the people Jackie expected to see at the cemetery were there, along with a few hundred people she didn't expect. The celebrity factor was making Cameron Clark's funeral the event to be seen at today. Even the mayor was here, probably saying good-bye to the income she had hoped Palmer's exposure to the filmmaking community would bring in. Jackie had to laugh. Jane Bellamy had only thought she had problems when Marcella's "thinly disguised real Palmer" story hit the doorsteps of the city last week.

Actually, Jackie hadn't expected Cameron to be buried in Palmer at all, but then why would he leave instructions to be sent back to Calfornia after his demise? Jackie had no doubt Sondra would be heading there soon—if she wasn't arrested first—to make herself known as the

widow of the late movie producer and wait for fame and
fortune to manifest themselves as the movie deals poured
in. Too bad Sondra had no idea how little loved her late
husband had been in the industry. Jackie didn't think for
a minute that it was her duty to tell her, either.

"Doesn't Sondra make a lovely widow?" said Lorraine
in a conspiratorial voice over Jackie's shoulder. She
pointed to the lovely widow in question, a vision in black
grosgrain and lace, with a little lace veil hanging down
from her hat.

"Stunning. I hope she's hired a photographer."

"Why should she? There must be two dozen of them
here already. The news crews are sort of lurking around
the outer edges trying not to be too disrespectful, but they
all want to know who's here, and get some footage."

Jackie could see that Lorraine was right. Even Marcella
and Werner were there, doing their best not to look obvious and failing. "Do you see anyone you know from
Hollywood?" she asked.

"A few. One of those guys over there by that tree is a
studio head, and the other one is Paul Canley, a director.
There are a few more around here somewhere, but nothing
like the turnout you'd see for someone who was liked.
But then it didn't take me this long to find out how little
people thought of Cameron."

"You're lucky you never worked with him, I guess."

"Yep," Lorraine said. "Lucky. That's me. Say, I tried
to call you on Sunday to see if you wanted to go to a
movie or something, but you weren't home. I didn't leave
a message."

"I was out of town," said Jackie.

"Really? How far out?"

"Los Angeles."

Lorraine looked shocked. "For a day?"

"Two days. I had to talk to a guy."

"This guy doesn't have a phone?"

"It's a long story," said Jackie. "A story within a story, actually. I was just trying to do something to help John. I think maybe I did, I don't know yet."

"So you *are* investigating Cameron's murder!"

"Well, someone has to. Somebody shot the *real* investigator."

"Not before you went to L.A., they didn't."

"I guess it's just become a habit," Jackie admitted. "I'm not bad at it, you know."

"I'll bet you're not."

"Oh, speaking of investigators, you'll never guess what I found in the video store this morning," Jackie told Lorraine.

"So don't make me try." She squinted against the sun, then pulled out a pair of dark glasses and put them on.

"Videotapes of *Eyes of the City* episodes," said Jackie. "Lots of them!"

"Oh, those! I'd forgotten when they were due to hit the stores." She laughed dryly. "If I had any shame, I'd be blushing."

"I saw a man buying eleven of them," Jackie said.

Lorraine sighed and shook her head sadly. "He's going to die of boredom, and it's going to be all my fault."

"I bought one myself," Jackie told her.

"You didn't! You should get your money back."

" 'High Crimes' and 'To Kill a Rat.' "

"You're kidding."

"No, really. Didn't that one win an Emmy or something?"

"Or something," Lorraine said, suddenly distracted. "Forgive me for being crass, but I'm going to go schmooze with these Hollywood types. A wise man once said, 'Never pass up an opportunity to kiss an executive's behind.' "

"Really?"

"On my word of honor. Find me after they plant Cameron, and we'll go have a drink or something."

"It's a little early for me . . ." Jackie began, but Lorraine was already walking away, putting on a big smile for the studio head and the director.

People were still arriving, and the ones that were already there were milling around like guests at a macabre cocktail party. Evidently the main event was not yet under way. Jackie spotted Ral and Mercy arriving and walked over to join them.

"Hi, Jackie," said Mercy. "Nice day for a funeral, huh?" She glanced up at the merciless summer sun and frowned.

"Nice day for a sunburn," Jackie agreed. "What's all this murder business doing to the Palmer Film Commission?"

"Oh, I've still got a job, or at least my key still worked this morning," said Mercy. "I'm going to be out there flying to L.A. and pushing Palmer as long as they sign my paychecks, and it's got to pay off, doesn't it? I mean how long can they hold one murdered producer against us?"

"Don't worry about it," Ral reassured her. "In Hollywood they only care about how well your last picture did. It's gonna be fine—you've already gone the better part of a week without murdering another producer."

"Don't tempt fate," said Mercy, looking around nervously. "There are a few of them here today."

Marti Bernstein walked toward them, looking decidedly unfuneral in a purple tie-dyed dress and leather sandals. Her dreadlocks were tied up with a pink ribbon. "Looks like Cameron had more friends than I imagined," she said, indicating the crowd. "Of course a lot of them could be here for the same reason I am."

"And what reason is that?" Ral asked her.

"To make sure the son of a bitch is really dead," said Marti.

Katie Nolan joined them, accompanied by a pale and slightly weak-looking Andy Fry.

"Andy, should you be up and around?" Jackie asked him.

"Probably not," said Andy, "but Katie .thought she ought to be here, and I was sick of lying around like an invalid."

"I'm going to take him home as soon as . . . you know."

"As soon as they finish burying our movie," said Andy sadly.

"We'll make another movie," said Katie, linking her arm through Andy's. "As soon as John's back with us."

The officiating priest could now be seen at the graveside, and the crowd started to gravitate toward the open grave where Cameron Clark's casket, an expensive looking dull silver with chrome-plated handles, waited to be lowered within. Jackie and her friends joined them. She wished with all her heart that she could bury all this grief and trouble as easily.

CHAPTER 25

"What do you say, Jake? Would you like to watch one of my new videotapes?" Like most dogs of her experience, Jake was indifferent to television, or to anything he couldn't smell. Still, it only seemed polite to involve him in the decision.

"I have to save the karate flick for Peter, and I really want to see *Sense and Sensibility* with Tom. That leaves *Eyes of the City*. Whaddaya think, Jake? Are you in the mood for a mystery?"

Jake whuffed once, probably because he thought it was expected of him. Charlie was not at all involved, being curled up in an orange ball behind Jake's front leg. "*Eyes of the City* it is," said Jackie. "Gosh, I haven't watched that in years!" She tore the cellophane off the cover and removed the tape. "Let's fast-forward past this first episode and watch 'To Kill a Rat.' Charlie, you ought to be able to appreciate that."

"Mrrow," was Charlie's reply to that. He didn't even bother to open one eye. He recognized his name, Jackie knew, but doubtless he didn't find it as interesting a sound as food hitting the bottom of his dish. That would get his attention every time.

Jackie sat back on the sofa with her remote control and hit the fast-forward button. She had arranged for this evening of solo video watching, her last before Tom and the kids came back, by turning down the lights, then pouring out a bowl of chili and lime tortilla chips, and opening a carton of sour cream. There was, in her opinion, scarcely a more heavenly combination of flavors.

She upended an open can of Guinness Pub Draught into a pint glass and watched it pour itself, magically approximating the real thing they poured at Bridget O'Malley's as it swirled into the glass in an explosion of golden bubbles. She picked the can straight up and let it pour the rest of the way, finishing itself off with a perfect half inch of creamy foam. She peered inside the can, but she'd never been able to see the little doodad that performed the magic, and maybe it was better so. Maybe magic shouldn't be examined too closely.

The counter on the VCR ticked over sixty minutes, and Jackie hit the play button. The jazzy, edgy theme music to *Eyes of the City* blared out of the speakers, momentarily getting Jake and Charlie's attention. Jackie adjusted the volume, then sat back with her chips and stout, put her feet up, and watched.

The episode started out with a man asking another man for money. It was obvious the first man was extorting the money from the second, threatening him with exposure of something in their past. "This is timely, huh?" Jackie remarked to her dozing pets. "There seems to be a lot of that going around."

The episode was certainly dramatic. The performances were good and the camera work classy. What Jackie really paid attention to was the script. It was terrific. It almost made her want to write for television again. If she could do something this good, all the bull might almost be worth it.

The doorbell rang. Jake gave her his usual expectant

look, and she paused the tape. The hiss from the speakers caused Charlie to jump up to all fours, ginger fur sticking up on his back like a Mohawk hairdo. Jackie pressed the button to mute the volume, and Charlie turned around and settled down just as the doorbell rang again.

"I'm coming," she called, and walked to the door and opened it. Standing on the other side of the doorway was Kurt Manowski.

"Oh!" Jackie said, the word startled out of her by her instantaneous reaction to Kurt's glowering features. "I'm sorry," she corrected, ashamed of herself but still cautious, "I wasn't expecting anyone."

"Can I come in?" he asked.

"Ah, the place isn't really fit for company . . ." she stammered, keeping part of the door in front of her as if it might provide some protection. Jake got up from his place on the couch and came to sit beside her, his expression alert.

"I know you think I killed Cameron," Kurt said without further preamble. "I know you followed me to Cameron's house the night after he was killed. I'm also pretty sure it was you who sicced those detectives on me."

Jackie didn't know what to say. It didn't seem healthy to admit to any of those things, though all of them were true enough. For that matter, it didn't seem too healthy not to be screaming at the top of her lungs and hoping someone out there would hear her and come to her rescue. Jake didn't seem to recognize the threat here, perhaps because there was no weapon in evidence, and unlike the kid in *The Boys from Brazil,* she didn't really have a secret word that would order him to turn someone into hamburger.

Headlights flashed as a car came down the block and turned into the driveway. Both Jackie and Kurt turned to look as the door opened and Lorraine Voss stepped out. "Hi, Jackie. Hi, Kurt," she said, slinging a handbag strap over her shoulder and closing the car door. "Is it a party?"

"I was just leaving," said Kurt, then to Jackie, "We still have to talk." He walked past Lorraine down the walk, then crossed the street and was lost in the darkness beyond the reach of the streetlight.

"Come in," Jackie urged her, and locked the door behind her, throwing the dead bolt and securing the chain lock for good measure.

"What was going on with you and Kurt?" Lorraine asked.

"Nothing, yet," Jackie said. She peeked out the curtains of the front window, but there was no sign of him. "I just felt sort of threatened when I saw him standing on my front porch."

"You still think he killed Cameron, don't you?" Lorraine asked.

"He's the most likely suspect besides the lovely widow," said Jackie. "Today I convinced Evan Stillman he needed to talk to him again. Kurt seems to have guessed that I had some part in that." She took a deep breath and tried to calm down. "I'm sure glad you pulled up when you did."

"I can stick around for a while if you'd like."

"I'd like," said Jackie. "I was just watching that video I bought today." She picked up the remote and pressed the play button.

"Oh, have mercy on me!" Lorraine exclaimed. She took the remote from Jackie, pressed the off button, and tossed the remote back onto the couch. "I've had enough of that show to last a lifetime. Of course I wouldn't mind if it got picked up for syndication. I could sure use the money."

"Would you like a Guinness?"

"That black stuff? I'll pass. Do you have anything harder?"

"I think there should be a bottle of Jameson's in the cupboard," said Jackie.

"That's great. A shot of that, neat."

Jackie went into the kitchen, poured Lorraine a glass of whiskey, and brought it back.

Lorraine pulled a chair up in front of the television and sat down, crossing her legs. "So I'm not saying for a minute I believe he did it," she said to Jackie, taking the glass, "but what have you got on Kurt?"

Jackie sat back down on the couch next to Jake and Charlie, who'd taken up their positions again. "There's a man in Hollywood who knows Leo Vanetti," she began.

Lorraine laughed. "There are a lot of people in Hollywood who know Leo Vanetti, but most of them don't admit it in polite company."

"Well, this man's sort of a friend of his."

"You travel in very interesting company, Jackie," said Lorraine, taking a drink of her whiskey. "Do go on."

"Leo Vanetti told him about all the people Cameron has blackmailed."

"Blackmailed!"

"He used to make a habit of it before he tried it on some relation of Vanetti's and had to decide between Hollywood and his life."

Lorraine nodded. "So he chose Ohio. Fat lot of good it did him." She laughed without much humor and took another drink.

Jackie took a sip of her Guinness and proffered the bowl of tortilla chips. "These are really good," she told Lorraine. Try them."

"Thanks. I will."

Beside Jackie, Charlie got up on all fours, yawned and stretched luxuriously, then took a few steps and jumped down to the floor. The picture started up again on the television and Jackie realized that Charlie must have stepped on the play button on his way across the sofa.

The volume was still muted, but the picture played on behind Lorraine's back.

"Oh, these are good!" Lorraine exclaimed around a mouthful of tortilla chips and sour cream. "Why didn't I ever think of this?"

"Feel free to take the recipe," said Jackie.

"So anyhow, to get back to Cameron, Kurt's younger sister was one of Cameron's victims."

"Sally? The one who committed suicide?"

"Uh-huh. Evidently Cameron hounded her too hard, and she just couldn't face it anymore."

"I never knew," said Lorraine, her face strangely sad. "I never knew what he was capable of."

"No one did," said Jackie.

"I knew Sally pretty well," said Lorraine. "She used to come on the set sometimes when Kurt was in an episode."

Lorraine continued talking about her friendship with Kurt's sister, but Jackie was distracted by the moving pictures on the television behind her. She tried to pay attention to Lorraine, but her eyes kept jumping back to the screen.

A man—the blackmailing "rat" of the episode's title—is walking down a dark, lonely road. Headlights come burning around a bend in the road behind him. Cut to the driver, his blackmail victim. He sees the man, but instead of slowing down he speeds up, and the car slams into the walking man, sending him flying into a ditch.

Jackie's eyes went wide. Her trembling fingers reached for the stop button, but pressed the pause button instead as she knocked the remote onto the floor, freezing a flickering frame of a broken body and a car speeding past it.

Lorraine turned around and looked at the screen. "That was always my favorite episode," she said, draining her whiskey glass. "Shall we go for a little drive? Without Jake, of course."

CHAPTER 26

Jackie kicked herself, mentally, as she drove Lorraine's car out toward the outskirts of town and beyond, into the countryside near Little Canyon. Why hadn't she figured it out a lot sooner? Why didn't these blinding flashes come to her *before* she was in danger of losing her life? She had made the connection between Lorraine's penchant for using material from her old TV show and the murder of the blackmailer in *To Kill a Rat* just a little too late to do her any good.

Lorraine must have been the "other business" Cameron had referred to that night, business he had to take care of before he went to confront John. He'd made his latest demand for payment, knowing that she'd just landed the lead in a big-budget feature, and she'd snapped. She'd let him get most of the way home, then sped down the road toward him like a bat out of television hell.

Jackie had felt like a total fool as she shut Jake up in the downstairs bathroom. He couldn't see the gun Lorraine had pressed up against her back through the leather of her handbag, and Jackie was afraid to risk his life by alarming him when Lorraine was so well prepared to shoot. So obediently as a schoolgirl she had called her dog to her, led him to the bathroom, and closed the door.

Lorraine had walked back into the living room with Jackie still in front of her, pulled a handkerchief from her pocket, and calmly wiped down everything she had touched that might retain a fingerprint. Then she led Jackie out the door and to her car.

Jake had begun barking his protest before they were out of the driveway. Jackie knew he wasn't capable of breaking down the heavy wooden door, but even if he had been, they'd be miles away and untrackable by the time he could manage it.

"So your name's really Ingeborg or something, isn't it?" Jackie asked her as she drove .

"Inge Nordahl, from Moosebutt, Minnesota," said Lorraine with a sharp laugh, "or someplace just like it. I studied theater and motion-picture acting for four years at Pasadena City College, but when I got to Hollywood expecting to be an overnight success, I was just another big-chested blonde with good looks and some ability, like half the female population of that miserable town."

"Big-chested?" Jackie glanced over at Lorraine's modest bosom.

"Enough money buys all the plastic surgery you can carry," said Lorraine, "and my father left me a reasonable heap of it. After I hired an actress to play my mother and fool Cameron into thinking I'd come clean with my family about my blue-movie career, I went to New York and reinvented myself as Lorraine Voss. By the time I was through, I was broke, but it was worth it. I wanted to be an actor more than anything in the world, and I did it. It took Cameron years to figure it out."

"But when he did, he still thought there was no point in blackmailing you anymore, didn't he?"

"By the time he figured it out, there was another reason," she said. "Mark was divorcing me and threatening to take my kids. The last thing I needed was Cameron exposing my unsavory past in the middle of a custody suit. And he knew it, the son of a bitch! He knew how desperate I was to keep his mouth shut, he just didn't believe how far I'd go to do it."

"So that's why John wouldn't tell anyone where he was that night! He was with you, wasn't he?"

"He came to my apartment. It wasn't the first time. I started putting the moves on him that day he took me out to lunch after I threw the tantrum. So that night I put something into his drink and he slept like a baby until morning. He never even knew I was gone."

"You used him! You threw him to the wolves! I don't believe it!"

"Better that than lose my children. Pull up over here. In among those trees, where the car won't show from the road."

"You don't have to kill me, you know."

"Jesus, Jackie, you sound like a character on a TV show! How many times do you think I've heard *that* line? Stop the car and get out, really slowly." Lorraine had removed the gun from her handbag once she couldn't be seen by Jake, and it gleamed dully in the moonlight—a .38-caliber, or Jackie missed her guess.

"You killed Piers Ackroyd, too?" The thought had just occurred to her—Lorraine in a blond wig, pretending to be a hooker and picking up the unpleasant little man in a sleazy bar.

"Yeah, you should have watched 'High Crimes.' That's the one where the murderer leaves hairs from a human hair wig to fool the police. Neat, huh?"

"Uh, yeah."

Jackie had already recognized where they were—perhaps a hundred yards from the site of Cameron Clark's violent demise. "You're getting careless," she told Lorraine. "There's no way you can rig an accident here and have anyone believe it."

"Why not? The cops must know you're obsessed with this whole Cameron Clark thing. If you came to visit the scene of the crime, fell over the bridge, broke your neck maybe—"

"It's a good thing you were acting on television and not writing scripts," Jackie told her.

"Oh, shut up! Start walking. I'll figure out the details as I go."

Moments later Jackie stood on the Little Canyon Creek Bridge, looking down at the rocks and brambles in the light of a waning moon. The light grew brighter.

"Get down!" Lorraine commanded. She shoved Jackie's head down and crouched beside her as a car went by and around the bend in the road that led to Sondra Clark's remote suburb.

When the car had passed, Lorraine pulled Jackie up again. "We'd better get this over with," she said. "Stand up on the railing."

"Are you kidding? I'll fall!"

"That's the general idea," Lorraine informed her. "Go on, get up there." She stepped back into the road and looked both ways for any approaching headlights.

Jackie clambered up onto the concrete bridge railing and stood, swaying, arms out for balance. What a ridiculous way to die, she thought. She didn't want to die, even if the manner of it would be more dignified. Her legs would barely hold her up, they were shaking so.

Lorraine started for her, arms straight out in front. Before she arrived, a dark blur shot out of the shadows and propelled her sideways. The gun went flying into the air and landed somewhere in the darkness with a loud thump. Jackie heard low, awful growling, and a choked scream.

"Jake!" she cried, and her foot slipped on the top of the railing. She flailed and tried to shift her weight, but she was falling.

A pair of strong arms caught her around the legs and

pulled her to the roadway. The pavement scraped her elbows and she was grateful for the pain. "Are you all right?" Kurt Manowski asked, pulling her to her feet.

"Fine," she said, and burst into tears. "Jake . . ."

"I let him out." Kurt handed her a handkerchief. "He's got everything under control now, so you don't have to cry." He pointed to Jake, who was standing on Lorraine's chest with his snarling face half an inch from hers. Lorraine whined feebly in terror.

"I'm not crying because I'm worried," Jackie said. "I think I'm crying because I'm still alive." She pulled one sleeve of the T-shirt out and wiped her face with it as she sagged back against the bridge railing.

Kurt walked over to where the moon revealed a dark glint of metal and picked up Lorraine's gun from the ground, then carried it back over. "You want this?"

"Uh, sure." She took the gun from him. "Then you weren't going to . . ."

"Kill you?" Kurt laughed. Jackie was pretty sure she'd never seen him laugh before, not like that. Not a bad-guy laugh but a real, heartfelt expression of humor. "No, I just wanted to explain to you why I took Cameron's safe, and offer you the papers that were in it in case you needed them to help John. Most of the papers, anyhow."

Of course he wouldn't have handed over the ones that concerned his sister. "I understand," Jackie told him.

"I kind of thought you would," he said. He pointed to Lorraine, who was still whimpering. "What should we do about her?"

"Do you have a cellular phone?"

"Are you kidding? I'm from Hollywood!" He put a hand into his inside jacket pocket and emerged with a tiny telephone that looked even tinier in his big hand.

"I've really got to get one of those things," said Jackie.

•   •   •

"So it looks like *Under the Dog Star* is a dead project," said Mercy Burdeau. "Your leading lady's in jail, and your budget's shot. What a tragedy!"

What was left of the cast and crew of John McBride's defunct independent film was gathered at Bridget O'Malley's for what John laughingly called an "unwrap party." *Under the Dog Star* would have wrapped that very day, according to the original schedule, and if things had gone differently they would have been celebrating a completed movie. Instead, John had a few cans of film in his refrigerator at home. Not one to let little details like that bog him down, he had declared a party anyway.

"Being in jail awaiting trial for first-degree murder is a tragedy," John reminded Mercy. "Just ask Lorraine."

"Compared to that," said Ral, "having to fold a shoot is like measles compared to bubonic plague."

"But we could recut," said Andy Fry. "We could shoot around Lorraine and make the movie anyway. Sure, we'd have to raise some more money, but—"

"No, let's let it die," said John, shaking his head. "Too much unhappiness in that film. Too much death."

"Besides," Jackie told them, "John's working on another script right now. He started it while he was in jail."

"He's letting me read it," said Katie. "It's wonderful."

"You're wonderful," said John, giving her a kiss on top of her head. "Why do you suppose it took me so long to figure it out?"

"Because you're a big dumb boy?" Marti volunteered.

"To big dumb boys," Mercy declared, raising her glass and giving a meaningul sideways glance in Ral's direction.

"Well, I'm a big dumb girl," said Jackie. "I was convinced Kurt was our killer."

Kurt Manowski laughed. "That's because I'm so damned good at what I do!"

"But haven't you ever wanted to play a good guy?" John asked him.

"Hey, look at this face." Kurt pointed to himself. "Would you cast me as a good guy?"

"I already have," said John. "In my new script. I'm writing it specifically for you. Would you like to read it when I'm finished?"

Kurt looked at John for a long moment without saying anything. Then his face broke into a wide smile. "Yeah," he said. "I would."

"And did you write in a part for Jake?" Jackie asked. "He and Kurt work together, you know."

"We sure do," said Kurt, taking a dog biscuit from his pocket and offering it to the big Shepherd. "Me and Jake are a team."

PENGUIN PUTNAM INC.
Online

Your Internet gateway to a virtual environment with
hundreds of entertaining and enlightening books
from Penguin Putnam Inc.

*While you're there, get the latest buzz on
the best authors and books around—*

Tom Clancy, Patricia Cornwell, W.E.B. Griffin,
Nora Roberts, William Gibson, Robin Cook,
Brian Jacques, Catherine Coulter, Stephen King,
Jacquelyn Mitchard, and many more!

**Penguin Putnam Online is located at
http://www.penguinputnam.com**

PENGUIN PUTNAM NEWS

Every month you'll get an inside look at our upcoming books and new features on our site. This is an
ongoing effort to provide you with the most
up-to-date information about
our books and authors.

**Subscribe to Penguin Putnam News at
http://www.penguinputnam.com/ClubPPI**